S. May

JOSHUA SON OF NONE

I wish to express my indebtedness to Dr. Robert Sinsheimer for the privilege of participating in his seminar on eugenics at Caltech.

And my sincere thanks to Leroy Hood, MD, PhD, of the Department of Biology at Caltech, for his advice and counsel.

JOSHUA
SON OF NONE

Nancy Freedman

Hart-Davis, MacGibbon London

Granada Publishing Limited
First published in Great Britain 1974 by Hart-Davis, MacGibbon Ltd
Frogmore, St Albans, Hertfordshire, AL2 2NF and
3 Upper James Street, London W1R 4BP

ISBN 0 246 10788 X

Printed in Great Britain by
Fletcher & Son Ltd, Norwich

to the future

to Benedict

and to those who stand under the windswept tree
Joie-Deame, Deborah, Michael-Sharon

Hope is a memory of the future.
MARCEL

The year was nineteen sixty-three. It was remembered. The month, November. It was remembered. The day and the hour were remembered. Every man, woman, and child in the country could relate their personal story, tell you where they were and what they were doing when it happened; how they got the news, who told them, what they thought.

Thor Bitterbaum had a special reason for remembering. He was completing a three-year surgical residency, and on this particular day, at twelve thirty, was working up Mrs. Lucille Webber whose complaint was that she could not void.

He glanced at his watch. He was running late. Still, if he hurried, there was a chance he might get a glimpse of the motorcade and possibly the President. It seemed to him extraordinary that someone so different from his predecessors had won the election. Not a ward heeler or career general, but a man schooled in the tradition of public service. He seemed aware of people, sensitive to problems, ready to consider solutions. Bitterbaum thought the man remarkable. In his opinion even the President's speeches were literature. Not since Lincoln had there been such documents.

The style, like the man, was crisp, energetic, and to the point.

Bitterbaum also was not lacking in style. He regarded himself as marked out for high attainment under the banner of his name. His mother had been an anthro major at Hunter College who did her thesis on Norse mythology. Her parents were appalled at her choice. Thor? Whoever heard of a Thor? Much less a Thor Bitterbaum. But she refused to see the incongruity, or perhaps secretly relished it, and Thor Bitterbaum he became.

The polarities did not combine smoothly in his character. He was a slightly incongruous, not to say improbable, person. A devout atheist, proud of being a Jew. A man who understood anything written down, but had no knowledge of people. His logical, well-trained mind could flood in a second with coruscating emotions.

At times he despaired of himself, but as the product of a complex and sophisticated society he found himself an interesting subject for study. It was curious, for instance, that his cynicism allowed such hero worship. *I'm a nut on the subject of the President;* he admitted it cheerfully. The dichotomy in his nature pleased him. He was Thor Bitterbaum all right and no getting around it.

He took his jacket from the peg, rammed his arms into it, and calling a last-minute instruction to the nurse, left. On his way out the door he was calculating the best route to avoid traffic jams and still see the end of the motorcade. A heavy blue convertible gunned down the driveway straight at him. Bitterbaum jumped back to the stairs. *Damn rich bastards. Think they own the world!* The blue Lincoln skidded to a stop; all its doors opened and hung there. Two men jumped to the curb, moving fast. They ran into each other, made false, uncoordinated starts. One of them was shouting. More cars raced in with the same disregard for life and limb, swerved onto the lawn, and emptied. Motors were left running.

A procession of cars arrived and were abandoned in flower beds, driveways, and lawns. It was some kind of full-scale disaster. The blue convertible seemed to be the focus. Bitterbaum made his way to it, pushing through the crowd. "I'm a doctor," he said, "let me through. Please let me through."

Someone grabbed him. "Doctor, doctor."

"Take it easy. What's happened?"

The man lurched against him. He's drunk, Bitterbaum thought, and then saw his eyes. The man was in shock. He made the diagnosis casually, not realizing he was to be the next victim.

The back of the convertible was a slaughterhouse. He saw the roses first, drenched in blood. The slight young woman in the pink suit was cradling the body of a man. They were enveloped in a froth of blood. The woman's stockings were bloodied, and clots of blood stained the pink suit.

She lifted a blank face, the face that had looked out from countless magazine covers. Then the man that she held—

As Bitterbaum made the connection, physiological changes occurred in him. His breathing became labored, his skin clammy, and his brain focused on a fly settled on the underside of the man's foot, cleaning its mandible. He became conscious of someone screaming. There were words mixed in the scream, the same words, repeated endlessly. "He's dead. What a terrible thing. He's dead."

A car radio was droning commercials. There was another wounded man in the jump seat. He recognized the governor. He observed multiple wounds, but the man was conscious. "Where's the stretcher?" he bellowed. "What's holding up the stretcher?"

The second-year resident was making a preliminary examination. Bitterbaum bent to hear the findings and saw that the top of the head was gone. The posterior cranium was quite destroyed.

"No pulse," the resident said. "No blood pressure. No discernible respiration. But he's not quite—" He looked at the young woman and didn't finish the sentence.

The stretcher arrived. Bitterbaum attempted to help lift the body, but the President's wife wouldn't allow them to take him.

Outwardly she was controlled, but the gesture of restraint was irrational. It was impossible to determine how she assessed the situation. With fragments of her husband's brain adhering to the upholstery, the matrix of logic disappeared. Hands reaching to take him must be pushed aside. She defended him. She would not yield him. Did she believe her husband still lived?

Someone standing by stripped off his jacket and handed it into the car. That's what she wanted. Wrap the head, hide the wound. It was a way of denying. Cover it and the wound was gone. She was hysterical in a quiet, almost sensible way. Now that her husband's head was swathed in the jacket, she permitted them to lift him onto the stretcher. Someone put the roses on his chest. It was a gesture of reverence and love, but they imprinted themselves in soggy outline on his shirt. His wife walked beside the stretcher. *For a tear is an intellectual thing.* He was taken up the stairs and through the scuffed double doors. They followed the broad red stripe painted on the linoleum tiles. Pediatrics, O.B., Gynecology, X ray, Triage. They stopped at Trauma Cubicle Number One.

The President was laid on the examining table. There was no window in the room; the overhead tubular light made the victim look not like himself but a statue of himself carved of translucent marble. They got him hooked to an EKG monitor.

It was amazing that the heart was still pumping. A tracheotomy was performed in an attempt to induce breathing. The body began making stertorous, agonized efforts. A nasogastric tube cleared the stomach contents. Bilateral tubes were inserted in both pleural cavities to suction chest matter and prevent lung collapse. They were attached to an anesthesia machine which had more sensitive controls than the respirator. The jacket slipped from the head. It had all been torn away. It was hopeless. Lactated Ringer's was fed into his right leg by catheter. The eyes deviated outward and were sightless.

The gushing from the top of the head ended. His wife knelt on the floor and prayed. The private doctor who traveled with them helped her to her feet. There were at least a dozen doctors around the cart, including the chief neurosurgeon for whom everyone made room. The tube in the incised throat wasn't working. The neck wound interfered. Bitterbaum attempted to free it. The trace on the EKG ceased. One of the doctors began to perform extrathoracic cardiac massage. He stood on the balls of his feet in an effort to get maximum leverage. "Get me a stool."

The neurosurgeon exchanged a look with the person on his right which plainly said, Why these heroics? The man is gone. But the doctor performing the massage wouldn't give up. He continued the rhythmic pressure.

Don't stop. We can't lose him. We have, I know we have, but we can't. No one in Trauma Cubicle Number One was normal. Bitterbaum fought the waves of knowledge spreading in him. He rebelled against what he saw and what he knew. This battle was done. *I haven't begun to fight. Another front, with other weapons.* The name Gurdon, that single name, spawned in his brain.

Someone said, "What's the story on the priest? We're not going to make it. This is not official, but the man is dead."

The neurosurgeon turned to the young woman with the wide staring eyes. "Your husband has sustained a fatal wound."

Her lips moved. "I know."

The private physician bent over the President and checked for a femoral pulse. He began to cry. And in a rage at his tears he thundered, "I want this area cleared."

A priest had been brought into the room, but he was standing numb and uncomprehending. The private doctor said, "Can't some prayers for the dead be said?"

The priest then stepped forward and gave absolution. "*Si capax, ego te absolvo a peccatis tuis, in nomine Patris, et Filii, et Spiritus Sancti, Amen.*" He unscrewed the vial of holy oil and pressed it to his thumb, anointing the President's forehead with the sign of the cross. *"Per istam sanctam unctionem, indulgeat tibi Dominus quidquid deliquisti, Amen."* He continued with the Apostolic blessing. *"Ego facultate mihi ab Apostolica Sede tributa, indulgentiam plenariam et remissionem omnium peccatorum tibi concedo et benedico te. In nomine Patris, et Filii, et Spiritus Sancti, Amen."* After this he said the Lord's Prayer, which the widow and the doctor murmured brokenly.

Bitterbaum was drowning for the third time in skeins of Latin. *The man still lived. Why were they saying prayers for the dead?* Cellular death had not yet taken place. Hope and resurrection lay under his hand.

1950.

That date was hanging in his mind.

I'm going mad, he thought. My President is dead in front of me, and I see a date. Why? What is the significance of it? What do I know about 1950? he asked himself.

Of course. It was the year Dr. Landrum Shettles announced in vitro fertilization of a human ovum. The embryo survived six days. In 1952 Briggs and King, working with the leopard frog, *Rana pipiens*, transplanted nuclear material from one embryonic cell to another. Over forty percent of the renucleated eggs underwent normal cell division to the tadpole stage. A year later, the double-helix structure for DNA was discovered by Watson and Crick. Life was a spiral staircase with banisters of linked sugars and phosphates, the steps complementary bases, adenine-thymine and cytosine-guanine. It was surmised that all genetic information necessary to reproduce an organism is coded into the nucleus of every living cell.

John B. Gurdon successfully demonstrated this with the African clawed toad, *Xenopus laevis.* Implanting the genetic material from an intestinal cell of one toad into the egg of another, he cloned an amphibian that grew to maturity. By a vegetative, asexual process an identical toad was duplicated from a single cell of the original. As far as Bitterbaum knew, no one had dared propose the step to higher animals. But only technical difficulties stood in the way. When Daniele Petrucci fertilized a human egg in vitro, destroying it on the twenty-ninth day after hearing a heartbeat, a furor followed. The Vatican intervened. The AMA called for a moratorium. Hysterical articles appeared in the popular press. Due to the pressure of opinion, both secular and ecclesiastical, work on cloning continued only in sub rosa fashion.

But the knowledge was there. And it seemed to Bitterbaum that while the widow and the personal physician were praying, a man of science, if he had resolve, daring, if he had courage, might run up that spiral staircase and create history.

The priest turned to the young widow. He had prayed, *"Si capax." If possible,* for he had jurisdiction only before death. "I am convinced the soul has not left his body. This is a valid last sacrament. I have given much thought to the problem and I have worked out a formula. I believe there is a direct relationship between the stamina of the body and the endurance of the soul to remain. If the person succumbs after a long illness the soul leaves the body within twenty minutes after pronouncement of death. But in the case of your husband, a man in the flush of health, I am convinced the soul lingers as long as three hours."

I *am* going mad, Bitterbaum thought. It was the world of the past speaking. Bitterbaum was not concerned with casuistry which belonged to the Middle Ages, or flat EKGs, arbiters of the present. He addressed his whole being to the future. Teilhard de Chardin said, "In the future man will meet God."

And the future was possible now. Life was possible instead of death. There was a viable alternative to the mumbo jumbo of medieval incantations. They turned off the machines and began the dismantling process. Bitterbaum stepped forward to remove the nasogastric tube. A man with training and knowledge takes the scalpel, that one lying there, and lifts a small amount of material from the wound and places it in a Pyrex tube, this one, and leaves the room.

No one noticed him, one more doctor walking down the corridor. The nurses' station had been taken over by the FBI. They commandeered the switchboard trunk line, controlling and monitoring all incoming calls. Outgoing calls were placed in an attempt to locate the immediate family.

The bustle of security, protocol, procedure, the chain of command, all was operational now that nothing could be done, now that he was dead. They were coding everything: the plane he had arrived in, the motorcade, the attack, the new widow, the corpse. Fun and games. He left them to it.

A reporter had taken down pages of notes and finally gotten an open line to his paper. He sat and cried into the phone. Nothing he had written was intelligible. It simply didn't make sense.

Bitterbaum passed this useless center of activity and proceeded toward the supply room. Here he searched through storage bins until he found a portable case of liquid nitrogen. He immersed the test tube and an immediate sense of relief and well-being flowed through him. The Thor part of his nature exulted. He had saved his President. The wounds were fatal, but he had saved him.

The strength and daring of Thor stood off and kept at bay the talmudic scholar grandfather, Jacob Bitterbaum, and the learned rabbi, Solomon Bitterbaum. They shook long unscissored beards and consulted Yekuthiel Bitterbaum, patriarch of the family. But he had never heard of anyone called Thor, who daily waded rivers to sit in judgment under Yggdrasil, the world tree, defending both Midgard and Asgard, men and gods, from the chaos of the giants. His belt doubled his strength. He had gloves of iron and could toss a thunderbolt. The red-bearded one swung his club, and goats and wild boar ran at his side. In the Ragnarok, in the forest of Thorsmorsk he would fight the serpent and it was recounted that both would die.

No wonder the old Jews shook their covered heads. Thor brandished the swastika, symbol of Mjellnir, his hammer, which the dwarfs, out of spite, had made too short. They drew back, these pious Jews, murmured ancient prayers and swayed in the face of the assertion that this hero could shrive and hallow the dead. And yet the dead was so shriven that he would rise up in strength and life.

Genetically he would rise. The nightmare of death was over. Man could live again and again, forever if he wished. Thor the Red Beard sat under the windswept tree and acquired the knowledge of runic lore taken from the world of death and set in stone. The megaliths told him the story of the dead. The giants were slaughtered. In this century he would kill death. In this century he had come out of the forest and majored in biology. The NSF supported his study. He graduated cum laude. There was a family conference. They voted for medical school. They weren't quite sure what a biologist was. Someone, they suspected, who couldn't make it into the ranks of the medical profession.

Thor was not opposed to the idea. He went along with it. He felt he would make a good doctor. But he kept up with what was happening in developmental biology. He dug into old journals and pored over the historic experiments of Hans Driesch, who as early as 1891 had carefully separated the components of a fertilized sea urchin egg at the four-cell stage and grown four identical sea urchins from one. Driesch was the last of the vitalists. But the mystic vital principle he sought was present in the spiraling steps of DNA. It was present in this case of liquid nitrogen.

As he walked out into the hall again it was amazing to Bitterbaum that the usual things were going on in Major Medical. A boy was bleeding from a fall, a man was admitted with severe chest pains, a woman came in and said she felt nervous. In Trauma Room Number One a sheet had been drawn over the prone figure. A nurse brought in two brown shopping bags in which to collect his clothes and personal effects. Two plain brown-paper shopping bags in which to remove all trace of the President of the United States.

From the nurses' station a radio blared details. One of the newscasters quoted an unidentified source as saying the body was to be flown to Bethesda Naval Hospital.

Let them take it where they wished. He carried living cells in a preservative solution in his left hand. It had been fascinating to him to learn that life, biological life, was also left-handed; polypeptides, amino acids, everything clutched to the left, grew and extended to the left.

Thor, tall stooped Jew in whom the Norse god dwelt, he alone of all the people that crowded the hospital was lighthearted, almost gay. He saw the President's widow with the now dried blood blotching her clothes and adhering to her hose. She seemed to be listening to a priest, a different priest, who was saying something in an earnest manner. But the wide-set eyes looked past him, looked past the rim of the world. It didn't occur to her to glance at the case he carried in his left hand. He wanted to go up to her and tell her.

Tell her what?

This stopped him. He had actually taken a step in her direction. But she stood on the other side of time, knee deep in yesterday.

Bitterbaum had belief too, and faith. His litany could be read under the electron microscope and interpreted by X-ray crystallography and through staining techniques by which it was possible to see twenty-three human chromosome pairs. Thor's new thunderbolt was the laser beam. With it he would lay about, slice surgically through organelles of the living cell. Faulty genes would be replaced by segments of DNA carried on viral genomes, reversing the clock of decay and senescence. His mass, like the great B minor, was a celebration of life, but in new terms. After two hundred thousand generations on earth, *Homo sapiens* had gained victory, biological life over biological death.

He wanted to reach out and touch that pink, bloodied suit. "Ma'amdon'tbedespairingThecellsofyourhusband'slivingbodywilllivebiologicallyHewillnotdieIamThorBitterbaumandIpromisethis." He could prognosticate the result of such action and such speech. The men at the Command Post would haul him off to a locked ward. But no one hauled the old priest off when he spoke of angels and gave the rule of thumb whereby one determined if the soul still inhabited the host body.

A collision of worlds had occurred in this hospital, precipitated by the assassination of a president.

The summer before, Bitterbaum had witnessed a cell fusion experiment employing Okada's myxovirus. It was rumored that in England Harris and Watkins had used the same virus to fuse HeLa and Ehrlich ascites cells. Genetic engineering was underway at a dozen centers. Much of it could be written off as futurology: ectogenesis, gestation outside the womb in *Brave New World* tradition; chimeras and cyborgs, man-animal and man-machine hybrids. But cloning he had seen with his own eyes. He had read the literature: Sambuichi, Briggs, Gurdon, King, Moore, Hennen. The technique was understood. Yet he couldn't say to the widow, "A cell of your husband lives. His biological double can exist in the world." She was conditioned to react to such tidings with revulsion, even horror.

The best schools prepared you to live in yesterday's world, while today's world was already past. And that young woman was a product of church and tradition.

Those were the forces that worked against imagination, that stifled initiative and restrained daring. Even the detonation at Los Alamos did not hold implications as frightening as cloning. Nuclear fission was something that happened out there in the world. This occurred inside. It was an interior revolution of such potential that no one could foresee its total effect.

He was sad to leave the young woman with wide, shocked eyes. A grief without size, shape, or dimension held her immobile. But Bitterbaum had thoughts to think and a plan to formulate. The atmosphere of shock and frustration was not conducive to this. He left.

He saw at once that he couldn't take his car; it was blocked in all directions by automobile carcasses. That was all right. He preferred to walk. He swung his arms, his left one too, the one with the case. He wondered briefly at the acuity with which he was able to focus. Was that sharp edge, that pleasurable tingle Thor girding on his belt of strength?

Even a cursory look at the history of science convinced him that once a process was conceived, men acted upon it. Sometimes the new was acquiesced to and accepted. Sometimes it took war and revolution to establish. But knowledge never lay fallow. It was used.

This was man's strength. It was also the factor that might topple him. But Bitterbaum felt free to take as a basic postulate the assumption that if not he, then someone else.

While the world was mourning the loss of the particular genetic combination which had just been senselessly murdered, he carried in nitrogen solution the possibility of a perfect replication. Avowed atheist that he was, Bitterbaum believed he was at the scene for this purpose, that he was the instrument by which this unique genotype would survive. He had been liberated from nightmare. He had been granted hope.

Only now, walking randomly through a city husked of its soul, did it occur to him that it might not work. What was the probability that one could clone a human being by cell fusion? Demsdale at Caltech was the man to undertake the project. He had successfully repeated the work on amphibians, but because of the outcry, his paper was privately distributed. The question was, why would Demsdale risk his career and reputation? Obviously he had to fire his scientific curiosity and enthusiasm. But even if he could manage this, even with Demsdale's genius guiding the venture, what chance was there of success?

When he lifted the matter from the wound and even when he froze it, there had been no doubts. First A, then B, and so on until the man was regenerated. There was no terminology to express this. The word *clone* was Greek, meaning *throng* or *crowd.* Implicit in this concept was the idea that nations would clone armies; employers, assembly-line workers. It was possible, he supposed, to involve large numbers in the cloning process, but he was interested in replicating one genotype: the finest, in his opinion, that his culture and civilization had produced.

What was the singular of clone? What was the noun? Could a cloned person be termed a clonee? The real question in this flood of subsidiary ones was whether or not the total person could be reproduced. Outstanding geneticists were at odds over this. To what extent did hereditary factors determine the phenotype?

What was the role of environment in reconstructing a man? Every living organism is modified by life. Although the human brain can grasp fifty bits of visual information at once, it cannot file more than ten of them. Four-fifths of all sense impressions are discarded.

How does the individual select? How does he categorize a nuance, a shape, a form? Would the same genetic material guarantee the same selection? That seemed doubtful. If a person selected differently, would he in fact be a different person?

Suppose the environment were simulated, programmed to resemble in essential details the background of the original? Could this be done?

To begin with, the time element was different, which meant the culture, philosophy, and mores were different. Parents could conceivably be chosen from the same faith, with comparable means, but they would be other people. Would the President have been the President raised by another family? Would any of us be the people we are, given other circumstances?

Science at this moment in time had no answer. Identical twins, raised apart, show remarkably close correspondence in standard IQ tests. But character traits, emotional equilibrium, these factors are more difficult to equate.

Of course the raising of a cloned human would provide incontrovertible proof of the precise interaction in these areas. The bizarre element struck him fully for the first time. Where, for instance, does one come by a womb? His mind boggled. Yet the experiment was of such scope that a way must be found. Man's knowledge of his own biological and psychological nature was at stake. The benefit to science was incalculable.

But he knew these considerations played no part in his initial impulse. He had not removed the tissue from the wound in the interest of science. He had acted to prevent the loss of a human being whom he admired and loved. Most people can be cut off without affecting the course of history. But Bitterbaum felt that the world could not afford the death of this man.

The will to save him by ordinary means was not enough; therefore, extraordinary means were justified. The clonee would be the first human produced asexually, the child of his race, a true orphan. A home, parents, siblings could be modeled on the past. But the problem was larger than that. Was it insurmountable?

The war, for instance. The President had lived through World War II. And the war had marked him. He attempted to enlist and was rejected because of a back injury. He spent months doing corrective exercises and wound up with a commission in the Navy. He was assigned to desk duty in Washington, but pulled wires and got command of a PT-boat.

Bitterbaum had pored over all available accounts. They were rammed while patrolling Blackett Straight in the Solomons. Over a calm sea a voice from the forward machine gun turret reported softly, "Ship at two o'clock."

They moved carefully to avoid making a wake. The hull of the Japanese destroyer loomed like a phantom. It was doing approximately forty knots. A wall of metal bore down on them, cutting them amidships. A gasoline fire erupted and in seconds the water was ablaze.

Three enlisted men and an officer were in the forward compartment which was airtight and still intact. The rest of the crew floated in their Mae Wests. Two needed help and the engineer was badly hurt. They stretched him on the deck which by this time was gurgling with seepage. The rest of the men crouched and crowded together taking turns in the water.

Daylight showed them islands identified as Vella Lavella, Gizo, and Kolombangara, all Japanese held. The long-range plan was to avoid capture; the short-range plan, simply to survive. The boat was swamping. The men could all swim with the exception of the wounded engineer. The commander spotted a floating spar and directed his men to hold onto it. Then he took the strap of the engineer's life jacket in his teeth and towed him. It was a five-hour endurance swim to an uninhabited atoll. They had been in the water a total of fifteen and a half hours.

Once his men were encamped the commander decided to try and make it to the reef where American patrol boats sometimes came within signaling distance. He rewrapped the lantern in its Kapok jacket, tied a life belt around his waist and a thirty-eight around his neck. His instructions to his men: "One flash, I'm in trouble. Two flashes, I've located a boat."

He swam out to the reef. The waves lifted him over coral and receded. He was scraped and cut. He waited, his body waterlogged and numb, forcing himself to scan the sea until its light seared his brain and he blacked out. He realized he couldn't get back without help. He began to propel himself, unable to actually swim. He moved with the help of occasional arm and leg motions toward the spit of land he had come from.

When he judged himself to be close enough he signaled. One light, HELP.

His men, groggy and not functioning clearly, misunderstood and let him drift by. His vest supported him. The current he was too weak to fight carried him. The phrase "swept out to sea" echoed in his mind. He thought of the carnivores cruising in these tropical waters. Drifting between consciousness and unconsciousness, was there a chuckle at the pile of books he had cracked, the careful honing of his mind? What a well-educated mouthful he would make for some dark shape.

By first light he saw he had been carried completely around the island. Streaks of dawn gave him strength for a final effort. His prayer was short—*If it be Thy will*—but it brought him to shore.

He found the crew in critical situation. There was no drinking water. It was decided to try for a nearby island where they could see coconut trees. That period in the water blended in nightmare fashion with the others. Again he towed the engineer. Being responsible for someone else helped him make it. They were by this time in such an exhausted condition that the coconut milk made them sick. But that night it rained, and they improvised catch basins of leaves and shoes, hands and mouths.

On the fourth day the commander with one of his men swam to Nauru Island which was inhabited by a contingent of Japanese. They managed to liberate a canoe, a keg of water, hardtack, and some sweetish sticky Japanese candy. That night they kept a lookout from the reef which they identified on their map as Ferguson's Passage.

Again no boat.

They decided on a return to Nauru to add to their store of provisions, but the wind freshened and the canoe swamped. They were rescued by natives who paddled out to them. The commander scratched their location on a coconut with his knife. The message was delivered to the New Zealand Patrol Command.

For him the war was over. There were serious complications with his back and a long period of recuperation.

Such a saga was proof to Bitterbaum of what this man could endure. Many men live and die without knowing themselves, without testing their resources and capabilities, without knowing what they will ask of themselves. But the man who had been commander, the man who had been President, knew.

Would the clonee know? Such an experience could not be manufactured. One could substitute mountaineering, caving, shooting rapids. Some of the components might conceivably be reproduced, but what would take the place of the Japanese navy? Or what induce the grief he had known when he lost his brother, a Liberator pilot flying daily missions over the Bay of Biscay? A robot plane had been designed to destroy the V-2 rocket-launch site in Normandy. The robot required a pilot to gain sufficient altitude for the mother plane to guide it. At that point the pilot would parachute to safety, and the drone with its ten tons of explosive lock into flight attack. It worked in theory. The trial run was successful. But at six twenty in the evening, directly after takeoff, the plane exploded.

There was no body, just medals: the Navy Cross, American Defense Medal, European-African-Eastern Area Campaign Medal. And a destroyer named for him. The future President was the second son, the next in line. After his brother's death he subordinated his other interests to one overriding goal. The actions he took from that moment prepared him for the office he would eventually hold.

Had he preserved this man, Bitterbaum wondered, the man himself? The basic question was: with unavoidably altered circumstances, would the same personality emerge? Or would that elusive quality, whatever it is that inhabits and makes us men, be absent?

The sun hung in one corner of the sky while the moon rode the other. Both were pale, both white. The sun gained intensity, the earth rotated. He was on a downtown street and an extra was out. The assassin was apprehended.

Was it one man? A crank? A fanatic? Had some poor schizoid, inflamed by the tensions in the city, done that deed? Or was it a conspiracy reaching to the highest places? If the truth were known, would it rupture the country? Was the headline story of a single assassin credible? He read the account. The building in which the killer made his aerie was along the line of march. Bitterbaum scanned rather than read. A careful reading would reopen the agony of Trauma Room One. He took in the essentials. A mail-order rifle purchased under an assumed name. An officer had also died, shot shortly before the assassin was captured at a local movie house.

Bitterbaum dropped the paper. He could not absorb any more of this reality. He preferred his own. The reality of frozen tissue, the reality of supreme service. If he could manage to bring it about, he would be rendering inestimable service, as had his namesake Thor, to gods and man. Did it really make a difference that his gods were the immutable laws of science and the logic of thought?

With his left hand, with his glove of iron he would nullify evil and restore what had been. Somewhere within the chains of his own genetic endowment, Jacob and Solomon and Yekuthiel Bitterbaum counseled that this was ambition and false pride masquerading as love. But the Thor portion of his nature stood scornful with mighty legs spread, arms flexed, ready.

The body had been moved to the seventeenth floor of Bethesda Naval Hospital and then to the basement morgue. The coffin had been damaged en route. Why did they bother to record such things? What did it matter? Life everlasting resided in the left hand of Thor.

———if he could hack it. If he could pull it off. He returned to his room to sleep, deferring final assessment. He dreamed of brown linoleum floors intersecting the light from open doors to form a gigantic cross. The litany for the dead, the Apostolic blessing flowed in black robes, "*Ego faculate mihi ab Apostolica Sede tributa, indulgentiam—in nomine Patris, et Filii, et Spiritus*

Sancti." "*Baruch atah adonai Elohenu melech ha olam,*" intoned a minyan of old Jews. But an older god, pagan and red-headed, has come from Thorsmorsk, world of night, to lift despair from the world of Midgard. Dashing, lighthearted, and without fear, he looks into the well of fate. In releasing the world of men from the despair of death, he will kill and be killed by the serpent.

The old Jews nod and concur in the death.

And the priest draws a cross in blank air and agrees.

It was a tree, Tyr, of runic magic. *And when man tasted of the tree he was banished from the garden lest he put forth his hand, and take also of the tree of life, and eat, and live forever. So he drove out the man, and he placed at the east of the garden of Eden, cherubims, and a flaming sword which turned every way, to keep the way of the tree of life.*

Thor Bitterbaum woke, remembering his dream. Wondering if it was a dream. Wise men of two world religions warned him in Hebrew and Latin. But the dancing God, the celebrant of life that dwelt in him, laughed. Out of what garden would he be cast, from which world driven? It couldn't matter, with such a gift, such possibilities under his hand.

He had moved from the personal love and devotion he felt for the dying President to a larger arena. He paced his small room, five steps in one direction, four in the other. To hell with forbidden fruits and the ancient fear of knowledge. Let man liberate himself. To this end Thor Bitterbaum drew up a shopping list.

That, in essence, was what it was. He was shopping for a rich man. At each stage the project would require tremendous capital outlay. He remembered reading that Demsdale had recently lost a large government grant. Normally, funding was not hard for a developmental biologist to come by, but Demsdale was pushing into territory marked off-limits by the AMA. A sizable donation enabling him to equip his laboratory properly and pursue his work might clinch things.

Bitterbaum admitted that he was thinking in terms of hundreds of thousands of dollars, possibly more. If the cloning itself succeeded and a live child was the result, it would take an equal investment to bring it up.

The problem was further complicated by the fact that not any rich man would do. Ruling out Republicans greatly curtailed the file, which shrunk further for reasons of age. Bitterbaum decided he must consolidate. The man to finance the effort would be the only other participant, the one actually to bring up the clonee.

Even Demsdale, who initially had the most important role, would not be let into the full history and would certainly be given no indication as to the real plan.

Security was essential. The clonee had to be prepared with utmost care to accept his origins. Premature disclosure would be disastrous. A two-man conspiracy could be kept. Provided . . . he eliminated a prominent name. There were rumors of a drinking problem. His man had to be reliable.

The shopping list begun with thirty names was reduced to a dozen. Of these finalists, all possessed unlimited wealth, all were under fifty years of age. Another name was struck—that man lived abroad. It was necessary that the clonee be brought up as an American, imbued with the American tradition.

Health was a factor. A name was question-marked.

He raised his pen over G. K. Kellogg and starred it. He had a line to Kellogg who was on the board of trustees at Caltech. Bitterbaum threw on some clothes and went to the library to check further. *Who's Who* read: "KELLOGG, Gerald Kirsten . . . Developed the first miniaturized transistor. Founded Kellogg Enterprises which became known for its slogan 'Information is money. Money is power.' At thirty-seven years of age his fortune has been estimated at forty million dollars. Married, Lynn Rollins, 1961. A son, Gerald, Jr., born 1962. Home, Latigo Canyon, Malibu Ca."

Bitterbaum closed the heavy red volume. If he had written the profile himself it could not have matched more closely what was needed.

The rest of the afternoon was spent with the chief resident, arranging an extended leave. Urgent family business required his immediate presence in California. He was licensed there and could make ends meet covering other doctors' practices. The resident accepted the story, and Bitterbaum was airborne that evening with his hand luggage beside him.

Thor Bitterbaum's efforts to contact G. K. Kellogg continued over a period of weeks. The reason for his failure became apparent when the AEI scandal broke in the press. Bitterbaum groaned when he read the account: corporate finagling, cost overruns, arbitrary cut-off benefits, unfiled proxy materials, pressure by lobbyists, campaign contributions in exchange for favors.

I chose him, Bitterbaum thought, I gave him three stars; *money, youth, interest in politics.* He was interested in politics all right, maneuvering behind the scenes for his own advantage. At first he backed candidates. Then he entered the play himself, conducting private polls, making contacts. And it had come unstuck. His starred chief contender had been totaled. Both the six o'clock and eleven o'clock news caught Gerald Kirsten Kellogg smiling affably and saying, "No comment." In each instance he was flanked by lawyers.

The morning edition of the *Times* carried an in-depth interview by a witness, a secretary through whom certain monies had been funneled. No wonder the man was too busy to see him. He was caught in a skein of his own devising, attempting to backtrack, destroy records, erase memos. Huddled with lawyers, receiving expert advice for which he paid enormous sums, there had not been time for someone with the improbable name of Dr. Thor Bitterbaum.

He thanked God for it, and at a lunch counter over a cup of coffee and a sandwich paged through his remaining prospects. Of the front runners, three resided in New York, there was a candidate in Florida, and two Californians, one presently in Saudi Arabia. Considerable investigation indicated that Mr. Douglas Tanner was well qualified as far as money and background went. But he was almost fifty, and the chance of bringing the clonee to his twenty-first year was only fair.

However, there were other factors to consider. Bitterbaum was low on funds, his sole job so far filling in for a Dr. Clemens on Thursdays. Also there was no reliable data on how long cellular material could be stored and retain its potency. And perhaps most important, Demsdale was here. If it worked with Tanner, the next step could be negotiated at once.

He had no access to Douglas Tanner. But by discreet questioning he was able to ascertain that his physician was associated with UCLA Medical Center. With this tenuous thread he psyched Tanner's personal secretary and emerged with a meeting scheduled the following day.

Bitterbaum woke with a nervous stomach, which he calmed by ingesting various self-prescribed pharmaceutical remedies. He took a cab to Century City and an elevator to the top floor of a black glass building. While he waited he went over his presentation.

When he was finally ushered into the inner office, he received a shock. Douglas Tanner greeted him from a wheelchair. He was a paraplegic. Nowhere in his biographical material was there mention of this. It was apparently a fact he did not wish publicized. Bitterbaum stuttered slightly as he claimed the man's doctor as a personal friend who insisted he must look Tanner up if he were ever in Los Angeles. He was just passing through. Nice of Mr. Tanner to receive him. He was back in front of the tinted-glass building in less than ten minutes.

Now what? He asked the question with more urgency than before. It occurred to Bitterbaum that he might have taken too harsh a view of G. K. Kellogg. The AEI matter seemed to reach to such high levels of government that it was unlikely one man had engineered it.

It looked to him as though Kellogg was the fall guy. The news media were pursuing him like a pack of wolves. His career was a shambles; whatever he hoped to accomplish via the political route was blocked, his aura of integrity shot. He could never inspire the qualities of trust and confidence that are a politician's stock in trade. But he was a gifted, energetic man; he would be looking for a way to pick up the pieces. Perhaps for the first time there was a real possibility of involving him in the scheme.

If he didn't go to jail, he might still be the right man. With everyone else backing away, this was the moment to drop by his office.

Bitterbaum's sense of timing was perfect. There was not a single meeting on G. K. Kellogg's docket, except for a Monday morning wrangle with his lawyers.

G. K. himself was acutely conscious of the lack of clutter on his daily appointment pad. When bad luck strikes, it strikes in threes. He was reeling under a private blow when the public scandal erupted. What more could happen, he dared not conceive. When the sky fell in, every segment of his life was blanketed.

The two years of his marriage brought an unexpected return: he was happy. Lynn had been his secretary. She was attractive and an almost standard affair took place. Simultaneously he escorted the usual bevy of debutantes. His object: marriage. He intended to merge empires and found a dynasty. The Kellogg dynasty. Until it occurred to him that he was leaving his dates early, phoning Lynn, dashing around to her apartment and complaining of boredom.

He was not bored with Lynn. She was quiet, but she had something that was lacking in the brittle, well-schooled young women he escorted, something his mother would have defined as horse sense, a knack of stripping away externals and looking at things squarely. G. K. began to wonder if he really needed a brilliant alliance. He'd gone it on his own ever since he could remember. Why not now?

He moved cautiously as befitted a man in his position. He hired an agency to run a complete check on her. She was born Lynn Cornelius Rollins. Her dossier was uneventful.

Born:	Riverside, California.
Religion:	Catholic.
Father:	Insurance agent, deceased.
Mother:	Elementary school teacher.
Health:	Good.
Graduated:	UCLA. Major: music, languages. Tried briefly for concert circuit. More coaching required to reach professional level.
Employment:	Departmental secretary, UCLA.
Affair:	Involving a professor. Broke up when she discovered he was married. Subsequently gained employment with the firm of Kellogg Inc., filling in as personal secretary replacing Miss Welty who was out with the flu. After an absence of two weeks Miss Welty paid generous bonus and transferred.

Lynn quite obviously was a talented person. G. K. knew her to be hard-working and responsible. Her good looks ran to the tailored side. She was an asset in the office, ladylike and capable. He decided she would fill the bill admirably as mother of his future brood.

One night he put it to her. "You work for me. You've seen me at my best and at my worst. You probably know me as well as I know myself. We get on. We find each other good company. I have decided to marry, and I'd like it to be you."

Her quiet eyes betrayed neither surprise nor pleasure. She asked simply, "Why?"

"Well, because, damn it, I'm a man used to the best. And I've become convinced that's you. You're quality, Lynn. I recognize it and I appreciate it. Also we pull in harness, we work well together. What do you want me to say? You know I find you attractive."

She smiled slightly. "Yes, I know. But I was sure you'd want a different kind of marriage, someone with position, that kind of thing."

"I thought so for a while. But those women aren't for real. They're manikins. I want something else."

"What do you want, Gerald?" She was the only one who called him that.

"Would you think I was crazy if I said I want to found a dynasty? I want a family, Lynn, a large family. I have built a financial empire. I can pass on wealth and power. I want to do this. I want to make the Kellogg name one to reckon with."

"Children are a condition of the marriage then?"

"I assumed being Catholic, you'd have no objection."

"I didn't know you were aware of my religion. Have we ever discussed it?"

G. K. could have fumbled this but he didn't. "Naturally I checked you out."

"Naturally." As his secretary she was aware of his procedures. Actually, it was eminently sensible of him to approach marriage in the same vein as his other contracts. She ignored the tug at her emotions over the absence of words like *love* and *need.* Looked at properly, he was promoting her from secretary to partner, from mistress to wife.

Lynn had enough experience of the world to realize she could trade in her limited tight little world for a new one of unbelievable dimensions.

Their first year of marriage was more fulfilling than either expected. The expressions of endearment he withheld from his proposal, he was soon showering on her. Lynn grew to fit her role. Her well-scrubbed face created a sensation, and her style of natural elegance was imitated from Biarritz to California. Her poise was heightened, her sense of humor reinforced. G. K. found himself in love.

The birth of their son was the culmination. It seemed ridiculous to call a newborn infant Gerald Junior. They agreed on the nickname, Jer. Who could imagine that in the second year it would all shatter? They were not perturbed when another pregnancy failed to materialize. But routine gynecological examination turned up a medical problem that prevented further conception.

Lynn was distraught. "I want you to divorce me."

"Don't be ridiculous. You don't fire a wife the way you do a secretary."

This was the moment the AEI chose to break. He left things up in the air with Lynn and flew to Washington. The insurance commissioner of the State of New York demanded an audit. He was called before a congressional committee to explain why there had been no announcement regarding discount lending rates. G. K. was not a man who liked to justify himself. The sessions were exhausting, acrimonious, and demeaning.

He recognized that he was a newcomer in the world of finance. He had forced his way by stock manipulation, process payments, consolidating holdings, dummy companies, the buying of defunct corporations for merger and tax purposes. Through this jungle of intertwined interests he had no difficulty threading a path. Where he had miscalculated grievously was in assessing the friendship, acceptance, respect, the proffered glass, the casual joke, the clap on the back. He believed he had paid his dues, that he was one of the elite. But when the ax fell, his head alone was on the block.

He was going to beat the charges. His lawyers assured him of this, and since he had not left it in their hands but plotted his defense with them, he knew for once they were right. But in a way it had beaten him. It did not matter that in the end he would be cleared. In politics it is reputation that counts. And while at the end of the first week it was certain they would not have enough evidence to charge him, his political ambitions were effectively destroyed.

He flew back to the coast, and checked into the Bay Club, turning up at his office because he had nothing else to do. He wasn't up to a confrontation with Lynn. He needed time to think their situation through. He didn't want to give her up. And there was Jer to consider.

Into this maelstrom Miss Naesmith announced that Dr. Bitterbaum, who had been trying to get in touch with Mr. Kellogg, was here.

G. K. waved impatiently at the intercom, meaning he didn't want to see him.

"Shall I set up an appointment?" Miss Naesmith asked.

"No," he said, capitulating, "send him in." In the interval before he entered he tried to recall exactly who the man was. He seemed to remember from an earlier message that he was connected in some way with Caltech. They probably wanted him to resign his position on the board. The door opened and Miss Naesmith ushered in the man who was to influence the future course of his life.

Miss Naesmith, stepping slightly out of character, allowed herself to feel for this gauche young man who didn't know how to tie his tie properly, or keep it from flopping.

Bitterbaum did not see himself as presenting an odd, somewhat rumpled appearance. He was a man with a mission. He enjoyed the drama of walls of glass with the movement of a city acting as mobile wallpaper. Instead of grass-cloth or wood paneling, moving vehicles were the decor, and people hurrying by, attending to their lives. The room itself was divided by a bookcase which held sets of morocco leather chosen for color coordinates. There were massive plants with deep inset lighting at their base. The chrome bar was austere and unobtrusive, although, he was confident, stocked with the best labels.

The human being occupying this showcase was somewhat dwarfed behind a kidney-shaped, hand-doweled desk. His face was not as massive as when framed by a twenty-three-inch television screen. But there was something leonine about the man, some quick and catlike quality residing in the heavy build.

Miss Naesmith withdrew and the man looked up. "You wanted to see me, Dr. Bitterbaum?"

The directive was plain, declare yourself and your business.

"Mr. Kellogg, I believe I have a proposition that might interest you." With that he launched into an incomprehensible diatribe on eugenics.

There was an expectant silence. Kellogg attempted to reconstruct the last sentence which apparently required an answer. The young doctor had said, "As a trustee, possibly you've attended Dr. Demsdale's lecture series on developmental biology?" "Demsdale?" Kellogg floundered momentarily. Then something clicked. "Didn't the NSF just cancel out a million-dollar grant from under him?"

"That's right. It was too bad. He's doing important work in genetics. I only mention it by way of background. It's necessary to fill you in a bit, so you're in a position to evaluate what I'm going to tell you."

G. K. had been looking for an excuse to terminate the interview. But suddenly he focused a laser-beam attention. What Bitterbaum was saying, once you stripped away the scientific terminology, was incredible. "You mean to tell me that you can reproduce a carbon copy of an individual from a single cell?"

"You are hearing me, Mr. Kellogg. Cloning assures the exact genotype. As though you Xeroxed the original."

His initial instinct had been right. Dr. Thor Bitterbaum was some kind of nut. He recalled him now. The usual preliminary check at the time of his first phone call disclosed that he graduated Caltech top of his class seven years before. Which in no way precluded

—and perhaps enhanced—the possibility that he was presently raving.

Bitterbaum pressed on. "At the time there was a good deal of publicity on cracking the riddle of DNA. Perhaps you saw some of it. Watson and Crick got the Nobel Prize. They phoned Linus Pauling and said, 'Forget it.' He'd also been working on the assumption that deoxyribonucleic acid held the genetic blueprint. The proof was comparable to splitting the atom."

"The fallout may be more disastrous," Kellogg said severely. "I mean, it's inhuman to produce a replica of a man."

"If human beings do it, it is not inhuman. It is an intrusion into other worlds, I admit that. But it seems to me you go ahead or you stagnate."

"Nothing has prepared man for such a role, absolutely nothing. He would be playing God, quite literally."

Bitterbaum nodded his touseled red head as though he agreed with him. But what he said was in disagreement. He was, Kellogg felt, a complex and difficult person. "I feel justified in going ahead. For one thing, the genetic load is increasing all the time along with increased mutation. Every individual now carries between five and ten deleterious genes to be transmitted by the present lottery method of natural selection."

Why was he listening to this? Why was he even discussing it? Kellogg pierced him with a dissecting gaze. "Tell me, Dr. Bitterbaum, do you believe in God?"

"Frankly, until recently, I didn't. Now I'm not so sure."

Kellogg rocked back in his swivel chair. "So you

want to clone someone? And you came to me. As an egocentric millionaire stereotype you figured I'd finance the possibility of my own perpetual life?"

"Not exactly." There was a pause. Bitterbaum couldn't get it out. The project had become so much a part of him that he hesitated to submit it to the judgment of another. He wasn't afraid of disbelief, he wasn't afraid of objections. But what if the man laughed? Laughed him out of the office and spread the story at his club over brandy? "Before I proceed, I must ask for your solemn oath not to reveal anything of what I will tell you."

G. K. nodded impatiently. He distrusted histrionics and he distrusted Jews.

"I was present at the death of the late President."

G. K. continued to nod. But suddenly he saw where this was leading. The whole elaborate prelude, amounting to a lecture on the current state of biology, and now this assertion. Alert and probing, he jumped to a wild conclusion. "You can't possibly mean—?"

"I have preserved living cells from which a biological duplicate can be replicated."

There was another emotion conjoined to amazement, a thumping excitement. "You're crazy, you know that, Bitterbaum? The President of the United States! I mean, you go from the African clawed toad to the President. There's nothing chintzy about you, Bitterbaum. I'll say this, when you go, you go all the way. You were right there? In the room? Jesus." He lapsed into silence but it was only to wind up again. "All right, we know enough, but are we wise enough to handle it? These are two quite different questions. Stop and think what you're proposing. The structure of society would be overturned. You'd have women hiring out as mercenaries, *rent a womb.* The family would completely disintegrate. I am an advocate of family. It's the one institution that gives security, the only place where one is accepted not for what he accomplishes, but simply because he is."

"I don't think it's fair to assume that a single experiment would destroy the family."

"The implications are inescapable. And what about the—the—what do you call him, the one who's cloned?"

"Well, clone means group. So I don't know if it's proper, but I use the word *clonee.*"

"Okay. Clonee. What about this clonee? I mean when he discovers he's someone's duplicate? Christ, that's the identity crisis of all time."

"Especially considering who he is."

Kellogg stared at him. "Good God," he said, then rallied to make his point. "After all, man isn't just a bundle of genes. He's a social animal, right? The product of his culture. This clonee wouldn't really *be* the same person. His background, his environment would be different. It seems to me that makes him someone else."

Bitterbaum nodded encouragement as one leads a backward child. "I've thought that out."

"Well, I'd be delighted to hear just how you propose getting around it."

"I've been doing extensive reading in clinical psychology. Both Skinner behavioral psychologists and the Rogerian ego psychologists, although they have different theoretical orientations, are generally agreed that it is the emotional and psychological experience that develops an individual. The externals that call forth the reactions are not in themselves crucial. Our clonee will love different people than his counterpart did. That's not important. The important thing is that he loves."

G. K. rapped his fingers rhythmically against the desk top. The game aspect was appealing. "The idea would be to provide the same type of family life. I can see managing the same sports, schools, curricula, travel even. But you're saying all down the line situations could be rigged to stimulate similar responses?"

"I'm saying it's a hell of an experiment. The experiment of all time. I'm willing to devote my life to finding out."

Kellogg looked at him sharply. "Which brings up another point. What exactly *do* you get out of it?"

Bitterbaum's smile was taut. "Knowledge. Satisfaction." He rocked back in his chair and the green flecks were at variance with his blue eyes. "But I must admit at the time I simply didn't want to let him go. I couldn't reconcile myself to it. I felt we needed him to steer us through the madness of nuclear threats and financial debacle. I still feel that. I think we may save humanity from extinction with him back at the helm."

"Jesus," G. K. said again. There was a long pause. "I tell you what, Bitterbaum, go away someplace. My brain's steaming. I can't absorb any more. I may call you in a day or two. I may never call you. Just go away. I've got to think."

G. K. approached a problem by tackling it head-on. If he became the financial backer he would insist on the central role, stipulating that he himself provide the atmosphere and conditioning for the clonee. The original had been raised in a liberal tradition. He could manage that. From childhood the original had been groomed for political office. That would be a continual challenge. He would have to bone up on everything from Keynesian economics to the working of the judiciary. The original had been invested with a sound moral and religious training. G. K. had no pretensions here, but Lynn could handle this aspect nicely.

The prospect intrigued him, yet he saw it must be viewed in a perspective that included his entire life. He was still living at his club. His wife didn't know he was in the state. He had simply deferred the hassle with Lynn. He had come to the conclusion that he didn't want to jettison her. He would rather jettison the plan.

And here was a replacement, a plan a thousand times more ambitious than the one he was forced to abandon. His decision was made. He phoned for a cab and pointed it toward Malibu.

Lynn was on the front lawn, a seascape behind her, the baby in a playpen, and petit point in her lap. She looked up.

"I'm home," he said, pretending not to see the weeks of tension in her face.

She submitted to his hug. "How did things work out in Washington?"

"What I predicted. It's all going to blow over. How have you been getting on here?"

"Fine. Just fine."

"How's Jer?"

"As you see."

He picked up the sturdy little fellow and swung him over his head. Jer chortled his delight. Lynn thought as she had many times in the past that her husband instinctively did the right thing.

He turned to her with a smile. "You know, Lynn, a large part of all this was sitting in a hotel room. A small part was outfacing the committee and strategy session with Hines and Alcott. Mostly it was reading the daily paper, looking up the Commodities Index, and thinking. God, a hotel room is a sterile place. I remembered how many there'd been before you. You know," he slipped an arm around her, "it's no big deal, this thing about not having more children. We've got a damn good start with number-one son here. We'll have our dynasty. We'll adopt the others."

Lynn's usual steadiness was shredded by this capitulation. She knew him well, and she had never known him to give up on a course of action. That he should do so now, with one that meant so much to him, affected her deeply. "I don't know," she regarded him with a searching look that made him feel she was looking with her mind rather than her eyes, or that the eyes were a mere intermediary. "I don't know if I should let you do this. Your own family, it's a different thing."

"I don't think so. We dreamed of a large family. We'll have it. You'd take the others under your wing?"

"Of course. I'd love them. You know I'd love them. But are you sure you'd feel good about it? Are you sure you want it this way, Gerald?"

"I want it this way," he said locking himself into Bitterbaum's game. And he did feel good about it. It had already brought him a dividend. His marriage was salvaged.

Lynn, for her part, seemed touched by his commitment. G. K. was aware he had racked up points. He suspected before he was done with this business he would need them.

Bitterbaum was not surprised that G. K. Kellogg was on the phone to him. The time element did surprise him. The man moved fast. He made decisions fast. They would get along.

They met for lunch, served in Kellogg's office, and worked out their approach to Demsdale. Kellogg agreed that he should be told as little as possible, and what he was told calculated to throw him off. Together they concocted a story that met the specifications.

Bitterbaum paved the way with a preliminary meeting. His purpose, he assured Dr. Demsdale, was to evaluate the present state of the work now going forward in eugenics, and furnish a report to Mr. Kellogg. Kellogg was interested in a million-dollar tax shelter. Because of his connection with the institute, he was thinking in terms of a grant or endowment. And the work Demsdale was doing had come to his attention.

Demsdale's extraordinarily fair complexion approached normal in a flush of excitement. The epidermis was so thin the course of each vein could be followed. "I've had difficulty with funding in the past. And I am the first to admit that we don't know just where developmental biology will take us. But man's always been in that position with respect to science."

"Mr. Kellogg is especially interested in the cloning process."

Dr. Demsdale's countenance regained its original drained look. The veins bunched at the indented temples and pulsed. "We've had a lot of hysteria to contend with, a lot of pressure to discontinue."

"Mr. Kellogg is anxious to see the work furthered," Bitterbaum assured him.

"The knowledge is here. The techniques are here. I don't think we can turn our backs on it. But we need guidelines, ethical, moral, and legal. They should be international. And hopefully, not of a repressive nature."

"I wonder," Bitterbaum said, "if there had been a set of rules, would the Los Alamos project have gotten off the ground?"

"There might not have been twenty years of cold war if agreements for simultaneous development and restraints had been worked out. And we would have avoided the pitiable self-recriminations of Oppenheimer. Or statements such as Einstein's, 'If I had it to do over again I'd be a plumber.' "

Bitterbaum nodded his red beard. "With a grant of this size we should be able to call on the boys in philosophy. I'm sure we could interest some very eminent people."

A certain wariness crept into Demsdale's expression. "What exactly is Mr. Kellogg's interest in cloning?"

This was the moment. "Naturally, being a layman he hasn't the objectivity that you or I have."

"Don't tell me he wants a clone of himself? No, I couldn't go along with that. Absolutely not."

"You are jumping to conclusions, doctor. Mr. Kellogg is not such an egotist." Now came the statement he had rehearsed. "He is a man who has suffered a personal loss, a bereavement. It happens that I was present at the end, and I was persuaded to collect some cellular matter, which I preserved in liquid nitrogen."

"You mean things have proceeded this far?"

"They have."

The tallow face seemed lit from within. The eyes burned like tapers.

I've got him, Bitterbaum exulted.

There were details to work out. "Because of the climate of public feeling, the project . . ."

Bitterbaum hardly listened. *He's going to do it. He's going to do it!*

". . . if I undertook the work, I would expect one day to be able to publish."

"That could be worked out," he heard himself saying.

Demsdale began writing on a piece of scratch paper. "The terms of the agreement then would be that Mr. G. K. Kellogg pay one million dollars in grant money to be administered by me. In return I will attempt a cloning operation by cell fusion from the donor material which you will give me." He paused and looked up. "I assume that Mr. Kellogg is aware, as I'm sure you are, that this experiment has not been done to date with human ova. The chance of success is, I should imagine, about one in four that actual growth and maturation of a viable human fetus will take place. Therefore the grant monies should in no way be tied to the ultimate success of the project. Is that agreeable?"

"That is agreeable, and will be stipulated in the letter of intent Mr. Kellogg will have drawn."

They shook hands on it.

A simple, straightforward account of the conversation with Demsdale was not sufficient. G.K. insisted on details. Eventually he pronounced himself delighted. But Bitterbaum was morose. It had gone too well. It was his experience that when things proceed with too much precision one should prepare for the unexpected jolt of misfortune. "Demsdale's ready. You're ready. Okay. One small item may hold us up. The mother. We need to locate a mother."

"Any ideas?" Kellogg asked.

Bitterbaum hesitated. "You employ a large staff. I thought perhaps . . ." He stopped.

G.K. did not deign to reply.

"Well, then, we might run an ad in the personal column."

G.K. was impatient of all this. "The source, Bitterbaum, the pool of young women to be tapped, is your female patients."

Bitterbaum bridled. "Is that a joke or are you in earnest?"

"I never joke when it's a matter of business."

Bitterbaum continued to look offended. Finally he said, "I don't even have a practice of my own. At the moment I am simply covering for other men."

"I understand that. It's an ideal position to be in. All I'm suggesting is that you keep your eyes open. After all, we can't proceed until we have the woman."

Bitterbaum nodded gloomy concurrence.

In the course of the next few weeks he persuaded himself that he had disregarded G.K.'s advice. But every once in a while, looking down a throat or palpating a spleen, the unbidden thought, *this one?*, would occur to him. In each instance he repressed it almost before he himself had made the conscious connection.

But Thursday afternoon, toward the end of the day, Miss Millicent Ash walked into his consulting room. She wanted a shot for poison oak. While he questioned her for possible allergic reactions he looked over the questionnaire she had filled out. She was a new patient, referred to Dr. Clemens by her office supervisor. She was twenty-four, unmarried.

Further questions elicited the information that she was from Evanston, Illinois, that she was quite alone and unacquainted. It was too good a bet to pass up. After administering the shot, as he turned to throw away the disposable plunger, Bitterbaum asked if she cared to have dinner. "Oddly enough, I'm from out of town myself. I'm not Dr. Clemens, I'm Dr. Bitterbaum. Thor Bitterbaum. I'm simply covering this practice while the doctor is on vacation."

Miss Ash told him that no one called her Millicent, that she was Millie to her friends, and that she would love to have dinner with him.

He chose an atmosphere that he hoped would connote solid values, nothing exotic. Japanese, Armenian, and French cuisine were ruled out. He selected an elegant but subdued setting with the same care that he took in ordering a half-bottle of rosé. A single cocktail proclaimed him neither a tightwad nor a swinger.

A steak dinner put Millie in a mellow mood, and she confessed that an unhappy love affair had been the impetus for her coming to Los Angeles. A new city, a fresh start.

Bitterbaum studied her. She was an attractive young woman, slightly bovine for his taste, with thick ankles. The finishing touches in a woman were important to Bitterbaum. He appreciated neat wrists and ankles, small hands and feet. However, her features were pleasant, her coloring fresh, and given an opportunity she could compete in the marriage market.

Having passed on her qualifications, he fabricated

an account of a South Pacific cruise. The passengers, he managed to hint, were mostly eligible males.

Millie said sadly that on her salary such adventures were only for hearing. But even vicariously, they were fascinating. Could she touch him, a person who had really done the things she dreamed of?

God, Bitterbaum told himself, I have an unsuspected talent: con man.

So far he rather enjoyed the ploy. But he was convinced that when he got to the crunch she would stalk out. To forestall public humiliation he suggested a spin in the hills above the Hollywood Bowl.

She exclaimed at all the right things, the lights of the city, the balmy evening. Bitterbaum began to zero in on target. He cast himself as sympathetic friend and family doctor. It was more like television.

He began to lay groundwork. He became quiet, abstracted.

"Anything wrong?" she said when his silence had grown uncomfortably prolonged.

I thought you'd never ask, baby. "No, not really."

She took him at his word and began chatting about a vacation in Yellowstone. He missed the connecting link, or perhaps there wasn't one, that led her into recounting the plot of every motion picture she had seen that year.

He was forced to reopen the subject. "Actually, before, when you asked if anything was wrong? Well, there *is* something that has been weighing on me. It concerns patients of mine who are also close friends."

"You've got to learn not to take your cases home with you, doctor. You should leave them locked in their filing cabinets."

"You're right, of course. But this is a very old friend. I was at their wedding," he elaborated, inspiration striking from he knew not where. "She's a good person, a homebody type. The problem is, she has a heart condition, congenital. They can never have children."

"That's not much of a problem. They can always adopt."

"No, that's not possible. They're of different faiths."

"Couldn't one of them convert?"

"It wouldn't work. They're each devout. You know, in their own way."

"Too bad," she smiled at him. "I don't know why we're talking about them."

"Actually I have a reason for bringing it up."

"What reason?"

"Well, it's difficult to explain. The wife, with the heart condition, wants desperately to bring up a child of her husband's."

She took out her compact and went over her lipstick. "Does he have a child?"

"No. No, you don't understand. Let's start again." He took a deep breath. "She adores him. Okay?"

"Okay."

"And she wants to have his child, but she can't."

"On account of the heart condition."

"Beautiful. Millie, you read me. But it's a real love affair. You have to keep that in mind." He was embarked on it now and his words had downhill acceleration and momentum. "He, the husband, will do anything to make her happy. So he came to me and asked me to locate a young woman who would be willing through artificial insemination to bear his baby. The couple want to contribute five thousand dollars to the woman who would do this. Tax free."

They were parked above the *H* in the hills that read HOLLYWOOD. Millie stared at him. "Is this for real?" she asked.

He started to trip over words in an effort to assure her.

"I can see it is. And you thought I might be the young woman. Why? What is there about me that gave you the idea that I—"

"Nothing, really—"

"But there must have been something. I mean you picked me to discuss it with."

"You're on your own, that's all, a free agent. If you wanted to, well, there are no external impediments. No family, no boy friend. And from my point of view, you're healthy and intelligent. I thought you might do something cool with the money, that it might take you out of a rut, open things up for you."

She leaned against the car door to take him in. "You really thought I might do it."

"Well—"

She could see he was going to apologize. "You know something? I might. I just might. Artificial insemination? That means I'd never have to see him, no contact, I'd just come to the office?"

"To the laboratory. But you're right, there's no contact with the donor at all."

"Fantastic."

"The monetary arrangements are five hundred dollars at the time of the procedure. Two thousand paid on positive pregnancy confirmation, which is when you sign legal papers giving up the child for adoption.

The balance is paid upon delivery. During pregnancy, running expenses, food, rent, etcetera, are taken care of."

"They really want this baby. Or else they're rolling."

"The couple is of moderate means," he said hastily. "This represents their savings."

"Have you asked anyone else?"

"No."

"I was just wondering what the normal reaction should be. I suppose I ought to get uptight and tell you to take me home. But I think I may do it." She seemed to be thinking over what she had said. "I'd be a little scared, going through it by myself."

"I'd be your doctor. I'd see you through it."

"Five thousand dollars," she whispered, staring at the night-shrouded shapes of boulder and trees, not seeing them. "I'd never get that kind of money together. No way."

She's considering it, Bitterbaum thought in sudden panic

"I mean, I could work all my life and never pull ahead. We were talking at dinner—" She stopped, looked directly at him. "Oh, I see. The island cruise. Of course. You were softening me up. Well, I've news for you, doctor, you've succeeded. I accept."

Bitterbaum's Adam's apple got in the way. He swallowed, it bobbed, no words got past.

"That *is* what you want, doctor?"

"Yes. Yes of course. Call the office in the morning for an appointment." Behind this routine sentence was an insidious Jewish despair. Phrased quite simply, it said: "What have you done, Bitterbaum?"

That evening Bitterbaum made two calls. They were short, businesslike, and since the pertinent things could not be said, the silences were electric.

Dr. Demsdale stressed the importance of a thorough work-up. "Take a careful history, Bitterbaum. And I want a complete physical. We're not going to take the chance of anything stupid tripping us up."

Behind such prosaic words they were zinging on a different level. Butterflies, shake the formaldehyde from your wings and fly! Man has beaten death!

Bitterbaum would do the procedure and Demsdale drill him in it. Biologically the dead President would live. Without memory of himself, it is true. But at some later stage conceivably this could be supplied and a continuum achieved. Real and actual immortality.

It would start tomorrow with a twenty-four-year-old girl, Millicent Ash, of whom in the normal course of events no one would ever hear. Her womb would nourish the first child of the race, the first cloned human introduced asexually with sterile technique into an enucleated egg.

Not since man descended from the trees had evolution heaved in such a throe.

Steady on, Bitterbaum told himself.

Perhaps only to a medical man could excitement

and suspense be generated by the taking of a sugar tolerance test. Prediabetes would contraindicate pregnancy. Bitterbaum sweated it out until the lab report was back. Negative.

He made his two phone calls and embarked on the next phase, the medical history. No problems were encountered. It was time to explain to Millie the importance of the temperature chart in determining her natural menstrual cycle. During the course of the month ovulation timing was regulated and superovulation produced by a dosage of 50 mg clomiphene citrate plus 5 mg prednisone per diem, which Bitterbaum gave for six days prior to the expected time of ovulation.

"Why superovulation?" she wanted to know. "What does that mean?"

He answered her questions conscientiously. "We want more than one egg. Remember we're working microscopically, an ovum could easily be damaged or lost. We don't want to perform the laparotomy a second time."

"Laparotomy? What's that?"

"Nothing to be alarmed about. It's simpler to work through a small incision in the abdominal cavity that allows for the insertion of the laparoscope, the instrument that locates and illumines the ovaries and fallopian tubes."

"But that's cutting. That's an operation. You didn't say an operation."

"It is the procedure of choice, the one with minimum trauma to the patient. We can do it under a local if you wish."

She was upset at this. "I don't know whether I wish

or don't wish. You're the doctor. You do what's best."

He changed his approach. Instead of explanations which made her nervous, he wrote prescriptions and issued orders. Millie relaxed. The night before the laparotomy he administered an injection of chorionic gonadotropin, gave Millie tranquilizers and a sleeping pill, and ensconced himself on the couch in the living room of the apartment. The place had done a great deal to allay her fears. She considered it the height of luxury. A bedroom, bath, kitchen, color TV, and private patio. Yesterday he wrote a check for five hundred dollars and she quit her job.

In the morning she was indignant over not being allowed breakfast. Bitterbaum administered more tranquilizers and escorted a subdued Millicent to Demsdale's lab. The scrubbed professional look of the room and the medicinal smell seemed to reassure her.

Demsdale himself was austere and forbidding, the qualities that most inspire confidence in a patient. He had her sign a standard release form, then asked her to undress behind a screen where she found a hospital gown laid out.

Bitterbaum had been meticulously coached and Demsdale was assisting; still, he felt unaccountably nervous. "The somatic donor cells are thawed?" he asked.

"I initiated the process twenty-four hours ago, so it would be as gradual as possible."

Bitterbaum nodded and began to scrub. Demsdale also scrubbed. Millie reappeared in the hospital gown looking scared to death. "Up on the table with you, Millie. We're going to make you drowsy. Don't fight it, that's a girl." When she was under Demsdale draped her.

Bitterbaum, working quickly, cut into the painted abdomen. Using remote-controlled scalpels and manipulators passed through the laparscope, he recovered five oocytes from the ovarian follicles. Demsdale grunted. Their timing was perfect. They had intercepted the eggs before their descent into the fallopian tubes.

Bitterbaum placed them in a sterile petri dish. The nucleus of each ovum was subjected to ultraviolet radiation, destroying the haploid set of chromosomes.

"Well," Demsdale said, "we have successfully removed Millicent Ash from the biological phase of the experiment. Her genetic contribution has been eradicated." At this point the biologist took charge. Treating the somatic cells from the donor's trachea, he prepared to fuse them with the enucleated eggs. The fusing agent was a culture of Sendai virus in allantoic fluid, prepared the previous day, maintained overnight at 4°C, centrifuged at 400g and again at 30,000g. The deposit was suspended in glucose-free Hanks' solution and irradiated to inactivate the virus. This step was essential, for as Demsdale observed, "We don't want to expose the clonee to the flu."

Although killed, the Sendai virus still retained the remarkable capacity discovered by Okada for softening cell walls and producing fusion. Demsdale bent over the microscope and with extreme care nudged donor cells into contact with the ova. With a fine micropipette he dripped virus suspension onto each pair. The cells seemed to melt into each other with a barely perceptible shudder.

Bitterbaum shuddered too. Genesis had taken place on a petri dish.

Demsdale looked up. "We lost one. Double fusion." He motioned toward the microscope.

Bitterbaum inspected the clutch. He saw the failure in the corner of the field, an egg fused to two somatic cells. But there were four left. He watched transfixed as they began to divide. Each ovum now had a full diploid set of chromosomes, exactly as if it had been fertilized, when in fact no fertilization had taken place or ever would. The genetic constitution of the dividing eggs was not the product of two parents. The total inheritance came from the nucleus of the donor cell, from that bit of matter he had fished from the neck wound weeks before.

Millie was sent home for six days. Although Bitterbaum had previously explained that the procedure was in two phases, she demanded to know why she had to go back.

"The main part is over," he assured her. "Next week it will be fifteen minutes under a local. Nothing to it."

"You mean, after all this I'm not pregnant yet?"

"No, but the chances are good that you will be."

Bitterbaum and Demsdale kept vigil. They locked themselves in the lab, taking turns sleeping on a broken-backed couch. Demsdale perked endless cups of coffee, and when they remembered, they sent out for food. The four dividing cells were maintained in an oxygenator in synthetic amniotic fluid under a CO_2 atmosphere at 38°C. On the second day mitosis broke down in one conceptus.

After extensive microscopic study, Demsdale said

finally, "Incompatibility. The donor nucleus was undoubtedly in prolonged interphase dissynchronous with the cleavage cycle of the egg."

Bitterbaum nodded anxiously. "The other three seem healthy."

"I'm not so sure," Demsdale said.

Bitterbaum bent over the microscope and observed what he considered typical mitosis. But Demsdale's intuition proved correct. During the next fifteen hours two of the three remaining ova had to be discarded as incapable of survival due to gross genetic damage, probably inflicted by the procedure.

They watched their single functioning blastocyte with increasing concern. Mitosis continued at the expected rate, and on the sixth day Demsdale pronounced it normal.

"Normal." Bitterbaum uttered the word with wonder and reverence.

"As nearly as can be determined, yes. But continue to preserve the original tissue until we know we are successful."

"Are we ready to go ahead with nidation?" Bitterbaum asked.

"Oh yes. Get the donor womb down here."

Donor womb, Bitterbaum thought to himself. Doesn't he remember her name is Millie?

Nidation was relatively simple. Under a light local the cervix was dilated and the blastocyte implanted in the uterine wall. From that moment the egg should attach and the fetus develop in the usual fashion.

Mighty Thor rose up. His gift of life stolen from Trauma Room One had taken hold. This was his triumph. In this moment he did not listen to the doubts, the questions, the fears that beset his counterpart, Bitterbaum.

Millicent Ash was pregnant. G.K., on hearing the news, uncorked a bottle of Piper-Heidseck in his office bar.

Dr. Demsdale could not contain his jubilation. "The first implantation. It's quite remarkable. I was prepared for half a dozen tries. Luck is on our side."

"If all goes well," Bitterbaum agreed. "And it will," he added hastily. "I predict that within the usual gestation period we shall deliver a normal, healthy child."

"That's got to be the understatement of all time." Demsdale's face assumed a good-humored expression that stretched the muscles in rarely used patterns. "We will have produced the world's first cloned human."

The months following seemed to confirm the prediction. Millie Ash's condition was classic textbook, even to her weight. Her spirits, too, were good. Bitterbaum visited her daily, bringing magazines, books, puzzles, travel folders, anything to keep her mildly occupied and pass the time. But the strain on his character of being constantly blithe and imperturbable took a toll. He had to fight a general feeling of irritation. At each visit there was a shift in her plans. Her first thought had been Hawaii and the more remote Pacific, with stops in Tahiti, Moorea, and Bora Bora. "They have these cottages built on a pier over the water with a glass floor. The water is illuminated by floodlights. You lie and peer down all night. Imagine all those bright tropical fish and the scary things, like sharks and manta rays. Imagine seeing it for yourself with a scorpion punch in your hand. Have you ever seen what they put into those drinks? Orchids, actual orchids, and tiny Japanese parasols and fresh pineapple, crushed ice and cherries. You're not listening."

"Of course I am." He assumed an expression of interest. But the worries continued without interruption at a different substratum. Had Demsdale been premature in his pronouncement? Were the fused cells still dividing and adhering in normal fashion? At the time of his direct observation they had been. But that was months ago in a petri dish. What was happening now in the depths of Millie's womb? She was growing large—but with what?

Next visit, a desire for culture motivated her. She ordered art books and histories of Greece as preparation for a cruise in the Aegean. Or perhaps the Mediterranean. She read that Ibiza was an artist colony, a haven for impecunious travelers. By stretching her funds she could live there a year, perhaps take up a craft, pottery or weaving.

No matter what her mood, Bitterbaum went along, helped in the planning of a dozen mythical lives. But besides the stress of his own fears, problems were beginning to surface with Demsdale. He demanded lengthy detailed daily reports on Millie, insisted on frequent examinations, and was anxious to perform an amniocentesis, at which Bitterbaum demurred, as the procedure was still in the experimental stage. It would be reassuring to karyotype fetal cells and rule out chromosomal abnormalities. But needle puncture involved a small but definite risk to the mother and an unknown risk to the child.

Of more concern than their divergent medical approach was Demsdale's growing obsession with the pregnancy. It occupied his entire attention. A graduate student who unhappily exploded the protoplast of a plant cell by failing to add sufficient quantities of osmotically active sugar alcohol was not reprimanded. He did not so much as comment when his secretary neglected to transcribe his lecture notes. He was interested in only one thing: the developing fetus.

Now that it appeared likely there would be a child, thought must be given to its rearing. He reiterated to Bitterbaum that things must be handled in a proper, responsible, scientific manner. A team of experts should be consulted. He himself was keeping a full set of records.

Certain questions also occurred to him. Which member of Mr. Kellogg's family had they duplicated?

To distract him, G.K. paid over the balance of the grant money. Demsdale appointed a committee to handle it. Not for a moment was he diverted from *the work in progress,* as he termed it.

"He's already wondering who the hell this clonee is," G.K. said, "and if he keeps poking about he's going to find out. It wouldn't be hard to trace you to the hospital on the crucial day. Then we've had it."

Bitterbaum agreed. "Millie's got to abort."

"What? Are you mad?"

"I don't mean actually abort. Demsdale's got to think she has. End of experiment. End of his interest. Right?"

"Not bad, Bitterbaum."

Bitterbaum made a wry face. He didn't like being praised for his ability as a confabulator. In fact it worried him that he was so good at it.

They always met in Kellogg's office. Looking down

at the pageantry of the streets Thor girded on his belt of magic, forging the old feeling of omniscience.

Millie was bored, and the prospect of a move delighted her. The new apartment had such features as a water bed and sunken tub. She complained that Bitterbaum ruined the decor by plastering the bath with decals as a safety measure.

George Rudolph Demsdale would be more difficult. To manipulate him elicited every ounce of Bitterbaum's histrionic ability. There was no use putting it off. He rang the lab.

"George, I've got to see you. Right away."

Demsdale asked predictably enough if something had gone wrong.

"I'll be right over." Bitterbaum hung up. By the time he arrived at the institute, Demsdale had worked himself into a state of nervous apprehension. "What took you so long? I've been calling the apartment. The phone must be off the hook. What's going on?"

Bitterbaum assumed the glum expression he had practiced. "She miscarried."

"What?" Demsdale was breathing all over him. He backed away. Demsdale followed, jutting his face into his. "But she was doing so well. I don't understand it. There was no sign of edema or eclampsia, no renal failure, nothing. Absolutely nothing to account for a spontaneous abortion. She must have taken something. You didn't prescribe anything, did you?"

"Of course I didn't."

"I mean something innocuous that taken in overdose could induce labor? Oh my God, this is terrible. Why wasn't I called? Why did no one call me?"

"There was nothing to be done. It was all over by the time I got there." He was rather pleased at the way this was going. Demsdale was supplying enough genuine emotion for them both. He was pacing and sweating heavily. His complexion was so waxen that the drops of sweat made him look as though he were melting.

"Where is the fetus? It's essential to do a P.M., to discover whether or not the fetus was normal."

"I'm afraid we don't have the fetus."

"No? Well, where is it?"

"It happened too fast. She had cramps. Called me. The cramping continued. She got out of bed to go to the bathroom. And—expelled it into the toilet."

Demsdale groaned.

"She flushed it down," Bitterbaum said, giving the final turn of the screw.

"We brought her along four and a half months and she does a thing like that. Can you believe how unfeeling that woman is? Well, there is nothing for it but to start again with a new mother. I insist on that, a new mother."

"I'm afraid we can't start again. I didn't mention it because there seemed no point, but in all my moving about the case containing the liquid nitrogen must have been damaged, a leak developed—"

Demsdale stopped pacing and faced him. "Incompetent!"

"There's no use getting excited. It could happen to anyone."

"No, it couldn't."

Bitterbaum shrugged. As a matter of fact, this part of his testimony was the truth. The remaining cellular material had deteriorated, and he had destroyed it. "You've got the grant money," he said by way of consolation. "Under the terms of the agreement, you keep that."

"You are correct there. That is a matter of public record. I also want to go on record as dissociating myself from you, Dr. Bitterbaum."

"Very well. But I don't see that it was my fault."

"She was your responsibility. My end went off without a hitch. It was up to you to watch her. You should have watched her day and night."

In reporting the scene to G.K., Bitterbaum said, "You know, he's right. We should have her watched."

"Why do you say that?"

"I don't know. A hunch. She's been moody. It is possible she may renege on the whole deal, try to keep the baby."

"She can't do that. That's an iron-clad contract she's signed."

"That's why she may run out on us."

"You really think she might try that?"

"Why take the chance?"

G.K. gnawed his pencil. "I'll put someone on it."

"The world is your wallpaper." Bitterbaum didn't bother to conceal a tinge of bitterness as he gazed down at the panorama of a workaday Monday.

The play shifted to G.K. Having gotten Lynn to agree to adoption was one thing. It was something else to break it to her that the child in question was his natural son. It wasn't the type of thing one looks forward to imparting to a wife. He chose his moment carefully, the predinner drink, over a plate of canapés.

Lynn looked provocatively aloof in a slit skirt. She had a habit of perching on the arms and backs of chairs rather than settling into them. He brought her a martini with double olives. It pleased her that he remembered her predilection for olives, and she smiled up at him.

"Regarding the Kellogg master plan that we devised a few months ago—"

"Yes?" And then as it occurred to her what it might be, she hastily set down the drink and took his hands. "You've found a baby? Is that it, Gerald? Have you?"

"Yes, I have. Listen Lynn, it wasn't a question of *finding.*" The words themselves, which were, after all, only syntactic orchestrations, produced a vascular constriction. His blood pounded. His chest was tight. He exhibited every evidence of guilt. This is ludicrous, he told himself, but the symptoms persisted.

"I guess I don't understand," Lynn said.

He tried to ignore the pounding in his temples. "There's no reason for me to tell you this, but I want to. The child I plan on adopting is mine. The mother means nothing to me. I hardly know her. It happened when I was in New York on one of those extended trips. Anyway, she doesn't want the child. And I do. So I've made the arrangements."

Lynn could be very quiet behind quiet eyes. Even the living room in her pupils was vacant. "You've been on several extended trips," she said finally.

"It happened last December."

"Then the child won't be born for another three months. Why did you decide to tell me now?"

"Because I don't want to raise him as an adopted child. I want to raise him as our own. You could do that, couldn't you, Lynn? I mean, you could still love it, knowing—"

"That isn't the problem," she said brusquely. "The problem is that these things are always found out."

"There'd be no possible way if you go along, cooperate."

"Haven't I always? That's the agreement."

"Don't be like that, Lynn." He attempted to put his arm around her, but her stiffened body indicated that was the wrong thing to do. "The girl means nothing to me."

"That's supposed to make it better?"

"It happened."

"It happened, yes, all right. You let me think you wanted to go on with me because of me, because of us. And now it seems it's convenient. That's quite a different thing."

"My feelings for you are the same. They're not different. I'm sorry about the girl, but I'm not sorry the way it worked out. Come on, Lynn. How about it?"

She made her decision; it caused a shade too much brightness in her smile. "Okay."

"If it's really okay, you've got to prove it."

"What a nerve," she said and liked him better for it. She actually felt tenderness for him because he was an impossible person that no one but herself would put up with. The more inconsiderate, demanding, and selfish he was, the more he needed her. No one else, including unknown girls who got themselves pregnant by him, would tolerate living with him or be able to feel the genuine affection she did toward him. "You're the one who betrayed our marriage vows," she told him, "philandered with some girl, got her into trouble, and I'm the one that has to prove myself. Honestly, Gerald, you're too much."

He caught her tone of indulgence. "All I meant was, I have to know that you feel the same about me."

"And how do I demonstrate that?"

"Go to Switzerland," he said without hesitation.

"Are you serious?" And instantly knew he was.

"I've taken a villa on Lago Maggiore. And when the time is ripe, you'll travel back with the child."

"What about Jer?"

"He'll be with you, of course. You won't take servants, but engage local people. I'll be with you part of the time. It will be a vacation."

She was watching him closely. "It's important to you that this child be raised as your own?"

"Yes. I can't explain it exactly. But yes, it is important."

"And you think it will work? There's no way it can ever come out?"

He shook his head and pulled her from the arm of the chair to his lap.

As her confinement approached, Millie became morose and noncommunicative. She didn't respond to Bitterbaum's sallies or laugh at his jokes. The magazines he brought were put aside or paged through listlessly. The travel folders had long ago joined the trash. She complained of being a prisoner, so he took her to dinner and the movies. But he was able to distract her only briefly. Physically she was doing well, but the mental depression worried him.

It was almost a relief when she came out with it. "I've changed my mind. You'll have to tell your friends I'm going to keep my baby."

Bitterbaum said as gently as possible, "You can't do that."

"I can. And what's more I'm going to. I know I signed papers. If it comes to a court fight, a judge always awards the child to the mother, the natural mother. And that's me."

"Millie—"

"No, don't say anything. I've made up my mind. It's my baby and I'm going to keep it."

He shook his head. It was amazing to him to observe her function in all aspects as though the child in her womb were hers. Gestation had triggered the hormones and the physical and mental responses followed predictably. Like a hen brooding a duck's egg, no evidence could persuade her that the invader of her womb was a biological stranger. She would go through birth, lactate, her own body completely fooled. But of course all such arguments were denied him. He was reduced to pleading the cause of his hypothetical friends. He dredged up every reason he could think of. He reminded her that they too had waited all these months.

"But they didn't have morning sickness. They didn't swell up like a balloon. They didn't have discomfort."

He abandoned that approach. "We'll discuss it when you're calmer."

"That will be never. I'll never be calm about giving up my baby."

"Millie, you're not in a position to raise a child. You've no money, no job. You'd have to work."

"I'll go home to my parents."

"Would they accept the situation?"

She began to cry. "I'll go on welfare."

"Is that what you want for your baby? When he could have a home, the security of two parents. And remember, he is my friend's son."

"I don't care about your friend. He thinks he can buy anything. Well, he can't buy my child."

"Don't upset yourself, Millie, please."

She sat hunched over her belly, glaring at him.

That evening the agency man phoned G.K. The subject was gone. She put a few things in an overnight bag and checked into a motel in the beach area.

"Keep on it," G.K. told him. "But low profile."

Bitterbaum was beside himself. "What do we do now? Should we offer her more money? Perhaps double it?"

G.K. pursed his lips. "That would be extremely poor business practice."

"She wouldn't go for it anyway." Bitterbaum slouched deeper into the hollow of the leather chair.

"I'd like to see the file you kept on her," G.K. said.

They met again the next afternoon when the documents had been sent for and perused. G.K. scowled at Bitterbaum across the printed form. "I am not interested in her mumps, her tonsillectomy, or her poison oak. You call this a file? I'm tempted to show you the one I've compiled on you, Bitterbaum. Now that is a file."

"So is this, a medical file. I don't know what you expected."

G.K. curbed the retort he had in mind and said instead, "In order to deal with Millie Ash, we have to know her. You've spent the better part of the last nine months in her company. Tell me about her."

"But there's nothing to tell. She is the most ordinary person I know, and if I had a choice I wouldn't know her."

"Come, Bitterbaum, don't be childish. I don't want your opinion. I want facts, details. She was born in Evanston, Illinois. Did she finish high school? Which high school? Did she go to business college? What jobs has she held? I want to know everything, hobbies, friends. Did she ever room with another girl? Who? Did she have a boy friend? Who is he?"

"I don't know."

"Of course you know, Bitterbaum. She must have

mentioned her family. Is her father employed? Where? Are there sisters, brothers?"

"I tell you I don't know."

"You've seen her every day. You talked about something."

"We talked about the marvelous, exotic places I've been, Tahiti, Ibiza, Zermatt." The sarcasm wore thin. "I swear to you I know absolutely nothing about her other than that she has gained twenty-four pounds and that her blood pressure is one hundred thirty over —"

"Why did she come to Los Angeles?" G.K. shot out the question and Bitterbaum replied in the same rapid-fire manner.

"She had a fight with her boy friend." He stopped, amazed at what he had said and known.

G.K. smiled at him.

"It was something she mentioned once in passing. Is it important?"

"I'd say so," G.K. replied mildly.

"But I don't even know his name."

"He exists," G.K. said. "That's all we need to know."

Bitterbaum hesitated. He had something to add and no matter how he phrased it, it was going to sound melodramatic. "I don't know how you operate, Mr. Kellogg. I wouldn't want to get into anything heavy. I mean, no rough stuff. Do you agree?"

G.K. took a moment to decide if he was in earnest. Then he laughed. He took out a handkerchief finally and wiped his eyes. "I'm not Mafia, Dr. Bitterbaum, I'm not Syndicate. I'm a lone entrepreneur on whom a hatchet job was done. I figure this to put me back in the running. Long range, of course. That's the way I plan, long range."

Ten days later Bitterbaum received a call. "It's me, Millie. Before you say anything, I want to apologize for splitting the way I did. I had to think things through, you know? And of course you were right. I can't possibly take care of a baby. I mean it's not possible."

"Of course. I'll meet you back at the apartment. Take a cab."

"Okay." Her voice was small and contrite. "I want to thank you for being so understanding and all." Subtly the intonation changed, or perhaps it was distorted electronically. It seemed to grow in confidence and assertiveness. "There's one thing that's important to me. After the baby, how long till I get my figure back?"

Bitterbaum smiled into the holes of his office phone.

"You see," she explained, "I'll be going back to Evanston."

No, he didn't see, not exactly, not the details. But it was plain G.K. had followed through.

Millicent Ash gave birth to a six-weeks' premature male child, and Mrs. Gerald Kirsten Kellogg returned from Switzerland that October with her two sons, Gerald, Jr., and Joshua Francis.

Uncle Thor strolled out on the porch. The immense lawn had been turned into a playing field. A game of touch football was in progress. The girls were included, even a couple of neighbor kids. He took no notice of the chaparral whose muted colors folded with subtle shadings into the shadow of the hills. He barely recorded the sight of an ocean bursting on him. The white-water view across the highway underpass to a private beach where sailboats bobbed was of no interest to him.

He was preoccupied, searching his mind for the right approach, the right words. He had come to the Latigo estate this weekend to confront G.K. and battle for Josh.

Thor Bitterbaum had never married. He admitted to himself years ago that Josh was the only person he loved or could love. He knew the tug looking at the newly delivered child, felt it as he drew mucus from his lungs and watched the first breath. His love was compounded of a strange mixture; seeing the well-known, well-publicized traits appear, he felt both awe and dread. From the time the boy's teeth came in he was in heavy orthodontic hardware. But the silver smile, while effectively altering a startling resemblance, failed to obscure the charm. He was a tousle-headed gangling thirteen, his shyness at variance with something purposeful in his nature. To Bitterbaum it seemed there were already glimpses of the man he would be.

G.K. had done a good job. The setting was perfect. So perfect that he sometimes wondered that no one guessed it was contrived. Perhaps it was natural he feel that, since he had helped devise it. Siblings had been added at the proper intervals. He himself had selected them according to age, sex, and as nearly as possible, heredity. They were a good-looking, robust, healthy bunch. Except for Ellen, the older girl, who spent most of her time in a nursing home, joining the family on holidays. The emotional imprinting simulated in all essential respects the former life of the clonee. Their success by now was a source of dread to him.

He had come to beg for an end to the charade. That was a well-adjusted boy charging and blocking with an all-or-nothing spirit. They should thank God, he and G.K., and forget the rest.

Over the years of their association, G.K. gained a prestige unknown to more than a handful of men in a given generation. Bitterbaum failed to distinguish himself. In an age of specialization, he never bothered to specialize. He was nominally the Kellogg family physician, but in illness or accident G.K. invariably overruled his authority and called in a battery of high-powered consultants. On the other hand, G.K. was scrupulous when any matter concerning Josh was in question. He listened to Bitterbaum's advice and most times followed it.

Not recently. Recently the point at issue was the

relationship between Josh and Jer. At first, G.K. congratulated himself on the chance that had given him a son the right age to take the role of the older brother who figured so prominently in the life of the President. Jer was to be a model for the younger boy and provide a constant challenge.

That was the script. But it didn't work that way. It was Josh who set the pace, carrying out his father's expectations with flair and style. He bent his mind and body to accumulating trophies, to coming in first. A runner-up, G.K. dinned into them, was a loser.

The sisters emulated Josh in everything. G.K. fumed. Jer was his son. He wanted him to have the qualities he was forced to admit he lacked. The boy was too much like his mother. The quiet, self-effacing attitude that was so becoming in Lynn was not what was required here. Finally he spoke to Bitterbaum about a scheme to bring in another boy to fill the bill. He was met with a conspicuous lack of cooperation.

In the two-week interim Bitterbaum's resolve against the plan hardened. The changing factor in his thinking was Josh himself. He could no longer expose him to a fabricated life.

He had come to demand cessation, an end. He considered Lynn as a possible ally. After Josh, the most important person in his life was Lynn Kellogg. The bond between them was the boy. In a curious way they shared him. While she and G.K. pulled together as they had from the first, it was to him she came if she had any concern for Josh.

Lynn ran a tight ship. She saw to the children's religious instruction, and while she did not insist on daily mass, she made it a practice to stop in every day with them at Our Lady of Malibu. And the activities she marshaled for the holidays were almost more than Bitterbaum could take in. Tennis lessons and matches were regularly scheduled, and a ladder had been printed on which he discovered his name near the bottom. Sailing, of course, played a large part in the summer fun. They launched sailfins through the surf, but the large boat was berthed at the cove. This was used for family outings and picnics.

The devil of it was, it was all working. That's why it would be difficult to convince G.K. If they were failing, that would be one thing. But they were succeeding. He dismissed the idea of appealing to Lynn.

Mentally he made sacrifice to Thor. Or perhaps it was Thor he sacrificed. He had stretched his life on runic stones. Practicing his profession, utilizing his skill, moving through the years, he was pinioned by concern for what he had done. Josh was deceptively tan and fit-looking. The exercise, determination, competitive spirit kept him from being frail. But he took everything hard, from colds to the usual childhood illnesses. Last year a bout with scarlet fever left him alarmingly weak. It was a fight to regain a plateau of health. He wondered if G.K. didn't push him too hard.

The youngsters caught sight of him. They shifted their game to include him. Outsiders were always puzzled by Bitterbaum's easy access to the Kelloggs. G.K. explained him as an old friend of the family. To the children Uncle Thor was a fixture and loyal supporter. The howling mob descended. Jer threw him the ball, Vicki intercepted. Bitterbaum ran forward and was immediately engulfed in a tangle of arms and legs. It was more than a game, it was an atmosphere he entered. Josh was in the thick of it, playing with his usual intensity. While the game was in progress nothing else existed.

"How are you, Josh?" he asked at the end of practice when he had recovered his breath. He had to bite his tongue to keep from asking specifically about his back. So far nothing abnormal had shown up, but it would. That was the hellish part of it, having to anticipate so much that the boy could not escape. It bolstered his determination to spare him if he could, years more of masquerade and ultimate unmasking. He didn't want that hour for Josh when the clock struck midnight and the harlequins revealed themselves.

He watched the swirl of children. Josh's particular pal this summer was Lefty, Leticia Compton, whose father owned several acres adjoining the Kellogg ranch. Displaying the independence of an only child, she showed up daily on her Indian pony, Dancer. Lefty's teeth also were in braces. Perhaps that was initially what sparked the friendship between her and Josh.

She resisted summer school by ignoring the biology assignment until the last minute, which, as she explained to Josh, was now. Josh offered to help her collect specimens and Bitterbaum watched them walk along the trail past the cleared section to the stables.

He turned back to the house, and inquiring of one of the servants, found G.K. in his bedroom suite. He had bet on Kellogg at a moment when his career was in doubt. G.K. had not only succeeded in rebuilding his professional credibility, his sphere of influence was increasingly impressive, his control in financial and political circles a modern phenomenon. This was the man Bitterbaum hoped to deflect.

He was supervising the packing of his grip in preparation for a ten thirty flight to Hamburg. Bitterbaum observed his color was high. He wondered if he had been watching his cholesterol intake.

G.K. looked up. He had just won a battle with Holt over the inclusion of a bathrobe that Holt felt should be retired. This victory put him in a good frame of mind.

"I've located the boy," G.K. said without preface.

Bitterbaum frowned. He had allowed the play to be taken away from him. Instead of attacking, he found himself defending. "What boy?"

G.K. ignored this. "His name is Lederer. Steve Lederer. He is fifteen, Jer's junior by a couple of months. He's an outstanding athlete, the type of boy we're looking for. His mother is a widow. Still attractive. In my opinion she feels hampered by a half-grown son. She'd be agreeable to anything we want to work out. We've talked on the subject before, Bitterbaum. Jer is a great kid. We both know that. But this boy Steve could be just what we need."

"I don't like it."

G.K. transferred his annoyance to the bathrobe. He took it out of the grip and began methodically unpacking his entire case.

Bitterbaum shot him an appraising glance. "It isn't a particular boy I object to. I'm sure you've checked him out, I'm sure he's qualified as far as that goes. It's the whole picture I wish you'd look at. Is it really necessary to carry things to the last decimal? Can't we let Josh develop as Josh? Be himself?"

By this time clothing was scattered all over the bed. "Unlike you, Bitterbaum, when I start something I see it through."

"We have an agreement, G.K. You can't go ahead unless I approve, and I don't approve."

"You're soft on the kid, Bitterbaum. That's your trouble. Your heart rules your head where he's concerned. Your opinion is no damn good. You're the one who's backsliding from our original agreement. It's an agreement I've put over a million dollars and fourteen years of my life into. And let me tell you—no man backs out on me, Bitterbaum, no man."

"I see," Bitterbaum said quietly. "Josh is an investment to you. And you want a return on your money."

"You're always sniping at my business interests. Your attitude shows a complete and total ignorance of the subject." Then, relenting, "You know I'm fond of Josh. I want the best for him."

"And of course you know what that is?" Bitterbaum knew he was beaten and that G.K. would continue to act on his own. All he could do was stand in the sidelines and attempt to parry the blows as they fell.

He watched G.K. refold and layer garments into the interior of the suitcase. The bathrobe went back in. Holt was called to witness his defeat and instructed to fit brushes and shaving materials into the side pockets.

Acres of wild mustard produced tangled haloes of seed stalks. Josh plunged into tubular-sectioned cane that grew waist high. "Do you have these?" He held out a pod like a miniature Japanese lantern.

"No, stick it in the bag."

"Look, you can pop them." Squeezed between thumb and forefinger they produced a pleasing staccato sound.

Lefty laughed and popped one of her own. "I hate having to collect the bugs," she said, putting a warty insect into the plastic bag.

"It's an abridgment of your rights under the fifth and fourteenth," Josh said. "If you feel things shouldn't die, you shouldn't be forced to kill them."

"I told Miss Garnett what you said. You know, that it was against my religion. And she asked me what my religion was. I told her I was a Buddhist with strong leanings toward Zen, and she laughed. She thought it was funny."

"Here's lupin, do you have that?" The blue-bearing stem was thrust into the bag. Josh said without prelude, "I'm thinking of joining the Fox."

"The guy who fights pollution? He's neat."

"He strikes without warning at factories, plants, refineries. He sabotages them, stuffs up their smokestacks, spreads garbage around to show them what they're doing. And he leaves a sign, *the Fox.*"

Lefty laughed. A moment later her attention was caught by the dip of wings and a flight. "There's that sassy jay."

Josh nodded absently, he was pursuing a flight of his own. "Then there's the billboard bandit in New Jersey. He comes along with an electric saw and cuts down road signs. One weekend he cut down fifteen."

"Your father wouldn't go along with that."

"I know." Josh looked uneasy. "But the signs were illegal. They'd been ordered down two years before. I'd bring it up at dinner, but I know what he'd say."

Lefty chimed in, "Two wrongs don't make a right." They laughed, pleased with each other, the day, the fullness of the plastic bags.

Lefty lifted a fuzzy black caterpillar on a stick and watched it crawl along. With sudden resolution she pushed the stick deep into impenetrable underbrush. "Miss Garnett's not going to have him. And now no one can find him. He's too beautiful."

"I think you meant it. You *are* a Buddhist. Have you ever meditated?"

"No, have you?"

"No. Do you want to?"

"You mean right now?"

He nodded.

She squatted down beside him. "Okay. But what do we meditate *on?*"

"You don't meditate on anything. You let your mind float free."

"*You* let *your* mind float free. I'm going to study the fungi on that elm."

Josh grunted to indicate he was already embarked on the meditative process.

Five minutes went by. Ten. Neither moved. Neither

wanted to be the first to give up. Another few minutes crawled by. The sun seemed to delve directly into his brain, the light exploded into crashing blackness. A midge flew persistently at his eye. He kept resolutely from blinking. It, too, was one of God's creatures. Suddenly Lefty knocked into him. In a panic he rolled her over; her face was flushed and sweaty and there was a smudge across her peeling nose. With sudden intuition he knew that nothing bad must happen to Lefty. He spoke her name urgently, repeating it. Then, on impulse, kissed her.

Her eyes flew open, a surprising shade of green like an aggie he once owned. "Josh," she said, "what did you do that for?"

"I don't know." His heart pounded giddily.

Lefty was in no hurry to right herself. She enjoyed the world at this angle. And it was interesting to observe Josh from this new perspective. She let out a whoop, which she half smothered, clapping both hands over her mouth. She managed to tumble from his lap into the thicket where she rolled around in convulsive mirth.

"What's the matter with you?" Josh asked.

She couldn't answer. Her hand flew from her mouth long enough to point at him. She was still laughing uncontrollably.

Josh made an effort to ignore this breach of manners. According to his mother you should never laugh at anyone and you should never point. Lefty was doing both and wouldn't stop. He collected the bags into one spot, pretending to be absorbed by their contents.

By now she was gasping and holding her sides. He couldn't keep up his show of indifference. "What's so funny?"

"You," she managed to splutter. "Now I know who you look like."

"Who?"

The tears rolled helplessly down her cheeks. She shook her head. "I won't tell you."

"Come on."

She caught her breath between paroxysms and held on to her stomach, but wouldn't tell him.

The dinner gong sounded and the four older children raced out of four upstairs doors, bumping against each other in the hall, jostling for front position on the staircase. They raced down the curved, stately sweep of steps, skidding to a stop in a huddle just short of the dining room. They were expected to enter this area with decorum which was made impossible by Josh sliding into Vicki, who fell against Ann, who caught hold of Jer to prevent him making a proper but solo appearance.

Throughout this rough and tumble they succeeded in maintaining complete silence so as not to provoke the wrath of either father or mother, who with Uncle Thor were coming in from the terrace. But Vicki gave them away by emitting half-swallowed snorts, and Ann developed hiccups.

Their parents glanced in their direction. Though engaging in some kind of mimicry, they were punctual. That was in their favor. Lateness was never tolerated. Their father frequently quoted Lord Nelson who claimed he owed his greatest victory to arriving fifteen minutes ahead of the French.

Uncle Thor gravely seated Ann, who smiled with her mouth closed. At a nod from mother, Jer seated Vicki, and Josh plumped himself down.

"Well, children," their mother said, "it's cotillion tonight."

"Tell the boys they have to dance, mother. Last time they stayed at one end of the room and told jokes."

"You were the joke," Josh said.

Vicki kicked him under the table.

"Any more of that," G.K. said, "and you leave the table."

"Where's Cindy?" Bitterbaum asked, although he knew the four-year-old had dinner with Nanny in the nursery. This was his form of protest. He liked all the children present at meals.

But G.K. ruled like a tribal chieftain. He turned his attention to the boys. "I've entered you in the Bay Shore swim meet," he told them. "Last year you won the intermediate division, Josh. But this year you made Senior. Which means you'll have to really work. I suggest since you're in Jer's section that one of you go out for butterfly or backstroke and the other, crawl. That way you can both place first."

Josh asked his brother, "Which do you want to go for?"

"Crawl."

"Okay. I'll take butterfly."

"Oh dear," their mother said, "all that splashing. I got soaked in the third row last summer."

The general attitude was that competition within the family was a dry run for the world outside.

Bitterbaum covertly watched G.K. He kept waiting for the announcement about the Lederer boy. Apparently G.K. intended to choose the moment, which was not yet. Instead he pitched into Josh for a badly spelled note he'd seen tacked up by the tennis court.

Lynn had to intervene. "*I* before *e*, Josh, except after *c.*" Bitterbaum blessed her; by no word or deed could one divine that of the six children, Jer alone was hers. Everyone believed the two boys to be their own, while it was accepted that the girls were adopted.

G.K. had been perceptive in his choice of a wife. And yet old habits persist. The secretarial relationship still underlay whatever else they had built. At her husband's insistence Lynn kept a card file on each youngster, noting inoculations, dental appointments, sports commitments, social dates, and lists of trophies and ribbons.

G.K. once told Bitterbaum that he began learning to handle people when he realized it wasn't necessary for them to like him. With the children he was caustic and irascible but never raised his voice. They were in complete awe of him. His model was the original father of the clan. But Bitterbaum felt the role provided the opportunity to indulge an innate dictatorial bent.

Lynn had made her accommodation years ago, backing his decisions and presenting a solid front to the children. She herself did not escape, however. G.K. was demanding of her as of everyone else. Under his aegis her tennis improved, and she took up golf. Bitterbaum wondered if she even liked the game. It was a life that exhausted him simply to contemplate.

She was forever setting up establishments in foreign capitals, furnishing apartments, renovating villas, attending to the hiring of servants, inquiring into schools, crating books, giving dinner parties, remembering names. She seemed to take it all in stride. At thirty-seven she was attractive, slim, efficient, and unflappable. Her pale, sandy complexion prevented her, in Bitterbaum's eyes, from being a beauty, but she was, as Kellogg frequently asserted, one of his chief assets. If she resented being an asset, she never showed it.

"Children," Lynn said, "let's have a little less noise. Your father has something to tell you."

Immediately they settled down, which was unfortunate as Ann's hiccups issued forth like a report from a gun.

"Ann," G.K. admonished, "leave the table."

"Go to the kitchen," her mother said, "and Delia will tell you how to get rid of those hiccups."

"Hold your breath and count to a hundred," Jer said.

"Twenty," Josh corrected. "A hundred and she's dead."

"Boys, that will be enough."

Once again they quieted.

G.K. made his announcement offhandedly, only a quirk at the corner of his mouth betrayed that he was aware of the furor it would cause. "Next weekend we are taking *The Buccaneer* to Santa Cruz." He hushed the commotion. "I have something to add that will concern you intimately. Your cousin, Steve Lederer, is going to spend the summer with us. He will arrive in time for the excursion."

"Our cousin," Jer said, "I didn't know we had a cousin."

Neither did I, thought Bitterbaum. He had been waiting for it. Still the announcement closed the possibility he clung to that somehow he had persuaded G.K. to abandon the project. Making the boy a cousin was a stroke of genius. It gave him immediate status as one of the family.

"How old is he?" Jer wanted to know.

"Wow," Vicki said. "A cousin. Too bad it isn't a girl cousin."

"We've got too many girls around here as it is," Josh told her.

Cotillion was a weekly event that took place in the gym at Our Lady of Malibu. "I don't know why we have to go to these stupid things," Josh complained. "Nobody has done ballroom dancing since the Middle Ages."

"You've got to develop social graces, my boy," Jer told him in his best take-off of G. K. Kellogg.

Josh refused to laugh.

Lefty joined Victoria with hardly a nod in his direction. In a party dress Lefty was delicate and curvy in a way that her usual floppy T-shirt concealed. It was disconcerting. He couldn't believe he had kissed that glamorous face.

She didn't act as though she remembered either. Whatever she had to say to Vicki must be hilarious. Could she be talking about him? Telling Vicki? Is that why they were laughing? He felt himself flush.

Why was he participating in an obvious puberty rite? He was captive to his culture as much as the natives of the Mauritania plateau were to theirs. Except they didn't tolerate the female at such gatherings. They were *tapu.*

Not here.

The girls were pointedly ignoring them, laughing together. Mrs. Lindstrum nodded to the pianist and the first bars were played. Josh avoided Lefty—*Leticia,* he thought—and asked someone else. After that it became impossible to ask her. Now he'd never find out about the resemblance. The episode weighed on his mind.

When it came time for Ladies Choice she stood in front of him. "Hey," she said.

"Hey yourself."

"Remember when we did that experiment in ESP at nine o'clock every night? I thought you were really tuned in. But you're not. I've been *willing* you to dance with me all evening."

He put his arm around her. It was a foxtrot and Mrs. Lindstrum was counting, *one-and two-and.*

"I thought you were mad at me," he said.

"Why? Because you kissed me?"

It amazed him that Lefty dragged everything into the open.

"I liked it," she said. And then laughed. "What if our braces had gotten stuck?"

The picture offended him.

"Mine come off in six months. Then I go into retainers. How about you?"

"They're talking about putting more on."

"Are your teeth really that crooked?"

"I don't know. I've never seen them." *One-and two-and.* "Tell me," he said suddenly.

"Don't you know? Don't you really know?"

He shook his head.

"All right. At the end of this dance when I don't have to look at you."

"Is it that bad?"

"It's not bad at all. It's peculiar."

Josh went back to counting under his breath.

"Vicki wants me to come to Santa Cruz. But I don't know what mother will say. She thinks the Kelloggs have too good an opinion of themselves. Like when you had the Shah of Iran at your house for dinner."

"You know he's very short, about as tall as Vicki."

"But he's a shah."

Josh nodded. "He plays a decent game of tennis. We had two sets before dinner, six–love both times."

"The point is," Lefty pursued the topic, "we've never had a shah at our house. And never will. That's the difference between our families."

"I suppose we're not like other families," Josh conceded.

"It's as though you believe, all of you, that there's some special destiny in store for you Kelloggs."

"That's crazy." Talk like that made him uneasy. It touched some deep, never-examined anxiety. "It's nothing mysterious. It's just that father expects a lot of us. And we're never to do anything that will reflect on the family. Because we'll go into public service, each of us."

"Does that mean politics? Peace Corps? What?"

"It's Jer's decision. He's the oldest."

"What do you think he'll choose?"

"I don't know."

"What would you choose if you were the oldest?"

"Foreign service, maybe. The diplomatic corps. I'd like something where you have a chance to influence things, bring people together."

"This morning you wanted to be a billboard bandit."

His silver grin flashed. "The important thing is not to get too tied into anything, you know? I mean, not to the point of forgetting who you are."

"And who are you, Joshua Francis Kellogg?"

The green wheel of her eyes threw him a challenge. "Me. That's what people forget, that's all they have to lay everything on, themselves." In his earnest effort to communicate a piece of his soul to this girl he lost the rhythm, stepped on her foot, and was swallowed in self-conscious misery. Until it occurred to him that she was looking at him in a special way, a private way that saw through the present bumbling to the great amorphous ideals that hovered ungraspable just out of reach.

The music stopped and she whispered fiercely in his ear. "How would you like to be President?"

"What?"

Laughingly she whirled away. "Figure it out, stupid."

Josh's first glimpse of cousin Steve was emerging from the station wagon. Uncle Thor had been delegated to fetch him. Josh eyed the newcomer with hostility. He was tall for fifteen, taller than Jer. Good-looking too, with a quirky smile. He was laughing at something Uncle Thor said, and seemed completely at ease. Josh resented him on the spot. Not for himself but for Jer.

Jer was not a natural athlete; he had neither coordination nor determination. And recently Josh had been letting him have points, calling them in his favor when they were in dispute. This was against the family code, the old *win* slogan. But it bothered him to have Jer continually bested, especially when such store was set on first place. Cousin Steve did not seem the kind to defer to anyone. And instantly Josh vowed to beat him in every game over the summer.

"Hi," he said briefly.

Steve looked into his face with interest. He had the reaction of so many people. "Hey, do I know you?"

It was a reaction that annoyed Josh. Since Lefty continued to tease him about the resemblance, he scrutinized his face repeatedly in the mirror. He saw nothing but an unkempt mop of thick hair and an assembly line of heavy-gauge disfiguring hardware. I look like the tin woodman of Oz, he decided. That's who I really resemble. But here it was again, that disconcerting half-recognition.

"Why don't you take Steve to his room?" Uncle Thor suggested.

"I'd rather look around first if that's all right," Steve said unself-consciously. "This place is super, like a hotel. Wow, look at that ocean."

Josh motioned toward the courts. "Want to play a set before lunch?"

"I don't play," Steve said. "I'd like to learn over the summer though."

Josh was mildly surprised; he thought everyone played tennis.

"I'll take you on at Ping-Pong," Steve said, spotting the table.

"Sure." Josh was elaborately casual to conceal his delight. He was the undisputed champ. The rest of the family refused to do more than rally with him.

They stepped up to the table. Josh slung the racket along the surface to his opponent. They rallied for serve. Josh sent a low one with a spin flashing toward his cousin. Back it came, even lower, skimming the net. He off-centered the next shot, but that didn't phase Steve either. In his effort to outmaneuver him, Josh slammed the ball into the net. It was Steve's serve.

Steve, it developed, had a mean offensive himself. They fought the game point by point. The girls collected as spectators. Jer also appeared. Their parents wandered by and stayed. There was lightning response from each player, weight ready to shift, feet to jump, arms to reach. Josh loosed several serves in succession that forced Steve to back off from the table;

four feet opened between him and it. Then Josh tapped the ball over the net. Steve flew forward to connect.

Josh, who hadn't expected a return, missed the point. And the game went to Steve. Everyone crowded around him. It was the perfect introduction into the clan. Father clapped him on the back, Cindy hugged his legs, Vicki decided she was in love. Jer and Ann enthusiastically went over every point verbally.

Josh stood outside this magic ring. He hated a post-mortem, even when he'd won. But to hear his shortcomings analyzed play by play was unbearable. He decided he hated Steve. And even as he decided, he knew that Steve's crime was to have beaten him fair and square.

"You're okay, Josh." Steve extended his hand and tried to pull him into the group.

Josh ducked under the proffered hand and rescued one of the balls which he pretended was in danger of falling off the table. Uncle Thor followed his performance with a quizzical expression. He watched as Josh walked away from the others and struck out at a brisk pace along one of the trails.

Instead of being five minutes early for lunch, Josh was almost five minutes late. He hoped his father would dismiss him. Instead he administered a mild tongue-lashing and told him to be seated. Everyone had been moved one place down.

The discussion was an animated consideration of what supplies to include on the camping expedition. This outing that he had looked forward to now held no pleasure for him.

After lunch the girls and Jer captured Steve for a

sail. Lefty appeared on her bike and was invited along. Oblivious to the fact that she had come to try his Apaloosa, Lefty declared she would love to sail.

Josh mumbled something about some reading he had to catch up on. No one argued with him or attempted to dissuade him. He felt alienated. He had tried to protect Jer. But Jer himself, far from feeling threatened, welcomed the newcomer and like everyone else responded to his high spirits. As he went inside he caught a glimpse of disappearing beach towels.

Who would think Lefty would so conveniently forget their riding date? But what rankled most was Steve, and the magnanimous gesture of including him in his own family. How generous of cousin Steve, the outsider, to extend a hand and pull him into the center of things.

A pier, a wharf, where boats dripped oil rainbows into water. There was so much that was unusual to sort out. Josh gave up on particulars, melting tar, a dead fish, salt spray, to concentrate on the novelty of each breath.

Their father referred to the boats tied up at the quay as old scows. Battered, with coiled ropes and anchor chains and buckets of live bait aboard, the sea seeped through the caulking and fish scales stuck to crepe bottom shoes. You knew these ships challenged the sea for their livelihood.

They could not get all the camping equipment on *The Buccaneer,* so G.K. chartered one of these work-horses. Josh elected to make the trip on *The Gull.* Lefty surprised him by saying she too wanted to cross on her. She gave him a warm, frank grin and his spirits began to rise. Not only was he heading into adventure, but the adventure was shared.

The Buccaneer got underway first, the gaily flying flags filled with wind. The family waved from behind picnic baskets and sunglasses.

They watched *The Buccaneer* until she cleared the harbor. Then it was *The Gull*'s turn. The engines, after a false start, reverberated through the planking. They cast off. Josh and Lefty leaned over the side watching their wake, and then watched it braid from the stern. A few strands of hair broke free of the ponytail. These whipped her face.

"Your cousin Steve is really nice," she said.

"Yeah."

"Why don't you like him?"

"What makes you think I don't like him?"

She brushed this aside. "Oh Josh, I want to have a wonderful time. I want it to be the best thing that's ever happened. So don't be mad at me, okay? I didn't forget we were supposed to go riding. But I wanted a chance to know your cousin. Besides, I thought you'd come along. Everyone else did."

"It's okay," he said.

She took a great breath of salt air which enabled her to sigh as she let it out. "Now I'll forgive you."

"For what?" he asked indignantly.

"For having the Shah of Iran to dinner, and congressmen and ambassadors and people like that. What do you do when you have such distinguished guests?"

"We play Monopoly or Twenty Questions."

"Vicki told me that Cindy spilled orange pop all over Senator Hartnell's wife."

Josh grinned. "She did."

They went below and looked at maps of the coastline. Several showed details of the offshore islands indicating reefs, shoals, and natural harbors. They admired the nautical seaworthy look below decks. And Josh threw in a casual "batten down." A barometer was affixed to the wall and a kerosene lantern swung overhead. The smell of fish permeated even here, and at close quarters it was harder to take. They raced up the companionway and the captain gave them a turn at the wheel. Josh had studied navigation and couldn't resist showing off with a bit of trigonometry.

"Too bad," Lefty pointed, "we don't need any of your figuring or even a compass. There's Santa Cruz dead ahead."

A bracing wind had brought *The Buccaneer* in well ahead of them. She was riding at anchor, sails shipped, and a party already ashore.

Reefs lay scattered as though a giant child had skipped stones. Seals basked on a partly submerged rock over which water broke and ran off in eddies. The creatures exhibited curiosity rather than fear, lifting their heads and watching as the boat moved past. "Do they really protect men against sharks?" Lefty wanted to know.

"I wouldn't count on it," Josh told her.

The Buccaneer fired a salute of firecrackers as they came in, and the shore party waved and cheered.

The plan was that they remain on the island until their rations were consumed and then, having less to transport, all return on the sailboat. The girls would sleep aboard, and the boys camp on the beach. Josh helped stow their gear in the dinghy as *The Gull* was to make the trip back immediately. Then, fitting on a face mask, he dived from the bow.

The water was cold and clear, his body immutably part of it, remembering with limbic race memory. He dived deep, feeling the water recede as he glided down. At first he didn't see the fish. They were in schools, feeding along the rocks from drifting vegetation. He began to make out forms, flat blue fish outlined in yellow, and a long pale variety that swam unconcernedly under him. A deep maroon specimen whose bulging eyes peered into his face mask swerved at the last moment. A translucent umbrella trailing long tendrils floated by. He reversed himself, not caring to tangle with those delicate whips.

World within worlds. And below this, igneous rock caught in molton flows. We know only the crust, he thought, the skin. And he thought it likely that was what men knew of other things as well. He turned on his back and squinted at diamonds of caught sun sparkling the surface.

Swells rolled and tossed him. These depths he played in had swallowed men and ships and belched storms and spawned hurricanes, and nurtured streamlined fins that prowled for food. He thought of these things because pain was radiating from his hip to his ankle. It was tying up his leg. He allowed himself to be washed onto the beach. The water slapped against rocks and poured itself into fissures. He stood, staggering in through the waves. Uncle Thor tossed him a towel and sweater. Cindy pelted him with sand.

A pit had been dug; potatoes and ears of corn wrapped in tinfoil were buried beneath coals. The steaks looked done, and those who opted for rare were congregating with paper plates. Mother heaped on salad, and the feast was underway.

The fine white sand of the cove arched inward along an inverted ellipsoid. A small froth of combers retreated. The rock outcropping was stern and steep. The sea had demolished its ranks and the encirclement continued in single rebel slabs. The waves upended to strike at these impediments, but only carved and polished them. The weather was mild, the moon white and near. A core of contentment spread. A family together, enjoying one another.

It did not seem odd to any of them that survival for the Kelloggs consisted of steak, lobsters, and fresh pineapple. Thor Bitterbaum smiled to himself. His only concern was that possibly Josh had gotten chilled. He was still in his wet trunks, but had put on the sweater.

G.K. slept on the boat with the girls and Lynn. The party in sleeping bags around the fire consisted of Uncle Thor, Jer, Josh, and Steve. They pestered Uncle Thor for stories of operations and the accouterments doctors had been known to leave in the incision, such as scissors and rubber gloves.

Josh liked the fire, liked the flush on one side of his face and the cold star night on the other. It even seemed to him all right about his leg. He had been wounded in battle during the day and at night he and his troops—he hadn't time to finish the story, sleep swept him away, an ocean of another dimension, where he wandered in dark chambers and floated free.

He smelled the bacon and eggs, heard the girls' treble voices, and lay with closed eyes a moment to savor it. Uncle Thor was trying his hand at pancakes which he insisted should be eaten with sour cream. The general consensus was, not when there was maple syrup. His mother threatened to roll him up in the sleeping bag if he didn't crawl out. His mother no longer kissed him since he was thirteen, but there were special moments between them. Like now, she gave his hair a tug that said, You great lummox.

He smiled into her face. She was a person who did not permit gloom or oppression. She banished them from her life and from theirs. Even illness was kept at bay, not acknowledged. She believed in health, activity, and the sheer power of will. When he scrambled to his feet Josh tried not to limp. He wasn't sure as to the source of the injury. It might have been a football scrimmage, or he seemed to remember last week jumping for a tennis shot and landing off balance.

Approaching the grill, he heaped his plate for strength and said nothing. Mother insisted that a full hour elapse before swimming. So the boys dug tunnels in the sand, a deep elaborate network down which you could thrust your hand and meet other wriggling fingers. They persuaded their oldest sister, Ellen, to play with them. She laughed like Cindy when her fingers touched theirs. Lynn took a walk with her up the beach on a shell-gathering expedition. All the prize shells they found were brought to her; even Cindy gave over her pile. Ellen loved to collect things. At home it was buttons.

The boys were growing restive. They buried Cindy in the sand, and convinced mother that a water fight was not the same as a swim. Each boy took a girl on his shoulder and attempted to duck the horse and unseat the rider which resulted in squeals and much splashing. Since this took place in the water, no one could tell Josh was favoring his left leg. As a matter of fact he upset Ann and ducked Jer before being defeated by Steve.

The hour was up and a race set for the large rock a quarter of a mile out. Father gave the countdown. They were strong swimmers and it was bound to be close. Josh prayed that his leg wouldn't tie up. He kicked evenly and steadily, passing Jer. But Steve was alongside him and slowly pulled in front.

I'm going to lose to him, he thought. *And it isn't on account of my leg. I'd lose to him anyway.* Steve touched the rock, and executing a racing turn, started back. He might still catch him if he could come by a second wind. Then something happened. His face was in the water but he laughed anyway.

Steve was losing his trunks. They had become untied and were slipping, impeding his kick. Steve tried to ignore his predicament, but the next kick brought them down around his ankles. He stopped to retrieve them and Josh shot ahead and came in first to the plaudits of those on the beach.

"Great swim, Josh."

"I knew you'd win, I knew it, I knew it!!!" Cindy was jumping up and down ecstatically.

Josh glanced at Lefty. She tossed her sun-streaked hair and smiled. *I should call foul, I should tell them.* Why wait for Steve to come dripping up and say it?

Some perverseness kept him from speaking. He watched Steve join them. Instead of revealing what had happened, he grabbed Josh's hand and told him he had a powerful stroke. He was going to let him keep his win.

Josh couldn't accept it. He was suddenly able to tell the story. Steve laughed with the others, but gave him a long look as though he knew him now. Later he came up and asked if he wanted to take the dinghy out. Josh shook his head.

"Oh let's," Lefty said, "we can dive off it. Come on, Josh."

Uncle Thor helped them launch through the surf, and at the last minute hopped in.

Bitterbaum rowed while the rest checked their scuba equipment.

"We're using the boat as a diving platform," Steve warned them, "so no distance swimming. Okay?"

He's giving orders, Josh thought, as though it were up to him. Jer was hung loose. It was his place as the eldest that was being undermined, but the usurpation meant nothing to him.

Why should I care if he doesn't? But it wasn't a reasoned thing. Steve had demonstrated himself a decent guy. That wasn't the point. The point was there was one older brother and that was Jer, and it was he who deserved first place. And Josh was here to see that one way or another, he got it. Jer couldn't care less, but damn it, he cared.

Lefty threw him a couple of speculative glances. Her face was smeared with goop and her freckles shone.

They dropped anchor past the breakers and paid out about fifty feet of chain. The bottom shelved steeply. The idea was to make a few free dives to warm up, then climb down the chain hand over hand to see who went deepest. Later they planned the same maneuver with scuba equipment.

Lefty was over the side before the boys. Josh jumped after her. She was waiting to duck him when he came up. He gave chase around the boat, but she escaped, diving under it to the other side.

Holluschickies, Bitterbaum thought as he shipped oars, remembering Kipling's description of the adolescent bachelor seal during its short period of carefree frolic. Bitterbaum treasured it for Josh, storing the shouts of laughter against—He paused because he didn't know against what. The boy had been nurtured and brought to this midpoint. The groundwork had been thoroughly laid. The charisma was there this time around too. The charm, the wit, and behind the disfigurement of orthodonture, the kid was beautiful.

But what was in store for the boy who shouted, played, and leaped like a young salmon? There were times when he couldn't sleep, when he reminded himself that the assassin had not been cloned. He was dead, gunned to death in an underground parking facility. There was no way he could harm Josh. But his imagination pictured other madmen. Would Josh, after all, take over the helm of government? G.K. believed this, planned it, counted on it. But Bitterbaum was not so sure. Perhaps this time his talent as a writer might emerge more importantly.

Speculation was endless with him. Old bachelor that he was, only two things interested him: medicine and his son. That was how he thought of him—son. But he was careful, always careful never to betray a glimmering of this. He did nothing to jeopardize his standing as Uncle Thor. Good old Uncle Thor could be counted on to show up weekends and holidays as well as for fever and mishap. Lynn alone suspected the extent of his attachment.

G.K. was in the driver's seat. He had put him there. Nonetheless, Thor did not assume too much, or show too much. G.K. knew he was fond of the boy, but he had no idea what Josh meant to him. And that's the way Bitterbaum intended to keep it. With Lynn, his guard was down. She adored her second son. And it was Bitterbaum she was on the phone to if he won a trophy or moved up the tennis ladder. For years he toyed with the idea that he might be in love with her.

Rather reluctantly he decided that the mutuality of their interest was the boy.

G.K. was more remote. His financial concerns put a good deal of strain on his time. He was frequently absent from home. How personally involved he was with Josh was difficult to determine. He expected a great deal of the boy on a day-to-day basis. And in the long run demanded a return. Steve's presence was proof of Bitterbaum's failure to convince him that they had already been successful beyond all reasonable expectation. G.K. saw matters differently.

And Bitterbaum knew fear. It was a kind of free-floating anxiety. He had nothing to attach it to. Not yet. Not now. Now the sun danced and the hollus-chickies disappeared beneath the surface.

Lefty was the first of the swimmers to break water. She ripped off her face mask laughing and spluttering. "How can they stay down that long?"

Jer was up next. "Thirty-seven hands," he announced. "Wonder what the difference will be when we try the scuba?"

"Thirty-seven," Bitterbaum echoed absently. He was beginning to be concerned.

Lefty fastened her mask in place and peered down.

At forty hands Josh passed Steve who pointed up. Five more hands, Josh told himself. He was conscious of a ringing in his ears from pressure. But he had experienced that before in deep dives. He reached a span lower on the chain when the leg went. It tied into a ball of pain. He doubled himself around the cramp, seizing it with both hands. *God,* he thought, *I'll never get up.*

He wasn't sure which way was up. In clutching his

leg, he described several loops. There was the chain, and there were two ways to travel along it.

The water should be lighter above. He tried to scrutinize it but agony got in the way. His body drew together over the cramp. He tried to detach his arms to make the motions of survival. But he couldn't let go of the pain. He held his leg in a vise that nothing could loosen.

He began to feel a tightness in his temples and behind his eyes. In a second or two he would have to open his nose and mouth and lungs. His body told him if he did that he would breathe and live. His mind told him the ocean would rush into him and flood out his life.

Panic invaded, preceding the rush of water. He struggled along the chain, up, down, he didn't know. He did know it was too late. The knowledge of his death came to him in a blinding cold enveloping light that exploded his senses. He was awash. His bursting lungs inhaled and death poured in. He coughed, choked, his sinus passages filled. There was no air in him, just water. It roared along his lungs, a tidal wave that poured into his stomach. We have to endure death, we have to endure. *It is given to each man once to die.* But today? When the sea captured the sun in prisms and his brother and Steve were up there and Lefty and Uncle Thor. Mother and father were sitting on the beach. Lunch would be ready.

How can you die when it's time for lunch and the sun is shining? And you haven't been sick at all? The spasm became his center. His body turned into a cocoon of pain, pain bent it to a new shape. And the chrysalis that radiated from it suffered a sea change.

His life wasn't going to pass before his eyes. That wasn't the way it happened. It was going to float out of him.

His insides mixed fatally with the sea. He was drowning. Every cell and tissue in his body expanded, seeking air. But water packed the passages, the orifices were relentlessly plugged. The pressure was expanding him, it would blow him apart. The tremendous light reached a new intensity. It pierced his consciousness and siphoned it off.

Motion. Grappling motion. He was choking on a stream of air. He knew Steve had him. And yet he wasn't aware of a person. Just the air reaching him, making him ill, making him breathe when all function wanted to cease, had ceased.

Steve used the buddy system, forcing the mask over Josh's nose and mouth, seeing that he inhaled and then clapping it against his own face for a breath that would carry them further. Josh was dead weight, curled over his leg, unable to help, unable to grasp the chain. He was afraid to bring him up too fast. He treaded water, shifting the breathing apparatus to Josh, looking anxiously into his face for signs of consciousness. His impulse was to shoot to the top, but he knew he must not.

The only chance was in a slow, stage-by-stage ascent. The ordeal was bounded by terror, the responsibility for a life. He wouldn't know down here. There, top side, it would be revealed. Life or death, he would know then.

Now it was mechanical, something to be gotten through, after which he would know if he had won or lost. Won or lost, those terms were of such significance in the Kellogg household.

Once more he kicked toward the surface. Bitterbaum was in the water, feeling his way along the chain. He reached them and took over, supporting the body of Josh. He adjusted the air tank and strapped it into place. The final ascent was completed, they hauled Josh into the boat. The face mask, when they peeled it off, was filled with blood.

Bitterbaum waved the others back, straddled Josh and kneaded his rib cage. An ocean seemed to erupt out of his mouth.

Before he opened his eyes he remembered what his body somehow knew: *Steve has me. It will be all right.*

For a month after the almost fatal mishap at Santa Cruz, Josh had trouble with his leg. Bitterbaum diagnosed a back injury. It had finally shown up. He treated it with a series of cortisone shots, hoping by prompt attention to avoid the insertion of a metal disk.

By summer's end Josh seemed fit enough and was participating as heavily as ever in the regimen of the sports-minded clan. Bitterbaum observed no special communication from Josh to Steve. But his acceptance was complete. Decisions were left to him and he made them. Josh competed against him and always played to win. But there was no rancor if he lost. It was like losing to Jer. When the game was on, they were opponents; afterward, the parameters changed, they were friends. A closeness developed that was apparent to them all. There was no question but that Steve would stay.

G.K. had won another round.

Bitterbaum wondered if the future could be controlled from this point on. The three boys were to be on their own. Josh was enrolled in Choate where Jer was a senior and Steve a transfer senior.

Jer was full of advice, which teachers to avoid, how to get around the syllabus, what to sign up for, which were the good dorms. They made a pact to leave their mark on the school, the imprint of the Kelloggs.

Before he had an opportunity to settle into the routine, Josh was stricken with appendicitis. He was operated on and sent home to recuperate.

Uncle Thor insisted on port wine which he grew to abominate, but drank dutifully. He also embarked on a secret program of physical fitness, doing isometric exercises in bed and push-ups when no one was in the room.

Nevertheless, he was slow to gain strength. The girls were boarders at a parochial school, and only Cindy was home. He looked forward to Lefty for company. But her family had moved. Looking back, he had an unsatisfactory feeling. She, who last summer held such a central place in his life, had dropped out of it.

You throw a stone, it disappears. And no one knows where. So with Lefty. Their last meeting had been casual. There was nothing special about what they did or what they said. He decided to write her. He spent a morning laboriously constructing sentences, reading them and crossing them out. He wanted to tell her how her skin and lips tasted.

The letter he finally sent expressed a formal hope that she would write.

She didn't.

Nowhere was there a record of such an early involvement. G.K. convinced Bitterbaum it was better to withhold the letter than risk an uncharted course.

Josh waited for a reply but the stone had dropped beyond his vision. He forced himself to be angry. Anger he was capable of dealing with.

Uncle Thor showed him card tricks. They played chess. Glancing across at the young clonee, Bitterbaum brooded on the future. Would the success with Josh inspire an army of Joshes? Would the great and powerful of this earth want to be succeeded, not by sons, but by themselves?

Done on any scale this would mean stagnation in the gene pool, with fewer regroupings and possibilities. The tremendous reserve of potential adaptability that was built into the race would be dangerously modified. Adaptability, the quality that enabled man to survive from the arctic to the equator, would be threatened, which meant the race was threatened. McClearn said, "A species that runs out of variability, runs out of life."

When he thought in terms of Josh, he was pleased. But when he extended the dimensions opened by Josh, the implications overawed and terrified him. Guidelines were needed. Otherwise the demonic fantasies of Huxley were prosaic fact. José Delgado, the Yale psychologist, believed man, like the dinosaur, is insufficiently intelligent to survive in a changing environment. And Sinsheimer of Caltech seemed to concur. "Men," he wrote, "are victims of emotional anachronisms, of cultural drives essential to survival in a primitive past, but undesirable in a civilized state."

Bitterbaum was in partial agreement; man must sharpen his intellect and curb his aggressions. The key to both problems lay in the DNA cistrons. A human being as superior to present man as this generation to *Pithecanthropus* could result. On the other hand, if man did not act on the discoveries of biogenetics, it was quite likely his mental inertia would destroy him.

Before answering the question, should man seek an optimum man? it was necessary to recognize the fact that one child in twenty is born with discernible or latent genetic defects. This represented a significantly larger amount than previously. He was reminded of Steiner: "My genetic structure is waiting in ambush for me."

Extensive research had shown that there are over two thousand ailments of genetic origin, and that twenty-five percent of patients are hospitalized with genetic diseases, which include sickle-cell anemia, cancer, heart disease, diabetes and scoliosis. Gene therapy was being used as an alternative to abortion. But enormous difficulties surrounded genetic engineering, due to the extreme delicacy of microsurgery and the polygenic nature of most defects. From the theoretical point of view the way to go was control of the genotype before conception. The frightening moral and ethical implications did not escape Bitterbaum.

Because he had been brought up in a home where Friday nights his grandfather read the Bible, there flashed through his brain God's warning against tasting the forbidden fruit: "Eat and you shall surely die."

But the serpent whispered: "Eat, you shall be like God."

He had gone beyond that, he had gulped down the whole fruit.

"Your move, Uncle Thor."

After several weeks Bitterbaum declared himself dissatisfied with Josh's recovery. He worried about the effect the smog might have. Even at the ocean there were days when the inversion layer hung, a heavy, static pall. Lynn no longer went into the city to shop but ordered by Tele-Purchase at home. Oxygen was sold on street corners to pedestrians who found it necessary to go into the downtown area.

He conferred with Lynn and she decided on a whirlwind tour of Italy. Within hours they were in Rome. And the next day Josh was riding a horse-drawn hansom around Florence, walking on the Ponte Vecchio, watching the searchlights pick out the famous landmarks, having lunch in the piazza in front of Maria della Fiore, looking up at the freestanding strength of Giotto's tower. Strolling the convoluted streets, he watched a glass blower. Suddenly he saw the headline LOS ANGELES. He bought the paper. Struggling with the Italian, the picture began to form and the emergency became clear. That morning two million people drew breath and found it inadequate. Coughing, feeling dizzy, they inhaled another. The second breath produced shallow respiration, in some cases cardiac embarrassment.

Switchboards plugged to hospitals and ambulance services jammed. People collapsed. The death toll among the very young, the old, and the infirm was four percent. The wire services and news media went on alert. Mass evacuation efforts were abortive. People expired on the freeways, arteries leading out of the city were blocked. It was impossible to reach the airports. Communication broke down. The telephone center was manned by the army. Gas masks were issued, oxygen flown in. But before supplies could be distributed, they were in the hands of rioters.

He made his way back to the hotel. His mother had just been notified that Ellen was dead. It was hard for Josh to take in. His mother's face made it real. Her nostrils smelled death, the shadows gathered in her eyes saw it. He slipped his hand into hers.

Italy was a sequence out of time. So was going home, attending the funeral. Time began again with the start of the new term at school. He watched with interest the steps taken to clean the air. Automobiles were banned in many areas, malls developed, and monorails constructed.

A sliding-scale toll was charged against single-occupant cars. It was prohibitive to use freeways with less than four passengers per vehicle. More and more people worked at home, in touch with their schools and offices on closed-circuit television. Not Choate; it continued as before.

His father was not always pleased with his academic record. He wrote some terse things about buckling down, bringing up his grade point.

Jer and Steve were graduated and went on to Harvard. It was Josh's fate to be two years behind, but to come to the fore, to catch up. He was building a framework to handle facts. Knowledge, he decided, was more than assimilating information. The important things no one was able to teach. He heavily underscored a passage in a book by C. S. Lewis: "Man's power over nature is really the power of some men over other men with nature as their instrument."

Bitterbaum noted the change in him, the new maturity. From one holiday to the next he observed the growing process. At seventeen Josh stood six feet, with thoughtful blue eyes and an Irish penchant, so close to the Jewish, of reacting with incisive humor as a defense against life.

If the decision were left to him, he would never disclose Josh to the world. There was too much hysteria on the subject even within the scientific community. It was charged that cloning would turn the human society into a stratified ant heap, that excesses would lead to clonees being kept as spare parts to replace organs. They would be the perfect donors with compatible tissue matches and no chance of rejection.

Had he, Thor Bitterbaum, opened Pandora's box? And what winged things would mount from it, assailing his senses, confronting his morality, calling him to account? In his more honest moments, he realized that only in a charged and emotional state would he have dared do what he had done. But it was his triumph, almost too great, almost too marvelous.

Josh was forfeit from the inception. There seemed no way to change that. The boy's life was as programmed and foreordained as a Greek tragedy. It would unfold. And his punishment would be to see it played out in all its inevitability.

Would his lamentations be the boundary of Josh's life—to this moment normal, undistinguished, but in five years, in ten? Was he to be studied and observed like a pin-pierced moth? Would he be torn apart by an incited mob? Or would he rise to command the world? The constellation of years was turning faster, aligning his life with that pivotal point, discovery.

When he discovered he was a duplicate, would the shock, the trauma never experienced by the original but an integral part of the nervous system of the clonee, differentiate him and make him his own man? Or would the mechanism falter, break down completely?

For the Kelloggs it was Easter; for him, the Passover. The first signs of budding ladened the trees; the bird life in Latigo Canyon was busy with straws and twigs. The older boys arrived the day before. Josh was expected. The family was gathered. It was arranged that Josh phone from the airport. Uncle Thor would pick him up.

A croquet game was set up on the front lawn. The sound of mallets striking wooden balls was discernible against laughter and the murmur of voices. The excited screech of a child was punctuation. Then the call he had been waiting for. Josh's miniaturized face appeared on the offset phone screen. "Uncle Thor?"

"Yes, Josh. I'll be right down to get you."

"I'm not at International."

"Where are you?"

"Well, it's like this, I bought a youth fare, you know? And I was waiting to see when I could get out, when this stewardess said, 'Why not come on my flight?' She's real coherent, her name's Pat. So here I am."

"Where? Where are you?"

"San Francisco."

"Well, you'd better get down here. I don't know what your father will say."

"I can't get down. I'm taking Pat to the Zen Freak Out. In fact I'm part way there. That's why I'm calling, we're stuck in a traffic jam on some back road. I figured I had time to do things like telephone and get sandwiches. You should see what I'm driving, Uncle Thor, a T.W.A. limousine. Pat wangled it. It looks pretty unusual. There's a bunch of kids in a rider-rig in front of us, and a modified snowmobile with a topless driver, female. And—"

"Slow down, Josh. What on earth am I going to tell your parents?"

"You'll think of something. I've got to go, the line is starting to move."

"Wait, wait—" But the phone clicked into place and the picture blanked out.

I shouldn't allow him to put me in this position, Bitterbaum thought. It was dangerous. Fronting for Josh could lead to direct confrontation with G.K., the thing he wanted most to avoid. But he knew he'd go along. Josh knew it too.

Such encounters had not fallen to the lot of Thor Bitterbaum. No attractive airline hostess had ever accosted him with the promise of a date if he'd take her flight. His face with its long, bony, slightly crooked nose and thin, sardonic mouth had never attracted the opposite sex. Perhaps that was why he vicariously enjoyed the escapade.

Also, Josh counted on him. The immediate problem was what to say to G.K. and Lynn.

No sooner had his agile brain posited the question than a dozen possibilities occurred to him. He selected the one that would have most appeal.

G.K.'s business kept him so constantly abroad that Lynn took an old manor, *Westwind,* in Hampstead Heath outside London. It was from here that he called a family council. Bitterbaum suspected it was part of the game plan. But he wasn't sure what episode was to be reenacted. He deplaned, slightly airsick.

The girls were a revelation. At their ages, a year made a great change. Cindy was a flaxen-haired ten. Ann and Vicki at fourteen and sixteen were bursting into femininity. Bitterbaum expected them to be charming; they had before them a perfect model in Lynn. It seemed to him they resembled her physically. He could not explain this phenomenon since he himself had arranged their adoption. Certain things they had the good sense to imitate, her carriage for example. The girls also had her direct method of speaking to the point. No beating around the bush for any Kellogg.

They had spent a long weekend riding and sailing at *Godset,* a restored farmhouse in Thisted, which was enclosed by pine forests and the North Sea. It was a property Lynn was in the process of buying.

The young people realized on this occasion they were not gathered to enjoy themselves. G.K. had summoned them from America, from Denmark, and he himself had flown in from Istanbul. It was the week of

Jer's twentieth birthday. They speculated among themselves whether this was the reason for the family conference.

Bitterbaum usually managed to stay a jump or two ahead of G.K. At the moment, however, he had no idea why the call was issued and the clan assembled.

They were at ease with each other. Although they could never be accused of being relaxed. They filled the room with wit and high humor. Bitterbaum was struck as always by their physical good looks and exuberant health. Jer was somewhat slight and lacked the height of the other boys, Steve would conceivably have to watch his weight, Josh still had a mouth full of braces—but they were all attractive in a vigorous way. They were at home wherever home was. And they enjoyed being together. Their evident pleasure in each other he attributed largely to Lynn. She had welded a close-knit family.

G.K. chose a deep leather armchair from which to address them. Bitterbaum decided he had worn well. It was now nineteen years since the start of their joint endeavor. At fifty-six he was in handball trim. He possessed a golfer's tan, and his face, while heavy, was remarkably unlined. Bitterbaum, eight years his junior, had a countenance as deeply etched as the lines in his palm. *I worry too goddamned much,* he thought.

Like now. We're probably here to wish Jer happy birthday. But the remote contingency that they were not, raised specters in his mind. In two years would they be summoned in just such fashion on Josh's account? *Don't cross bridges,* he admonished himself. *Sufficient unto the day* and today it concerns Jer. He didn't like thinking in platitudes. Association with the Kelloggs had done that to him. His sources had once been more literary. But the Kelloggs were happy with *a penny saved* variety, and they had slipped into his own thinking.

G.K. waited for the conversation to die away. He had the knack of waiting. Bitterbaum often thought it was that which had brought him his fortune. While other men gave up, G.K. was still encamped. Gradually the young people, conscious of nonparticipation from the occupant of the most imposing chair in the room, fell silent.

"We Kelloggs," G.K. began in a rambling, almost absentminded way, "are here at *Westwind* to celebrate the twentieth birthday of Gerald Junior. It is an occasion to be marked when a boy enters the most important decade of his life. Most people regard the *twenty-first* birthday as signaling adulthood. But the example of Lord Nelson applies doubly here.

"Jer's future will be decided now. By next year it will be implemented. I will have had a year in which to interview colleagues, run down leads, talk to people, and when Jer graduates from Harvard the right slot will be waiting for him. So, Jer, as the eldest, you have the floor."

Bitterbaum surveyed the intent young faces as they turned to Jer. Josh in particular seemed tense.

"Well, sir, it's pretty much what I said last Christmas. I like the academic life. It's not pressured. There's plenty of time off, a three-month vacation."

Vicki giggled. But her father's expression quelled her.

"Then your proposal is to go on to graduate school and earn a Ph.D.?"

"Yes, sir. I'm interested in the history of political science."

"Admirable. I find myself in complete accord with your aims. Wilson came to the Presidency of the United States via the academic scene."

"Excuse me, sir, I'm not interested in national politics. I think I might concentrate on the Darwinian influence in nineteenth-century political life."

If G.K. was disappointed he gave no sign of it. "You know your own mind. And you have five years of work cut out for yourself. I would say offhand that it would be wise to stay with your alma mater, but I will make inquiries as to where promotion is most rapid. Let me be the first to wish you happy birthday, son, and a good year."

The others clapped and chimed in with, "Hear! Hear!" The sisters surged around him with kisses, and Cindy tried to get in twenty spankings, but he laughingly held her at arm's length.

Their father called them to order. "Now we come to my nephew, Steve."

Steve. Naturally it would be Steve. He had provided himself with a bench warmer. Steve could not afford Jer's independence.

"Two months from now you will also reach the twentieth milestone. Will you tell us, Steve, where your ambitions lie?"

"Yes, sir. You encouraged me to go into politics."

Of course. That was the script, written a generation ago. Steve had obviously been nudged in this direction.

Bitterbaum looked glancingly at Josh. The presumption was that he harbored the same ambition. Was it true? This time around, could he be guided into the old channels? He tried to bring his attention to what Steve was saying.

"Law is the traditional route, so I'd like to go on to law school."

"Excellent," G.K. said with hearty approval. It was evident he would have preferred this for Gerald, Junior. But a son is not under the same obligation as a pseudo nephew. "I'll look into Boalt, Princeton, Yale, Harvard. We'll see that you get into the best school. Just keep your grades up." He leaned forward and fixed his eyes on Josh. "You see why I am insistent on grades. They play a large part in opening doors. In two years we will assemble in your behalf. And I shall expect as creditable a showing as your brother and cousin made today. They have set goals for you to shoot for. Remember, competition within the family hones and sharpens one for the world outside. It is a competitive world and a winner's world. That's what I want of my children. Top dog, no less. And you can do it, all three of you."

Lynn added, "What your father didn't say, because he assumes it, is complete rectitude in all your dealings. Others may need to circumvent, cut things fine, but not a Kellogg."

That's probably true, Bitterbaum thought, but only because the old man did their circumventing for them. It was nice, he supposed, to keep the hands of the second generation clean. But Bitterbaum firmly believed the maxim that every great fortune is based on a great crime. And in the last thirty years Kellogg had made four or five fortunes. Shipping, oil, the Shuttle, banking, Wall Street. He'd had a seat on the Exchange since he was hardly older than the boys. Bitterbaum took pains to remain unfamiliar with the details. Even so, he wondered at so ingenuous and naive a remark from Lynn. After all, she had been his secretary. But people believe what they want to believe, even what is convenient to believe.

He had been dense not to have guessed the purport of the meeting. And he couldn't afford to be dense where G.K. was concerned. He had to stay ahead of him.

Bitterbaum tried again to read Josh's reaction. Had Steve's decision been a blow to him? It was impossible to tell. He was in animated discussion with both boys, questioning them keenly on the details of their choices. However, when the others left the room, Josh stayed behind. He didn't notice Bitterbaum slouched in one of the wing chairs.

He walked to the window and stood looking out. Turning slightly, he reached both arms stiffly toward the wall, and when his palms touched, lowered his head between them. It was a gesture of utter weariness. It seemed not to belong to an eighteen-year-old.

Bitterbaum's private despair overwhelmed him. G.K. had another victory. The inevitability they had created in Josh marched on. Before him he saw the effect of the emotional imprinting he had once so glibly outlined. How smug he had been, how erudite with his Rogerian attitudes and Skinnerian premises, etched here before him in this defeated figure.

Josh excelled so frequently and so casually, that it had not occurred to Bitterbaum that he might feel he had to win his place in the family continually. He was resilient, but not that resilient. His training was to bounce back, to get in there and pitch. There was no alternative in this success-oriented family. The boys were pushed hard, the sights always raised. You train a high-spirited horse that way.

What about a boy?

You clone a frog.

What about a boy?

He approached Josh and touched him gently. "Well, Josh, what have the two older princes left for the younger?"

He started. And then said easily, "I've got two years to think of something."

"They did rather preempt the field."

"They'll both be presidents, Jer of Harvard, Steve of the United States."

"That leaves business. You could head up an empire."

"Business doesn't interest me." Josh spoke almost violently. He seemed to realize it himself. "I'd like to do something different from the others. For once I'd like not to be compared." The heresy was out. They were both stunned by it. "I may write," he said defiantly, as though he expected God to strike him.

"Why not?" Bitterbaum tried to control the spark of hope. All he said was, "You've got a good background."

Josh shook his head. "Father wouldn't approve. He'd think it was all right as a corollary of something else, some other career. But not as a primary goal. You know how he is, Uncle Thor. I'd feel I'd be letting him down, and the family. So I don't know. I really don't know." That sudden grin flooded his face. "That's not accurate. I *do* know what I'll be doing. My job will be to provide back-up for Steve. I'll be his adviser, that's an okay role. And that way I'll fit into the organization. I've often thought we're sort of an Anglo Mafia."

Bitterbaum regarded this rebound of spirits with suspicion. He believed the disappointment to be real and deep. But he went along with the put-on because that's the way Josh wanted it.

Josh made a discovery. He discovered that he too was adopted. The possibility had never occurred to him because his parents were so open and casual about the fact that the girls were.

He had come across his mother's sewing and her prayer book in the conservatory. It was a lovely cool area with domed glass ceilings, furnished in wicker, with plants clustered in pots and hanging baskets. There was a smell of earth and growing things in the room and it looked into a rose garden. In summer it was separated from the garden only by screening, so that in a sense it was a continuation of it. Josh had a special fondness for the room and many times brought a book and curled up while his mother worked on her embroidery frame. It was companionable, something they both enjoyed.

They rarely talked, or only in a desultory fashion. But there was a bond between them that showed itself in their ability to be quiet and get satisfaction from these moments when each pursued his own thoughts. The wordless rhythm of early morning spread the sun's light, tipping the roses with shafted color.

Josh wandered in from the breakfast table. His mother had been called to the phone. He bent over the embroidery. She was working something for Vicki. Her name was entwined in flowers and leaves. A gym bag was his first guess, no, a pillowcase. It was too fancy for a gym bag. He picked up the prayer book. A satin ribbon held her place. In the frontispiece of the book was Jer's name: *Gerald Kellogg, Jr. Born July 6, 1962. Weight 8 lbs. Height 21 in.* Under it, as expected, was *Joshua Francis Kellogg.* But the words that followed went out of focus.

He closed his eyes and opened them to read what he thought he saw: *Natural son. Born September 2, 1964. Adoption papers signed September 12, 1964.* The writing was his mother's.

Not his mother's.

Lynn's.

He had always felt himself more her son than his. Natural son. *Bastard.* That's what she should have written. An other-side-of-the-blanket Kellogg.

Who was his mother? Someone the great man was playing around with? An actress? Call girl? One of the international set? Or a below-stairs servant girl?

Hang in there, Josh, he told himself, *hang in there.* His thoughts, no longer bound by his mind, were circling it, watching it function, watching the ten billion nerve cells generating energy—not thought, he wasn't thinking, but a meld of perceptions jammed like the keys on a typewriter when they fly up together and everything stops. You have to unjam them manually, pull them down with your fingers. One of the stray nerve cells remembered the shoji screen in the Latigo Canyon home and the fantasy.

As a young child he imagined the butterflies would someday wrench themselves loose and fly away. This was the day for it. Another of the billion cells simultaneously transmitted a line from Albert Schweitzer: "Abnormal life begins with the loss of one's own field and dwelling place." One's own.

One's own mother.

Mother, it's your writing. You wrote, *natural son.* You knew every time you kissed me, scolded me, pulled my hair in that mock-fierce way you have. You knew I wasn't your son. And yet you let me believe it.

Why?

If I'd grown up like the girls, knowing, it would seem all right. *Between the idea and the reality falls the shadow.* That's me, the hollow man. They opened my head and stuffed in lies.

Mother, I want you to be my mother.

But you're not. You're someone called Lynn Kellogg who never leveled with me, not once. You put your arms about me a thousand times. But there was no honesty.

You really were a mother to the girls. You'd say to them, We chose you.

But I didn't come to you that way. Father got some girl in trouble and then did, quote, "the right thing." I was foisted on you, the result of G.K.'s infidelity.

Yes, it must have been that way. Father was cheating, playing around, and when she found out mother —Lynn—took me in. She's that kind of person, stray cats, too, and lost puppies.

Eighteen years, that's a long time for a game to go on. Calmly. The wolf eyes circled, watching the crazy thing called grief foul up the mechanism. He heard his mother—he heard Lynn Kellogg—come back into the room.

He moved away, and trapped himself against a window. He'd have to turn around and face her or else live and die in this corner. He could see himself sauntering from the room, "Hi, Lynn, old girl, how's every little thing?" Or would he burst into tears like Cindy? That would be pretty ludicrous, a freshman at Harvard crying for his mother. Not *for* his mother, *because* of her. Which her? The one who abandoned him or the one who played a game with his life? A strange sound dribbled from his mouth. He turned it into a cough. But he could feel her glance.

"Are you all right, Josh?"

"Yeah. I choked on a piece of toast at breakfast."

"I wish you wouldn't bolt your food. Get a glass of water."

He was dismissed. The task of devising a way out of the room was solved. He rushed by her and through the adjoining room. He ran up the stairs, meeting no one on his way to his room. He closed the door behind him, walked to the mirror, and took a long look at himself.

Another thought was squirreling out a place for itself. It was possible that he wasn't Kellogg's child either.

Who are you? he asked himself.

What are you doing in this family?

Do you belong here or somewhere else?

Are you an orphan?

Are you a bastard?

Why did they play this hoax on you and none of the others?

Natural son. The natural son of G.K.

There was certainly no familial resemblance. They hadn't a feature in common, not even coloring.

Suddenly blood engorged his temples, pounding behind his eyes. Lefty. Long ago Lefty. Lefty who'd run out on him, never answered him, was turning his head, rotating it slowly with her hand against his jaw. First in one direction, and then in another, very slowly. "Of course. You look just like him. It's bothered me ever since I first saw you. I kept asking myself, 'Who does he look like?' But it's obvious. You're the spitting image of the President they assassinated. It's amazing. It's really amazing. I bet with those braces off your teeth you'd be a dead ringer. It's more than a resemblance, I mean once you've seen it, once you're conscious of it, it's sort of spooky. You're not related, are you? I mean are your family cousins or something?"

He had just laughed. But that night again he studied his reflection and saw what she saw. Then at school there was always somebody who brought it up, or sometimes it was a visitor to the house. Once a taxi driver commented on the uncanny resemblance.

Natural son.

Yes, but whose? He went to the encyclopedia and looked up dates. It was physically possible. He had been born nine months after the death of the President. He remembered the Walt Whitman poem that served as epigraph to one of the books on his life: *O powerful, western, fallen star.*

Was it possible that he was the son of this man? The clamor, the surge in his head subsided. He opened the bottom drawer of his desk and began rummaging through it in a systematic search. He found what he was looking for, a pliers he'd used to align his bicycle wheels. He took up his position once more in front of the mirror and spreading his lips, began working at the wires holding the metal caps of his braces. One by one he uncurled and wrenched them off.

Confirmation. The face that looked back at him was a famous face. Perhaps the best-known face in modern history. He had expected to see that. No, what he expected was to see nearly that. What he expected was an approximation. But this was extraordinary.

He was his double. He remembered an old German folk tale in which it was related that every person in the world has his doppelgänger, that each man's exact replica exists somewhere in the world. He stared in fascination at his face, touching it with his hands.

He *was*, he *must be*, the son of that man.

He was brother to the Man in the Iron Mask, the Dumas story of a twin who was kept hidden away all his life in a dungeon behind a mask welded to his face. Wasn't this a modern version? The mask was the braces he had just pried off. Was the dungeon *Westwind*? He began to laugh silently. This would all be some kind of nonsense except for the reflection radiating from a thin film of metal backing deposited on the surface of a glass showing him that face.

It wasn't his own. It was a face that belonged to the world. It was minted on half dollars. There was no question as to who he was. Even disowned, he knew his father. What did it mean? Was he himself some sort of state secret? The implications were too far-fetched. Still, Camus defined life as the limits of the possible. This was not only the limit, it was the bloody end.

Not a state secret, an embarrassment, that's all he was. He smiled at the glass. His teeth, large, straight, and strong, completed the likeness. There was nothing wrong with his teeth. A dead-ringer Lefty had said.

He leaned toward his reflection. "Ask not what your country can do for you, but rather what you can do for your country."

He wondered if the President's family knew of his existence. He doubted it. The affair that culminated in his conception must have been during the fall of 1963. She could have been anyone, a secretary, or a college girl on leave, a senator's wife, a newspaperwoman, one of the celebrities or artists who performed so frequently at White House parties during his administration.

Well, the odyssey was ended. He knew. For eighteen years he had been hidden in the midst of a family, unknowing and unknown. G.K. of course knew the story.

Did his mother? What about Uncle Thor? Why had he entered into this elaborate subterfuge? Was there any thought of grooming him for the number-one slot?

No, of course not. The American people would never go for a bastard. Besides there was a legitimate son, his half brother. It was he who would eventually be put before the electorate.

The secret couldn't have political overtones then. It was kept to protect the reputation of a great man, and leave his family an untarnished memory. He was an uncomfortable liability, nothing more.

But this conclusion did not please him. "I am the son of a great man." He remembered an underscored passage in Teilhard de Chardin: *Seize the tiller of the world.*

It was a possibility, with this face, with these antecedents.

He was nakedly now who he was; the braces were off. The lies, too, were flung off. He phoned the airport and arranged for a flight to New York. Then he called a taxi. He would stop en route and clean out his checking account. The note was harder.

Dear Lynn and G.K., I know. Maybe that's sufficient explanation. I need to get away and think. Don't try to find me. When I've sorted things out and decided what my course of action should be, I'll be in touch. Josh.

He threw a few things into a Pan Am bag he found in the closet and took a pair of sunglasses from a bureau drawer. He put them on and studied his appearance.

They helped. He tried combing his hair differently, but it was wiry and not pliant about lying in a new pattern. He gave up on that, but hesitated over the braces. He probably should put them back on. Just to get out of the house it might be necessary. Sorting through the pieces he picked out several, pushing them up over his front teeth. He looked like himself again. He would have them rewired in place.

His immediate task was to slip out of the house without meeting anyone. The taxi was waiting for him at the west entrance.

He had no coherent impression of that trip. It was an inward journey. From New York he caught a plane for Washington, D.C. It must have started there.

He was familiar with the city. The current President himself had conducted his father and the three boys on a tour of the White House. He had been bored that afternoon. Priceless bric-a-brac, ancient portraits of ancient people, chandeliers, red rooms, green rooms, blue rooms, the East Room, didn't interest him. He amused himself trying to spot Secret Service men.

Today every detail was important as he tried to reconstruct a link to the past. There was a guard at Pennsylvania and Lafayette Square by the north portico. Josh inquired when the next tour was scheduled. But he had missed it for the day. He was told to come back at ten the following morning. It didn't matter. He had figured it all out on the plane, alternate moves, different approaches. Nothing could deflect him.

He proceeded past the Capitol to the library. He sat the entire day concurrently reading three lives of the late President. One dealing with his early years convinced him.

The President slept with a board under the mattress of his bed because he suffered with a bad back. Josh had a weird sensation, almost as though he were reading about himself. He looked up dazed when he discovered the President wore a quarter-inch lift in his left shoe.

Every doubt had been erased. The physical parallels could not be denied. They matched his own with such exactitude that it was uncanny. One book was filled with small, gossipy facts. The President didn't like ice water. He had to remind himself how many millions of people must share that idiosyncrasy.

Josh closed the books. He closed his eyes. They were all there, the emphasis on sport, on winning. The same maxims he had been brought up with: *A contender is a loser, there is only one winner.*

There was no coincidence here. G.K. had read these same books. There had been a definite attempt to duplicate the early environment. Why? What was the plan?

Knowing the swift culminating tragedy toward which the man's life raced invested everything with a sense of drama. Or was it his close identification that made him approach the last pages with such dread? He had stopped reading before the motorcade was attacked, before the President reached the intersection where he was to lose his life.

The blood that poured out of him, that clotted on his wife's suit and on the bouquet she carried was O, Rh positive. The same type that rang in his ears and turned his skin clammy.

He went back to the account. The state where it happened led the entire country in homicides. More murders were committed there each month than in all England.

By that date, November, there had been a hundred and ten murders in that city alone. There were warnings, premonitions. A national committeeman had urged those around the President not to allow him to enter a city where swastikas were smeared on Jewish shops, where billboards carried the text IMPEACH EARL WARREN, where Christian Crusaders and Minutemen sang, "Stevenson is going to die, die, die. His heart will stop, stop, stop. And he will burn, burn, burn."

Hate oozed like pus through the city that oppressed its minorities, that feared black men and education and liberals and intellectuals. There was an old saying that in the Southwest, a man who stopped to think before firing his weapon was dead. That tradition persisted. Posters were put up with the Chief Executive's picture and the caption: WANTED FOR TREASON.

The *Morning News* ran a scurrilous editorial. Responsible local citizens were alarmed at the climate of smoldering rancor. An eminent evangelist attempted to transmit his fears. A member of the President's party was upset when he saw the forty-five minute, open-car route published in two papers.

And a thwarted and confused man, who had previously made an abortive attempt on the life of a U.S. general, walked the streets and saw the posters and read those papers. He had defected to Russia only to discover he was the same ineffectual misfit there. His wife took their two children and walked out. The day before the presidential visit he pleaded for a reconciliation. His wife permitted him to spend the night, but laughed when he made overtures and jeered at him as incompetent, impotent, not a man.

It was incredible that this shabby creature and his marital difficulties were inextricably intertwined in a drama involving a man of such eminence. Had the wife relented, turned to her husband in the night, the President of the United States would have lived.

But instead, a rejected human being, feeling himself inadequate, took off his wedding ring and left it on the dresser in his wife's room along with the contents of his wallet, a hundred and eighty-seven dollars in creased, rumpled bills. Then going into the garage he put a hidden mail-order bolt-action, clip-fed, 6.5-mm Mannlicher-Carcano rifle with a four-power telescopic sight into a brown paper bag.

Josh slammed the book shut with a violence that caused heads to turn. In the stillness of the room it might have been that fateful shot. He spent the afternoon at a dentist's getting the braces fitted back into place. At first the man didn't want to do it. Josh had to convince him it was a practical joke.

Once again he was semidisguised. He put his dark glasses on and was ready to face the world. He checked into a hotel, stocked up with the daily paper, *Time*, and *Global Report*. He read until two A.M. and then dreamed he wasn't able to sleep. The reason was, he was driving in an open Lincoln, a target held stationary by a back brace. He turned into a canvas ringed red, white, and blue, and felt the bullet hit a bull's eye. Bells rang. He cried out and it was morning.

He had put in a call with the desk for eight thirty so he could have breakfast. But he didn't want breakfast. Instead he walked up Pennsylvania Avenue and stood waiting as tourists assembled for the first guided tour of the day. The next seventy-two hours were to be a pilgrimage into his own past. The father who in all likelihood had not known of his conception was his only link with himself.

He speculated that, had his father lived, it would have made no essential difference in his life. He was not a private person, he could not be expected to acknowledge a bastard son. The result would have been the same, to hide him away with some suitable family.

The puzzle was why had the circumstances of the President's life been grafted to his own? If there had been no other issue— But there was a son. A legitimate son, four years older than he.

Perhaps his position was heir to the heir apparent. Insurance, just in case. From time to time he had seen pictures in the paper of his half brother and sister. Neither of them had the strong resemblance to their father that he had.

The tour got underway, past the Ionic columns of the main floor, the salons, and the great State dining room. He had forgotten that there was a doctor's suite and dentist's office. They inspected the TV broadcasting facilities, were told of the bomb shelter, large enough to accommodate all White House employees. A pervasive air-conditioning blotted out the exterior heat. His father had utilized these rooms, walked these corridors, scribbled autographs for sightseers, grasped extended hands. But beyond this, who was the man he sought?

The private moments were not recorded, the intimate times when he played with his children or dined with his young wife. What had been lacking in that perfect Sunday-supplement romance? Why had he turned for companionship to—whom?

Who was his mother? These marbled floors and

satin-draped windows and imposing balustrades said nothing. They had known four first families since.

He was brought up short before a full-length portrait. He looked into his own face. He had come full circle. But the well-defined, half-smiling lips held no special message for him. It was an impersonal, benign glance that fell on all alike.

The tour went on, the guide droning facts and dates. Josh was left behind, bemused in front of the man he was determined to know. A guard touched his arm. The intrusion brought him to the present. He did not rejoin the others. He'd had enough. The identification he wanted was not to be found here. He proceeded with his plan.

The plan took him to the airport. He had a belated breakfast and by noon was airborne, heading for the city where his father had been assassinated. He deplaned at a field with an ironically pacific name, just as nineteen years ago his father had. He arrived by commercial flight: his father had used his favorite Boeing 747, the flagship of the presidential fleet.

Everything had been coded that day. The plane, the flight, the man. The Secret Service was so busy with their games that they had let him die. The President, as nearly as he could figure out, was only there because of the incompetence of the vice-president whose territory it was. John Nance Garner once said, "Being vice-president isn't exactly a crime, but it's kind of a disgrace, like writing anonymous letters."

It seemed to him from his reading the day before that factionalism had split the party in the vice-president's back yard. The President became convinced his own healing touch was required. And he put forth an effort. His wife, representing the haute couture of the East, rode beside him. Sheer personal magnetism was to weld the factions together.

A blazing sun struck Josh's face. He flagged a cab which he took into the downtown area and dismissed. He wanted to follow the route on foot. The façade of buildings that had borne witness jumped at him out of context. Thom McAn Shoes, Hallmark Cards, Hart Schaffner and Marx, Walgreen Drugstore, the Neiman-Marcus department store. Plate glass, manikins, tubular neon signs, these things remained.

He came to the marker in the plaza. At first glance it appeared to be an ordinary testimonial to the achievements of the city. Then the statement: *This site unfortunately became the scene of a tragedy which plunged the world into a state of shock.*

He walked on, turning onto Houston. He wasn't interested in the killer. He didn't want to know where he had his warren of a room, or where the house was that his wife lived, or where the theater he hid out in. But his eyes searched the sixth-floor window of the corner building which presented a clear unobstructed view of the motorcade as it rolled slowly by.

Slowly, so the President could be seen and waved at and called to, so the eyes of the crowd might look into his. So that the young wife in her French original might be gazed at. On her lap was a presentation bouquet of red roses shortly to be soaked in blood. *O rose, thou art sick! The invisible worm that flies in the night, in the howling storm, has found out thy bed of crimson joy, and his dark secret love does thy life destroy.* It was to shed blots of blood instead of petals.

Why had no one listened to that national committeeman who knew the temper of this city, who cried Cassandra-like warnings with the voice of a thousand years?

Why did no one apprehend the man the FBI had in their files, who was a known defector and who worked in a building along the route the President would take? It seemed an elementary precaution.

As the cavalcade proceeded down Main Street and along Houston, the President's outgoing charm seemed to win the crowd. The people cheered him. Were they the same housewives who three years before had sprayed the vice-president with saliva? Was the smiling crowd the same that assaulted Adlai Stevenson on United Nations Day?

A man at the curb touched his wife's arm and pointed to the sixth floor of the building opposite. "Look honey, if you want to see a Secret Service man." He assumed the figure leaning forward taking a bead with his rifle was covering the presidential party. They watched him squeeze the trigger.

It was twelve thirty. The car had just made a sharp one-hundred-and-twenty-degree turn into Elm Street. The big Lincoln slowed almost to a stop and proceeded at eleven and two-tenths miles per hour. The President was shot through the neck, but not fatally. The bullet bruised his right lung, tore through his windpipe, and exited his throat carrying away a piece of his tie before passing through the body of the governor and cutting a swath through his back, chest, right wrist, and left thigh.

The President was held rigid by a back brace. Everyone else in the car threw themselves down. The President remained an upright target. He started to raise his hand toward his head, the gesture was never completed, the top of the head was no longer there, the second shot blew it off. Band-tailed pigeons rose in alarm forming an unfinished V overhead.

The beautiful woman in beautiful attire flung herself across her husband. She bent over him, cradling him, holding the mangled head against her.

Carnage is red. Slaughter is red. But it is also viscous and thick. A sheet of blood poured over everything; the upholstery was drenched, the carpeting, the roses. Gobs of blood as thick as hunks of liver lay on the pristine pink suit, splattered the stockings. And matter from the brain stuck against the leather trim.

The heart still labored, pumping out enormous quantities of blood which continued to gush from the top of his head. The brain was destroyed. But the body, trim, healthy, young, made continued, strangled efforts to breathe.

The hospital was four miles away. Josh kept walking. His own respiration was spasmodic. The heat pounded on top of his head like a wound. Why was he putting himself through this? Why couldn't he stop?

Compulsion had taken over. How far away was Calvary? Concentric circles flamed behind his eyes. Buildings and vacant lots and the concrete of the road swirled, mixed, joined each other's forms. He walked through it seeing the heavy cars racing this street, hoping through speed and sirens and horns and belated efficiency to undo what had been done, hoping to mop up the blood that still spurted and sprayed over everything. Stuff back the membranous tissue, bandage and cover and pray. But shock still paralyzed them. The car radio couldn't be made to work.

When they arrived at the hospital at twelve thirty-six no one was ready. There was no stretcher, no doctor, not even an ambulance attendant. No one was functioning. A reporter wrote reams of notes that later he was unable to read.

That time, nineteen years past, was tangential to present time. His mind reconstructed the scene through eyewitness accounts, yet at a deeper level experienced the dead tragedy. It was almost as though it were he himself who after the first shot remained stiffly braced, awaiting the second.

In some odd way there was symbiosis; he *knew* the searing pain in the throat, *remembered* the feeling of helplessness as he sat unable to move, waiting for the second discharge.

It was a strange kind of memory, it didn't seem to be located in his mind but in his body. His throat recalled the rapid tearing of tissues, saliva disappeared from his mouth. The sun must have gotten to him. He felt himself blacking out, dead. He leaned against a tree, breathing deeply until the world righted itself and appeared with normal and accustomed contours, no blurring, no running together; sky was sky; fence, fence; and hospital, hospital.

There it was directly ahead of him, a drab, rambling three-story building. An incongruous spot for a great man to have breathed his last. *Holy Mary, Mother of God, pray for us sinners now and at the hour of our death, amen. Eternal rest grant unto him, O Lord. And let perpetual light shine upon him.*

He stood a moment longer. His pilgrimage was almost complete. He would return to Washington, kneel at the Eternal Flame where the rest of his family had knelt, and much of America. And then it would be done. His orientation toward his new self could be accomplished.

For ten days he sequestered himself in a downtown Washington hotel suite. He was so familiar with the striped wallpaper that he knew exactly where it was seamed. He was growing a beard, and the curly stubble considerably altered his appearance. He felt he would be able to dispense with the braces permanently. He went to the same dentist and had the job done.

Returning to his bed-sitting room, he wrote a brief note to Bitterbaum asking to see him and requesting that he say nothing to his family. He was not able to forgive Lynn and G.K. They were the principals in the charade. Especially Lynn who had been his mother and whom he now called by her first name.

He saw no reason to cut himself off permanently from his brother and cousin. He was convinced that they were as ignorant of the whole affair as he had been. And the girls of course had known nothing. But the more he thought of it, the more he was positive that Uncle Thor held the key to the mystery. He had been instrumental in the girls' adoption. It was conceivable that it was he who arranged and manipulated events to bring about what he considered "the best" for that unwanted but potentially important child.

Josh had been slightly uncomfortable all his life with the great surge of affection that Uncle Thor displayed toward him. He knew that in Uncle Thor's eyes he was special. Now he began to understand. He understood too the cause of his, at times, uneasy response. He was loved in a context, a framework, almost as though he were a young prince. That was it, the mystique forbade the very thing that would have made them close. Now he could use that affection to get at the truth. He had to know it all. He had to know who his mother was.

A maid discovered the letter propped on the dresser and brought it to Lynn. She remained calm. She went to a phone and dialed the forty-sixth floor of the Rockefeller Plaza, New York, which was headquarters and clearinghouse for the family. The secretary there would know where G.K. could be reached, and reroute the call.

She misdialed a number she knew better than her present address. This small mishap unstrung her completely. Her hands began to tremble and she felt tears at the back of her eyes.

She had known this would happen. She had told Gerald at the beginning. One way or another those things always come out. But he wouldn't listen, he was adamant on the subject. She supposed he was afraid that if Josh knew that much, he might deduce his illegitimacy. And of course it would be as awkward for Gerald to acknowledge a bastard, as for Josh to be put in that position. Just as it would be embarrassing for Josh to know that his mother had been her rival and his father's mistress.

Lynn had given much thought to this. She always wondered when her husband was able to fit in a serious affair. At the time she had no intimation of such a thing. She had imagined that if it ever happened, she would know. She hadn't. They had been married at that time only two years. Gerald had been extremely devoted.

But one could not deny the child. She loved this second son. There had been a rapport with him that existed with none of the others, not even her own. Perhaps because her love was mixed with trepidation and fear for him. As a natural child he was exposed and vulnerable. And she constituted herself his shield. She found a special sweetness in his response. He was shy and introverted by nature, and she took delight in drawing him out. No matter how busy she was, there were always moments in the day reserved for him, that special tug of the hair in passing, a private look, a joke.

She dialed again, taking care not to contrapose any of the digits. New York answered. "Henry," she said without preliminaries, "please locate my husband. It's urgent."

Henry suggested that she switch off and Mr. Kellogg would get back to her. She did, setting herself the task of going over the weekly menu. But she couldn't concentrate. She read Josh's note again. *"I know."* Dear God, how dreadful to make such a discovery. And he addressed her as Lynn, not mother, Lynn. She had been racking her brain to figure out how it had happened. There were no overnight guests. It was too early for visitors. She reconstructed the morning. It was the anniversary of her mother's death fifteen years before. She had taken her prayer book to the conservatory. She read several prayers thinking of the woman who had been her mother. Wondering how well she had known her.

She had looked at the morning paper, then picked up her embroidery. She was doing pillowcases for both girls to take to school, working their names into a rosette design. She occupied herself with this for maybe half an hour when she was called to the phone.

Wait, wait—the prayer book. Her heart began expanding, expanding like bread rising. Except this was heavy, a growing weight. Hopelessness was its leaven, despair its yeast.

She saw it now. Josh must have wandered into the room, idly picked up the prayer book, absently riffled its pages. The handwriting on the flyleaf caught his eye.

How could she have been so careless, negligently careless? Was it similar to a Freudian death wish? At some level had she wanted Josh to know? To love her anyway?

Love her? He called her Lynn. He must hate her.

She and Gerald had set up a lie and lived it every day for eighteen years. There had been no honesty. Josh couldn't forgive that.

The phone rang. It was New York. She switched on

the off-set screen. Reduced to a three-by-five frame Gerald did not look imposing. But he came through confident, strong.

"Hello, Lynn. Henry said urgent. Is everything all right?"

"No. It isn't. Josh has left home. Gerald, he knows."

"What did you say?"

"He knows, Gerald."

The transatlantic cable seemed to groan. It whispered *Christ.* He rallied. "How do you know? Was there a scene? Did he walk out, leave a note, what?"

"He left a note."

"Read it." The peremptory quality of his voice helped steady her. She read the note. "Christ, Lynn, this is worse than you know."

"What do you mean?"

"I can't explain now. If Josh should contact you, let me know immediately. And try to find out where he is. If Bitterbaum calls, have him phone me. You don't know how it happened? How he found out?"

"No," she said with the mental proviso that she would amend her lie at some later time. "Gerald, you said it was worse than I know—"

"Lynn, not now. I'll get back to you. Sit tight." He rang off to arrange for a detective and call Bitterbaum in Los Angeles. His answering service said he was not expected until Monday. Henry, on another line, reached him at his beach house. He plugged G.K. in. "Bitterbaum, he knows."

Bitterbaum said, "G.K.? Is that you?"

"It's me, damn it. Josh found out. He knows."

"Wait, hold on. I've got to lower the hi-fi." There

was a moment's pause, then he was back. "Did you say Josh knows?"

"That's right. He left. He's run off. Bitterbaum, are you there?"

"*What* does he know? Exactly what?"

"Everything."

"It isn't possible. Think a minute, G.K. It isn't possible. Tell me what happened."

"I just talked to Lynn at *Westwind.* Josh left a note that said, *I know.* He also said not to try to find him."

"All right. He's found out something. Enough to put him into a tailspin. He probably found out he's adopted."

"You think that's it?"

"I think it has to be."

"God. I hope you're right. All I could think of was that the whole thing had blown wide open. I couldn't figure how. But I figured it had to be. When he wrote, *I know,* I panicked. So help me God, I panicked. But you're absolutely right, Bitterbaum. If I'd stopped to consider, there's no way he could know except I told him or you told him."

"And you thought I told him?"

"I don't know what I thought. What he said in the note was, *I know.* But that's it, he's found out he's adopted. It's a shock to a kid of that age, I guess. He's crazy about Lynn, always been close to her. I think I'll call off that detective."

"What detective?"

"I'm telling you, Bitterbaum, I flipped out. But I can see Josh needs to work it through alone. Right?"

"I'd say so."

"I'll be in London this weekend. If you hear from him let me know."

"Try to calm Lynn down. I imagine she's pretty upset."

"Will do. Take care of yourself."

Bitterbaum flicked off the phone and poured himself a Scotch. He had received more of a jolt than he let on. For one horrible moment the whole elaborate structure was shaken, a crack appeared, widening as he looked. He cast ahead to the next moment, the moment when it would crash and bury him.

But common sense held it together. Josh couldn't know the truth. The calamity had been staved off. But it was only postponed, deferred. It would topple and sweep his life away.

And Josh?

He kept that hatch closed. It occurred to him that Josh might try to get in touch with him. He phoned his secretary and asked her to drive out to the office and check on his mail. He fixed himself another drink. This time he added soda. He took it out on the porch to watch the sunset over the water. Half an hour went by. The color deepened and gradually faded. A white moon separated sea and sand. The waves lunged at the shore with reverberating shocks. Miss Oakes phoned to say there was no mail.

It was nearly two weeks before the letter arrived. It was postmarked Washington, D.C. He turned it over in his hand. It had to be Josh. But what was he doing there? The family had never lived there. It had been a place to pass through en route to somewhere else. Why pick Washington? What affinity could he have for the place? Was it coincidence? Did the twin resemblance cause him to guess? But how could you guess a thing like that?

He read Josh's curt, formal request for an interview.

The apprehension he had succeeded in lifting from G.K. settled over him.

Bitterbaum primed himself for the confrontation by reminding himself to listen. *Don't assume too much. Listen. Let him tell it.* He had discovered this worked very well with patients. Many of them knew much better than he what was wrong with them. And they certainly knew better what helped them.

He chose the beach house for the meeting, hoping the relaxed, informal atmosphere would subtly influence the course of things. Toward this end he made sure there was a six-pack in the refrigerator and cold cuts. But when Josh arrived it was plain that all such extraneous considerations were worthless.

In the first place Bitterbaum hardly recognized him. His hair was long and his features semihidden in a sprouting beard. Another item did not escape his attention. The braces were gone. He masked his anxiety with a friendly tap to the boy's shoulders. "How are you, Josh?"

"Okay." He glanced around the room. "Can we talk on the porch?"

"Sure. Why not?" He led the way. Did he think he had the room bugged? "How would a beer go?"

Josh shook his head. There was impatience at this introduction of trivia. "You know I've left home?"

"Your father called me." *Listen,* he reminded himself. If there's a silence, don't mind. Wait for him to reveal himself.

"I left a note explaining."

Bitterbaum said mildly, "I don't think your folks considered it much of an explanation."

"In the first place they're not my folks. We both know that."

"I don't know anything of the kind," Bitterbaum said.

Josh looked at him for the first time with anger. "I'm adopted."

"Yes," Bitterbaum said, "so are the girls. That certainly hasn't made them less loved or wanted. I don't see them running away from home."

"That's right. But they weren't lied to. I don't have to ask you why they lied to me. I know. I know who I am."

Bitterbaum felt a sense of displacement. The waves rolling in on the beach crashed and breathed inside his head.

"All my life," Josh went on, "people have told me who I look like. Of course, the braces were clever. Did you think of that, Uncle Thor?"

The first rocks were loosed and sliding by him. He waited for the avalanche.

"Once I knew the Kelloggs weren't my parents, the resemblance became important. I was able to figure out who I am."

Bitterbaum straightened and let go of the railing. What's the good of clutching a wooden railing when you're about to be clobbered, when a lifetime of machination is going to pour over your head, sweep you away? "Well?" The word didn't come out clearly. He repeated it. "Well, so tell me. Who are you?"

"You know goddamned well that my father was the former President of the United States. He was assassinated in—"

"All right, all right, all right." His relief was almost a prayer, a palpable thing.

"What I want from you, Uncle Thor, are the details. Who is my mother? Does his family know about me? Who arranged for the Kelloggs to bring me up? How much do they know?"

"Hold on, Josh. I can't satisfy you on most counts because I don't know. I can tell you that Lynn Kellogg was told you were G.K.'s natural son. She could have no more children and she welcomed taking you."

He thought there was a momentary softening in Josh. But almost immediately he was back on the track. "But Dad knew?"

"And I knew. To answer your other question, as to your mother, there is simply no record. It was handled before your birth. Dr. Clemens made the contact. I was covering his practice at the time. He's dead now and there are no records except of the adoption itself. G.K. was eager to have you."

"Why? Why was he eager to have me? Looking back I have the feeling I've been programmed to follow the same course as my father. It seems to me my life, my family, my religion, even the emphasis on sports and competitive games, was an effort to reconstruct my father's early environment. Why? I have a brother. His legitimate son. Am I the extra string to the bow, held in readiness in case anything happens to him? That just isn't realistic. Doesn't G.K. realize that the stigma *bastard* can't be overcome?"

"Steady on, Josh. No one's programmed you for anything. You're the adopted son of wealthy parents who have given you the best. Okay? I don't see anything sinister about that. Were you, for example, brought up differently from Jer or Steve?"

Josh leaned his tousled head into his hands.

"You've had a shock. A double shock. But don't be too hard on us, Josh."

Josh lifted his head and looked with intense directness at Bitterbaum. "I'll tell you what, Uncle Thor, I'll put everything in the balance. If you answer one question with complete honesty, I'll feel that perhaps there's a basis for trust."

"What's your question?"

"You'll think it's odd, but I really want to know. Remember that girl, Lefty, that lived near us in Malibu? She moved away about five years ago. I wrote a couple of times. She never answered. I want to know, did she get my letters?"

"No, she didn't."

The blue-gray eyes never faltered. "Thanks. But can you tell me why?"

Bitterbaum wet his lips with his tongue.

"No," Josh said, "I'll tell you. It wasn't part of the program. There was no place for anything that I arranged for myself or did of my own volition. It's what I said before, my whole life was laid out." He had been pacing, now he came to a stop opposite him. "Look, I appreciate your leveling with me. I appreciate the fact that G.K. wasn't sitting here when I walked in. What I'm saying is, it's okay between us. And I'll write mother. But I won't go home. I can't ever go back to being some kind of pawn."

"You're still reacting emotionally, Josh. Go ahead,

take time to think things through. When you do, I believe there are opportunities that G.K. provides that you can't turn down, one of which is Harvard in the fall."

"I don't want anything from him," Josh said violently, "not Harvard, not anything." He fished a piece of paper out of his pocket. It was an IOU in the amount of fifteen hundred dollars. "It's what I took from my bank account when I left. I've dated it this time next year. He'll have back every penny by then."

Bitterbaum smiled, his thin lips always managed to twist into a rueful expression. "I don't think G.K. needs fifteen hundred dollars. I do think he may need a son."

"I was never that. He had me waiting on the sidelines, just in case. He was hedging some bet, playing a long shot. How do I know what was in his mind? But I do know I was part of a scheme. The thing with Lefty proves it."

"Can you tell me where you're going?"

"No. This has got to be on my own. I've got to scratch the surface and see what kind of a guy is there—you know, beneath the tennis and the sailing and the golf."

"And the beard," Bitterbaum amended.

Josh grinned.

That flashing, dazzling smile grabbed at his heart. When he was alone again, Bitterbaum asked himself if he had listened well enough. He hoped to God he had. He recalled Paul Tillich's phrase, *a listening love.* That seemed to him the best kind of love one could give. And this boy who had gone in search of himself needed the stoutest and the best, especially if, God forbid, he should succeed in his quest.

Due largely to Bitterbaum's intercession with the family, Josh continued on his own. It was another world than he had known. Previously he had jetted over it, zoomed through it, hopped from hotels to villas to clubs. He was, however, a stranger in the world of all-night diners and pizzaburger joints. And he had never heard of Chicken Delight.

He got a job delivering orders. He invested in an electric mobile and rented a room in Venice. This was a beach slum they were upgrading by getting rid of old buildings and old people, as well as clearing out the blacks and zippies. Half the places he served had eviction notices plastered over the doors. But no one seemed to bother about them. The wheels of justice creaked. There were so many cases bogged down in the lower courts and small claims division that squatters sat on for months unmolested.

One of the places on his route used captured souvenir flags from all the guerrilla wars the country had engaged in, as window curtains. Exterior and interior walls were often done in pop art, some with Oriental motifs. In one building stained-glass windows were in the process of being welded into leaded frames.

He got used to accepting tips from paunchy, florid men in undershirts and frail old ladies in paisley dresses. A couple of college girls invited him to join a pot party. He, who had met people only in a formal context, now caught and returned frisbies, was asked his opinion on how to set out a tomato vine, was consulted on arithmetic, asked for help in locating a free clinic.

Many of these people didn't include cooking in their life style. Or possibly they were addicted to Chicken Delight. He made as many as three or four calls at one address in a single week. In fact, when a day went by, he would wonder what old Mr. Larson was doing about dinner. Between calls he stopped to find out. Mr. Larson was watching the fights on cartridge television and drinking beer. He insisted Josh join him.

From the beginning he was conscious of a curious acceptance. There were preliminaries. "You're new on the job, right?" And a few more probing queries. "You in school, son?" These he turned aside easily. They didn't really want to know. It was a way of saying, *Where are you at?*

Josh thought of the nameless hands into which he had pressed coins all over the globe. He hadn't actually considered that they were people leading lives. The first time he took a tip from a black, he noticed. My life is really upside-down, he thought.

Poverty was a mulch which spawned night prowlers and human shapes rolled under billboards. *Orange Julius. Vita-C Cola. There's an Electrocar in Your Future.* But is there a future in your future? Tribal tattoos, the witch doctor of Habit puncturing arms and thighs and stomachs. The dark wasn't dark enough. It didn't hide, it didn't cover. The low riders, black princes of the night, inflections reaching falsetto highs. "Move, white boy, or you get cut. You surely get cut."

Laughter.

The comedy of the street. The Anglos. White pimply faces. They don't come singly. They were born in packs. A drunk doesn't make it, he goes down. Funneee!

A kid steps in puke. Hilarious!

Two rutting dogs can't uncouple. Man, look at that! The male pulls and pulls, running with the yipping female. He stands still and heaves, pulling her insides out.

Josh put the animal in the back of his mobile. But it hemorrhaged all over the seat and was dead by the time he got to a vet.

Again laughter. "Heard you got yourself a dog." He began to understand. It wasn't that they were subhuman, cruel, and devoid of compassion. They couldn't do a damn thing about it. Laugh or you cried, you swore, you got stoned and screamed.

Little girls his sisters' age, turning tricks. "Like, get with it." Even the ocean was unclean; orange peels and cellophane floated in on a sludge of tan waves, and yellow froth gurgled with scum at its edge. Old men sieved the sand, and if they found anything, younger ones took it from them.

Speech was scatological, the body and its functions were the reference point for every known situation and condition. Raucous, dangerous, exploding in a second, this was the culture of the inane drunken laugh, the alley rape, the war between hogs. Knives were neat and lethal, bottles messier. He saw a human eye plop on the boardwalk where it quivered like an undercooked fried egg.

He thought of the entire population as the disposables. Disposable wrappers, disposable bottles, disposable people. Their prey were themselves.

His attitudes were changing. He saw reclamation projects as legal means of ejecting and evicting, driving the disposables from the bit of territory they held. Once an area was reclaimed, they could not afford it. He began to look on the hovercraft speedway that bisected Venice as alien. With the other disposables he watched the playboys in nautical attire jetting just over the surface on their way to the marina for a day's pleasure cruising. Once he would have been among their number. Now he regarded these sportsmen from another life and distant perspective.

The transformation that occurred in him was profound. Lynn always said if he was in trouble, call an officer. That was the last thing you did. Pigs rousted you, hauled off the little guy, letting the big wheels alone. They were on the take with the local merchants. It was a microcosm, small-time stuff. But Josh began to extrapolate. Certain stories G.K. told at table came back to him. The world of international power politics was not that different. The scale was different.

When the door opened, he saw that the room across from his was filled with stripped car parts, bicycles, and television spheres. The kids that lived there were about fifteen. Where did you start when the robber was fifteen or younger? Was there a way to recycle people?

In a way Josh was more naive, with less experience than any child of the neighborhood. The kids were ferrets, they'd dug out hiding places in the rubble. When the old man was on the rampage or the old lady brought home some guy, there were places they could hole up. They were swift to see a blow coming, quick to elude it.

Josh walked into things. Things he had never dreamed of and didn't know about. The bathroom was down the hall. The door was left open when it was not in use. The cubicle revolted him and he always brought paper to spread around, and even to stand on. The stink that issued from the encrusted toilet made him retch. As much as possible he used the bathroom at work. But when he came home at night he needed a shower, which was in the tub, an arrangement he had never seen before.

This particular evening he took his towel and a bar of soap down the hall. The door was open so he went in. He was attacked by a nude male who had been standing behind the door in a state of erection, waiting. Josh's habits were regular and the man had not waited long.

Josh's personal integrity, the clean-cut quality of his appearance, his assumption of fair play had been a shield and buckler. He walked among them, but he was not one of them. They stole covert glances. He was slender but athletic, striding past with boxes of Chicken Delight. Sometimes they called in orders to see him again. Young god, with a friendly smile that made you feel good. Venice accepted him, ghetto, barrio, whorehouse, he walked in innocence and safety, because it pleased them. It pleased them that he wasn't afraid. It amused them that he didn't know enough to be afraid.

But even among criminals, there are outcasts. His name was Merle. An effeminate name but no one laughed at it or made jokes. He had been a boxer, the big top had known him. He worked out at Muscle Beach, lifting weights, lifting boys. He had observed Josh two weeks ago, followed him, clocked him, checked out the rooming house. He smeared his body with oil so it was impossible for Josh to get a hold on him. His hands slid around, his fists glanced off. They struggled, and finally crashed against the tub. The man struck the base of his head and lay stunned.

Josh turned on the light. One naked bulb showed him the thick torso, the thick features. The eyes were blue like a doll's and almost at the surface of his face.

Josh said, looking down, "I've never killed anyone. But I could kill you. And I will if I ever see you again." He kicked the man's flowered shirt and sleazy trousers into the hall. The man got up off the floor keeping his eyes on Josh and went after them.

Josh locked the door and had his shower. He was trembling. He had seen into his own nature. It was true what he had told the man: he could kill.

Weekends were busiest. No one wanted to cook on the weekend. He was the supernumerary with his box of deep-fried chicken parts walking through lives and scenes that in no way touched his. One call he made frequently was to an old lady whose old children came every week to visit her and tell her she should go into a home. But the lady refused to budge from the place she had spent forty years. Each week her old children determinedly reopened the long-standing argument. Josh thought of the old woman as the wallpaper lady. Her dress was similar in pattern to her wallpaper, both were lavender and flowered. She looked as though she had just stepped out of it.

She always had a task saved for him. He was to come

in and adjust her television, or would he look up a telephone number, or locate her glasses? He decided she wasn't as delicate as she appeared, as she ate her Chicken Delight with Tokay and butterfingers. One weekend she didn't send for her usual order. So Monday he dropped around to check on her. The house had a FOR SALE sign in front. He went so far as to ring a neighbor's bell and ask after her. But they knew nothing other than that she had gone away with two other white-haired people. The description matched that of her children. So he supposed they had won and she was placed in a home after all.

For some reason this depressed him very much. It was the start of a bad day, the worst in his life. The evening that began with the capitulation of the old lady ended when he opened the door to his room and saw Uncle Thor.

His hundred days, the hundred days that had passed since he left *Westwind,* he had been on a long string. He could hear G.K., *Give him his head.* That had been the reasoning, the consensus. His sense of freedom was illusory. Every move he had made was known and reported.

In a hundred days Napoleon almost won back his empire. And he had delivered Chicken Delight.

So the family decided he had had his fling and now he was to be carted off home. He set his mind and will against the involuntary pleasure at seeing the angular stooped frame. The familiar features, the high-bridged nose that overhung his face, and the kindly myopic eyes belonged to another life, the one he had abandoned.

Josh didn't inquire into the mechanics of being

spied upon. It amused him to think of some high-powered agency man making out a report on his activity—*delivered fried chicken to 110 Maple Avenue at six thirty, then proceeded* . . . It was ludicrous. At least he told himself it was, so as not to get angry. He didn't want to quarrel with Uncle Thor.

Then he noticed what he had been too preoccupied to see, that the long pretzel-like figure stooped and twisted itself further to avoid looking at him. Josh placed himself directly in front of him and the multi-toned eyes slid past his own. Apprehension replaced anger. His stomach tightened in spasm. The ancients believed the liver was the seat of the emotions. But with Josh the stomach was the indicator. It absorbed a knowledge still hidden from his mind. What had he seen? He didn't know, he couldn't analyze the look. "Is everything all right?" he asked.

What happened next was so surprising to him that he forgot to be dismayed. Uncle Thor turned away and began to cry.

Josh was beside him in a moment. "Uncle Thor!"

He nodded to indicate he had hold of himself. "Josh. It's heavy. Steve was killed in a car smash-up yesterday, just outside Lugano, Italy. He was driving the Porsche. It turned over three times. It was totaled."

Totaled? Steve was totaled. Heavy, Uncle Thor said. Heavy, heavy, hangs over thy head. What shall the owner do . . . "What shall I do to redeem him?"

"What?"

"Does mom know?"

"Yes."

"Where is the family?"

"At Malibu."

"Let's go." He kept thinking, it's a mistake. The Porsche was a birthday present, green and drawing-board sleek. How can a birthday present kill you? "How did it happen?" he asked.

"It wasn't a collision. No other car was involved. I thought those lousy bastard Italian drivers, but it wasn't that. They think he fell asleep at the wheel. The car went off the road."

"Who saw him? Who reported it?"

"It was handled locally. But apparently he died instantly."

"That's what they always say, isn't it? To make you feel better?" *How can we be talking about it? It didn't happen. Steve is tough. He can tackle like a pro. And diving, there's nobody like him, half-gainers were his specialty. Were. Were? So I do believe it. No. He was tough. He had a great tan. You couldn't die with a great tan.* "Was he thrown clear?"

"No. He was pinned under the car."

"It didn't . . . catch fire?"

"No."

He was glad it didn't catch fire. Which was kind of crazy, dead is dead.

"They performed an autopsy."

Josh held up his hand. He didn't want to hear. They open you up, they catalogue your organs. They decide were you smashed or torn open. What suffocated, what strangulated, what bled. But it didn't matter. Steve, with his jokes, his sense of humor, his golf handicap, and his plan to go into politics, was dead.

It surprised him that he hadn't thought of God, of Jesus, in connection with Steve's death. He quickly said a *Hail Mary.* Death. Thanos. What was it? When he was a kid he thought it was being removed—like from a game. You lose a checker piece, you take him off the board, he's dead.

His game would have to be played from now on without Steve. No more conferences on girls, or plans for camping, or shooting the rapids in Colorado, or trading books on the north face of the Eiger, or hand-wrestling, or outdoing each other with push-ups. Steve held the record with sixty. He'd been getting into shape to better it. Now it would stand.

Steve had saved his life. Why couldn't he have saved him? Suppose he had been there instead of delivering Chicken Delight for three months? He would have talked to him, kept him awake, taken a turn at the wheel. He had been ringing doorbells of people he didn't even know when Steve died.

That seemed to him grotesque. People he didn't know had been saying, "Thanks, son." And Steve . . .

He followed Uncle Thor downstairs. He didn't take anything. He knew he'd never be back, but he didn't take anything. Toothbrush, comb, socks, underwear, a few paperbacks, the things he had acquired were shucked off.

Uncle Thor paid the two passenger toll on the Coast Hyway. He was returning to Elba in the heart of The Malibu, seventeen miles of dazzling sea pressed into a narrow border by the hills. On certain days the smog still reached this far.

This was one of them. It hurt to breathe. Your lungs expanded and drank in the yellow shroud that hung along the coast. And your chest cavity sucked into it alien things that burned and irritated. Your chest ached. It felt hollow and it ached.

Uncle Thor turned up the drive. "Okay, Josh?"

"Yeah." It was a grunt. Speech hadn't been invented yet. Death came first, before speech. And there were still no words for it, nothing adequate to describe it or what it does or what it leaves. He thought of Ellen. Two gone out of seven.

Just inside the front door Cindy threw herself at him. "I knew you'd come home. I knew it. I knew it. Oh, Josh." She had the bony angles of adolescence and her grief looked comic. He kissed her forehead opposite his face. "Where's mother?"

"In her room. It's awful, Josh. She doesn't say anything. She hasn't said anything since it happened. Vicki threw up. And we all said prayers. A letter came just yesterday saying he would be home next week. That's what makes it seem so funny."

"Is Jer here?"

"Yes, he's here."

"Tell him and the girls I'm home. I'll meet you in the upstairs study. Okay?" He went up the oak stairs, his hand gliding the banister. He knocked on his mother's door and entered. She looked up. Her face was composed. She hadn't kissed him since he was thirteen, but she got up, went over to him, and kissed him now.

They both knew it meant that she took him for her son, and that he was her son. That disposed of, she said, "I'm glad you're back, Josh." She said it casually as though he had returned from the movies.

"Is there anything I can do, mother?"

"Try to devise things for the girls to take their

minds off it a bit. And tell Delia not to bring any more flowers up here. I hate them like this in pots and tinfoil."

Josh noticed them for the first time. The calla lilies looked obscene with their bursting stamens. There were cut flowers too. The water was clear but tomorrow or the day after it would be brackish and dank. "Oh God," he put his hands across his stomach and bent in half. His mother, whom he meant to comfort, held and comforted him.

For the months of summer that were left Josh asked the questions that have no answers. Ellen's death had touched him. But it wasn't exactly unexpected. Everything about Ellen had been special; that she should die was sad, but reasonable. This was unreasonable. Until Steve died, no one had died. Now he opened his mind to his own death and the dissolution of all he knew. He began to work on a pastiche of death, a collage of verses.

I, who exulted in sunshine and laughter,
dreamed not of dying—death is such
a waste of me.

Death, the sable flame where vanishes
the smoke.

He added Webster's common sense: *You cease to die by dying.* And Kahlil the prophet: *What is it to stop breathing, but to free the breath from its restless tides.*

He was not comforted. He could find no meaning in Steve's death. What was an accident? If death could be an accident, why not life? They were one fabric, death was the twist in the Moebius strip. If death was senseless, so was life.

He would not be reconciled to this. He felt as though he were in some kind of trap. He must think his way out. In the meantime he acquiesced in everything, was agreeable to everything. But no wish, desire, drive, push emanated from him. The family decided he would go to Harvard in the fall.

He read books not to prepare himself but because he wanted to communicate with other men and yet not talk to them. He didn't know what he thought or believed. He floundered in a morass of uncertainty. But it was important to him to discover what conclusions other men had reached. Through them he hoped to pull himself from the quagmire.

He went back to the Greeks asking, "What is it all about?"

Thales answered, "All is water."

Not too helpful.

"Number rules the universe," Pythagoras said.

Interesting, but hardly pertinent.

He looked at Eastern mysticism. "The Tao that can be spoken is not the true Tao." He concluded his soul was not advanced enough to understand.

"Vanity of vanities, saith the preacher." And again, "He that increaseth knowledge increaseth sorrow."

If that was true, why was he going to Harvard?

"There is no science of human willing and doing

and there never can be," another source told him. Is there no purpose then to anything? Was life itself the original accident?

He could not accept that. His religious training was too early and too deep. Its fiber was part of his nature.

To complicate matters he fell in love three times over the summer, always from a distance. When he got close, the girl was never what he had imagined. A shadowy face lived in his mind but he was unable to match it with flesh and blood.

How different this young man from the boy who was voted his last year at Choate most likely to succeed.

Most likely to succeed at what?

Bitterbaum waited anxiously the change of outlook he anticipated college would bring. It did in fact bring a totally new life.

Bitterbaum was pleased when he heard Josh had joined St. Paul's Catholic Club, pleased that he made both the golf and swim teams. When news reached him that he was also Junior Varsity, he was upset. It was too much. And there was the danger of reinjuring his back.

Josh had thrown off the introspection that preoccupied his summer, and the activities into which he plunged left Bitterbaum with a new set of worries.

What was he doing in something called the Hasty Pudding Club that put on musical revues? And why the Spree Club with its emphasis on socially prominent members? Was his charge turning into a jet-setter?

Josh ran for class president but didn't make it. He was elected, however, to the business staff of the undergraduate paper, the *Crimson.* Bitterbaum recalled with a certain satisfaction that Franklin Delano Roosevelt had been chairman of this same publication. Still it added up to too much, a kind of hyperactivity.

An inkling of what lay behind it began to prick Bitterbaum's subconscious. He went to the school records, and then to the Harvard Library. Of course. The volumes he looked through had all been recently checked out. Josh was consciously patterning himself on the man he believed to be his father.

Bitterbaum had an attack of gooseflesh. He was living his life again. What impelled him to do this? What led him to it? Was it to create a link with his supposed father? An effort to identify with him? Or had the instinct to be his former self been cloned into him?

It seemed to him the course Josh was embarked on was unhealthy and wrong. He brooded a long while before calling the dorm and asking to speak to him. He was informed that Mr. Kellogg no longer resided in the dorm. He had taken an apartment. Bitterbaum copied down the address, recognizing it as he did so. It was in Bowdoin Square in the west section of Boston, where the former President had lived during his undergraduate years.

The rooms Josh received him in were a typical bachelor's establishment, the only personal touch a golf bag and books. "Well, Uncle Thor, you've tracked me to my lair."

Did he feel cornered, trapped by his presence, Bitterbaum wondered. The joke made him sad. "Josh," he said, "did it have to be Bowdoin Square?"

"Why not Bowdoin Square?" Josh asked, outfacing him.

"When are you going to start living your own life?"

"When people stop asking me, 'Don't I know you?' 'Haven't we met?' When I no longer need a beard to protect my identity."

"Haven't you been able to make your peace with that, Josh?"

"Uncle Thor, I was brought up to do what I'm doing. You must know it. You were probably one of the policy framers. The parallels with my father's career are no accident. I couldn't have gone anywhere but Choate. And Harvard, that was decided when I was born. What you object to, what you really object to, is that I know."

"What I really object to, Josh, is your bitterness."

"Why should you, any of you, care about that? The important thing is, I'm doing what I was brought up to do. And I'm doing it well. I want you to know that I'm not going to disappoint anybody, G.K., or mom, or you. So you can go back to G.K. and tell him it's going to pay off."

"What's going to pay off? What are you talking about?"

"His investment in me, what else?"

"Josh, be fair."

Josh turned away. "Mother's the only one I don't have to justify my existence to." But as though he were afraid of this small chink in his armor, he added, "Even so, she was part of the charade."

Bitterbaum shook his head. "Don't you think that after eighteen years pretense becomes real?"

Josh shrugged off the hand that dropped to his shoulder. "I don't know. But I do know what's scheduled for me. Nothing like being able to look into the future. Paris, Uncle Thor, that's my next trip. I'm keeping a step ahead now. I find that amusing, don't you find it amusing? Not only am I front runner, but I know where I'm running to, every step of the way."

Bitterbaum felt uncomfortable with the boy. He was at a loss how to console him. If a half-truth was this caustic, what would be the result of stark fact?

Josh's senior year at Harvard presented a major problem. Since he insisted on patterning his career on his father's, the choice of a thesis that would win literary recognition was important. His father had made cum laude in political science with his analysis of England and the Munich Pact. The family had promoted it into a best seller and it was chosen Book of the Month.

Having set this goal, Josh began with characteristic thoroughness to study the possibilities open to him.

His world, the world of 1985, had recovered from the moral and financial debacle resulting from the guerrilla wars of the seventies. The last few years, progress had been made in removing the global pollutants, radioactivity, lead and insecticides. It took the choking death of 1979 in the Los Angeles basin to bring this about.

The technology had been known for a dozen years, but not until the sprawling communities from Orange County to the San Fernando Valley, from Pasadena to Santa Monica were trapped in their atmosphere like fish out of water, did government act.

The emergency situation lasted three days. Casualties ran close to five thousand. But for him it was always Ellen. He remembered her at each family gathering, each holiday. He recalled her sunny disposition, her button-box and shell collections, and how real dolls were to her even though she was older than Jer.

If only he could write *in memoriam* for his sister and those needless dead, looking to the future, uncovering the threats to human survival. If his book could do that then it would no longer be necessary to justify his existence in terms of a dead father. If he himself could make a contribution, his life would be vindicated, his adoptive father repaid. He could, as Uncle Thor urged, begin to live his own life.

Josh roused himself from the daydream. He had no patience with this trait of his. He punished himself with an exhausting day at the library. As he pored over periodicals and journals, a conclusion formed. The more deeply he became involved in his research, the more significant the financial thrust of the People's Republic of China into Africa appeared.

They were undercutting the American and Russian trade commission. It was a situation that could flare into crisis. He mulled it a long time. There was no question he had hold of a strong senior thesis. But he saw no way of expanding it into a book that would make the kind of stir he was determined on.

Regretfully he put it aside and went back to the library. Slowly the outline of a new project began to take shape. The articles he checked out became more technical. He realized he had made his decision.

His book would deal with the history of the Space Corps, an outgrowth of the Peace Corps, which it superseded and replaced. He became so engrossed that he forgot the bitterness that had driven him to it. The anger that was behind his determination to succeed drained away.

He made the resolve that upon graduation he would give two years to the Space Corps. This was where the action, the idealism, the imagination of his age resided. This is where Steve would have put his energy. The project had been conceived fifteen years previously by Dr. Ehricke of North American Rockwell, not in its present form of course, but the idea of discharging pollutants into space had its impetus there. Ehricke envisioned the moon as a repository of heavy industry. Not having atmosphere, it was not subject to the pollution that blanketed the globe in the seventies.

Technology had moved in that direction. A fleet of low-orbiting trucks developed from the original Space Shuttle concept made regular trips into space. A two hundred thousand pound boost propelled their cargoes of waste into Jupiter's gravity field, which acted as a slingshot to hurl the chemical garbage into the sun's corona where it vaporized.

Continued funding for this operation was coming before Congress. It would run into opposition from those who wanted to slice appropriations from the Space Corps for defense spending.

Josh looked up from the printed page. He saw his book. In a flash he had the solution. And it included the People's Republic of China and the situation in Africa. Instead of gearing for a confrontation, a triumvirate must be formed, the United States and Russia including China in their space programs: manned lunar bases, the no-gravity hospital under construction, the chain of communication and weather satellite stations presently in orbit. As many as twenty different experiments were mounted on separate booms extending from a single craft, exploring the earth's magnetic field, the radiation belts, cosmic rays and energy particles in the transition zone between the ionosphere and space itself. Past these were the lunar plants, factories, and mining operations. The work of the world was being done *out there.*

The theme of his book: siphon off China's expansionist policies, give her energies a direction, invite her to join what would become a global effort. He saw the earth as a garden, a place of domicile. The world had outgrown wars and territorial struggles. When countries needed more room they would build it, manufacture it, prefabricate it. The space to do it was endless. It was no longer a book he was embarked on, it was a crusade. He saw his future as one with that of the world. His voice must exhort, his hand point the way, his shoulder give what push it could.

The book, *Space Conquest,* climbed to the number-one slot on the best-seller list and stayed there. Everyone pronounced it *hyper.* It was translated into twenty-two languages, serialized in the press, condensed in the *Digest.* It sold a million copies in hard cover and went into paperback.

Overnight everyone knew of Joshua Francis Kellogg. He adopted air-force sun glasses which he wore as further disguise. They were instantly the rage of five continents.

In view of his new status, a family caucus was held, preceded by a private meeting with Bitterbaum. G.K. conceded that as long as Josh moved in the right direction it was better to make no disclosures.

In the forum of the living room G.K. argued for the political arena. Josh was already, his father contended, a name to reckon with. But Josh explained he had a commitment to carry out.

"Commitment?" G.K. was nonplussed. "To what? To whom?"

"To myself," Josh said.

"Hear! Hear!" Bitterbaum got to his feet in his excitement.

Josh grinned; he had come to know that what weighed most with the old boy was the welfare of Joshua Francis Kellogg. This strange red-headed, red-bearded scarecrow really was fond of him.

"Perhaps politics *is* the answer for me," he told G.K. "But it's an ultimate answer. Right now I want the basic experience of working in the Space Corps, getting to know it from the inside. I've signed up for a two-year hitch. I've passed the examination and the physical for active duty, and put in for pilot training. I may even make it. I'm waiting to hear."

His father shook his hand, all objections withdrawn.

Now that the debt was paid, Josh thought perhaps they could approach each other on a new basis. There was much to admire in this bluff, stern man. For years he had stood in such awe of him that it had prevented knowing him.

But at this first test of strength the old wolf capitulated. He did so with flair, a characteristic that he had imparted to the whole family. *Don't lose. But if you should, do that well too.*

"You're quite right to want to get a feel for this thing," he said to his son. "During your two years of duty, get to know every aspect of the operation, make yourself personally acquainted with all the details: fueling, manning, loading, docking, the works. Then you'll stand before Congress, my boy, and be able to implement the reforms necessary for the allocation of funds. It's the new frontier, and you had the vision to see it. This is just the start, Josh, just the start."

Josh looked at the circle of faces, all beaming, all

proud. Three years ago they had looked that way at Steve. The focus shifts; that's life, that's living. He didn't feel the need any longer to distinguish himself. But the law of inertia was invoked. His career, once set in motion, would continue. He agreed with G.K. that this was just the start.

Liftoff. The first hundred seconds and you were home free. Slammed back against the foam cushion, with $\bar{q}$ building to a maximum 650 pounds per square foot, the real pressure was getting past the abort decision points. Launch tower cleared at plus 5 seconds.

One down.

ASRMs jettisoned at plus 29.

Two down.

Max $\bar{q}$ at plus 54, 35,000 feet and 1313 fps, and a half minute later, burnout.

Three, four down.

Dump the SRMs, check energy dissipation on the cathode display, check the on-board Block II landmark sighting computer, select manual flight control mode, and prepare for orbit insertion. Plus 115 seconds, not much could go wrong now.

Smitty at dual controls was making the identical review. The Shuttle would be inserted into an elliptical orbit at 50 nautical miles, 25,853 fps. Separation of the external tank, orbit circularization at an apogee of 100.1 nautical miles polar, and from then on a buggy ride. Ground Control suggested they switch to hands-off mode, the automatic electronic guidance and navigation subsystem. This was the moment Josh seemed to feel the spacecraft relax, and he with it.

There was no question that he enjoyed his command. From an altitude of a hundred miles he looked down on clouds lighted from below. He forgot Smitty at the adjacent controls, forgot George and Al, the cargo handlers in the avionics pod directly below the flight deck. There was only himself orbiting the beach ball out there with its splashes of seas, its greens and its browns.

Was it really a world floating in a sea of space? Or was it an inflatable ball bought on Tele-Purchase, delivered and tossed into the pool? A vast pool, pool without end, in which clouds grazed. When he was a child he believed heaven must be located at just about the altitude he cruised at.

Man had always looked up. He raised his arms, he raised his eyes. He raised spires and towers, skyscraping pinnacles. He had placed God on top of all that space. One had the choice now of placing Him in farther galaxies or bringing Him close into the mind and heart. If God *did* dwell in man, that set up a symbiosis. God, then, needed man, as man needed God.

Strange, up here one thought such thoughts. He supposed it was because looking down there was no trace of man or his civilization. Did too much perspective eradicate everything? Or was it his position as outrider? He had clocked 1,780 man-hours in space. Seventeen hundred and eighty man-hours as guardian, sentinel, scout of the world.

This mental trajectory sent him back to the telemetry records in front of him. The vehicle was equipped with twenty-nine hundred data measurements.

Block I had an erasable memory capacity of over two thousand words. *His* memory bank was not so easily emptied. He had spent the two weeks since the last flight at *Godset* with a weekend in Rome. He always remembered Rome that first time when he was eleven. The many fountains stirred a wildness in him that he had to release. He broke away from the family. He ran to the closest fountain and then ran around it. He ran on without pause until he was at another fountain which he circled at a dead run.

His glorious plan was to circumnavigate every fountain in Rome. It didn't matter to him that he had darted away from his parents, that he was lost on cobblestone streets, in crowds of people speaking another language. His only thought was of the fountains and the excitement of racing around them as they splashed water into water. On their account he had been punished. His father spanked him only when he considered it necessary. On that occasion he considered it necessary.

His mother asked him again and again, "Josh, what got into you?" He didn't know. He hadn't words to explain. It was an impulse toward freedom and a test of himself. Could he do it? He had always asked himself this. Could he run around fountains, could he command this craft?

Two weeks ago they scouted for wheat blight with sensors built by one of G.K.'s companies, scanning whole regions in a single pass, the miniaturized transistors on the console recording as G. K. Kellogg had planned. The mission before that, observations were made of icefields by infrared and microwave. Subsurface flows of water were charted; snow packs, glaciers, and ice accumulations mapped for the hydrologists to study.

The job today was surveying great swathes for data processing and transmission of pictures. The target, the so-called ring of fire, the major volcanic belt running the entire length of the Rocky Mountains and extending to and encircling the Pacific Ocean. Onboard sensors detected discrete sources of heat in bedrock formations. From these findings a geothermal energy map for natural steam would be developed. At present the United States, Russia, Japan, and Italy were major producers of electric power from geothermal sources. Back in the seventies the earth itself was likened to a spaceship as its limits were first recognized. Since then it was referred to more often as the Tight Little Island, parodying the old description of England.

Josh's generation was the first inculcated with the notion that survival was possible only by reaching out for support systems. Of course, careful husbandry of internal natural resources was also essential. It pleased him that his job encompassed both. His sense of adventure was satisfied, and at the same time he was taking part in the wider crusade of adapting the environment to sustain man. He had put in eighteen months of intensive training at the S-4 Orbital Workshop in zero-*g* laboratory in Phoenix, subsequently serving as a copilot on a lunar run.

This was his first command, and he had held it just three months. Smitty, his co, was busy at the work station behind him. "When you get a chance, Smitty, check out the cabin humidity-temperature control. Maintenance was supposed to modify the heat exchanger. It's been stamped off on the squawk sheet, but you know how those things go."

"Right."

He himself consulted the CRT display, noted all liquid H_2/O_2 fuel gauges registering, and ran a circuit integrity test on the emergency power supply. Smitty fiddled with the thermostats, singing, "Around, around the sun we go. The moon goes round the earth. We do not die of death. We die of vertigo." Josh smiled and noted all systems OK in his log.

There was a spluttering from Ground Control, and a certain amount of static. But suddenly it was barking loud and clear. "Condition Alert! Alert!"

Smitty, who had started on the next chorus, broke off to listen.

"Come in, Orbiter. Acknowledge transmission."

"This is Shuttle Orbiter SSO-11. Over."

"Voice contact has been lost with Sortie Module XSM-2. Abort present mission and proceed on Rescue. Last known XSM–2 orbit parameters are being fed directly into your GN&C I/O buffer. Switch tracking to rendezvous mode. Prepare for a 7.7 fps burn at 1532 hours. Confirm navigational data and guidance commands for insertion into cis-lunar rendezvous orbit."

"Got you, Houston." The moment he heard "Rescue," Josh switched tracking modes, and the on-board computer already showed the same figures coming by RF. "All parameters confirmed. We'll take over."

Josh viewed the transition of the orbiter's trajectory on CRT and monitored the roll angles following the burn. He locked into the flight-path vectors indicated by GC. This was his first space rendezvous and he knew he had to stay within tight tolerances.

Smitty was trying to raise the noncooperative spacecraft, but its frequency band remained silent. The atmosphere within the cabin was tense and expectant. Their routine earth orbit had turned into a mission penetrating deep space. What was the reason for the disability aboard the Sortie Module? Was the commander ill? Injured? Some accident had taken place, but what?

More information from GC. Commander Parker had completed a five-day solo trek and was headed for docking with Skylab Irma. His mission: monitoring the Dubna discontinuity in the inner Van Allen belt, discovered the year before by the unmanned Soviet satellite, Intercosmos 37.

"That accounts for the high-eccentricity orbit." Josh turned to Smitty. "Do you know Parker?"

"Not directly. If it's the same Bill Parker, he was a couple of years ahead of me at g Workshop. He had a rep as an og-og boy. You know, if you can't go, then og. He got things done, but kind of ass-backward, if you know what I mean. He was supposed to be hyper with the ladies."

"Shut up, Smitty, I think I've got a blip on the CRT."

Lynn had moved back to the States and opened the Latigo house. She felt most at home here. She was enjoying the windy front garden with its farflung view of the sea, at the same time essaying a new link-stitch on her petit point and wondering about putting in a Japanese rock garden. Her interest in such a project stemmed from a vacation last May on the Kona Coast. They stayed at a Japanese inn, the exterior built around a pool of *koi* which flashed and darted, a living gem collection, coming to the side when she appeared for a conversation.

They did seem to talk. They fastened their bulging eyes on her, came to the surface, their mouths opening and shutting as they sipped air. It would be lovely to have *koi.* She had spoken to Gerald, who liked to please her in such matters. The project grew as she considered it. The pond would be at the foot of Mica Mountain, set into a rock garden. She would have a landscape designer create a waterfall to empty into it. There'd be a bridge, perhaps two off-centered concrete castings. And the blue water lilies she'd seen in Kyoto.

Delia interrupted to say she was wanted on the phone.

"I'll take it out here," she said, reluctant to go indoors.

Delia returned with the phone and plugged it into the exterior jack. It was Mabel Wilson. She sounded distressed. "I want you to know that we're all with you. We're all pulling for him. Try not to worry."

"Mabel, what are you talking about?"

It was amazing to her that she'd had no premonition, that she'd been dreaming about *koi,* about a rock garden and a waterfall. "Excuse me, Mabel, I want to tune it in." She dropped the phone and ran inside.

Josh's voice came on, along with the CBS commentator. Josh was issuing directions to his copilot, Smitty. She knew Smitty, he'd come to dinner several weeks ago when they were still at *Godset.* A devoted friend, she thought, and liked him. She always liked people who liked her children.

She heard his voice next making a technical reply, the state vector update was something or other. Then the commentator cut in. "You have just heard Commander Joshua Francis Kellogg and his copilot, Albert Smith. Commander Kellogg is the author of the best-selling *Space Conquest.* He is also the second son of G. K. Kellogg, inventor, philanthropist, and chief negotiator at the Icelandic Talks. The Space Shuttle Orbiter commanded by young Kellogg has been ordered to abort its geological mapping survey and to proceed to a possibly disabled Sortie Module. The Shuttle is equipped to retrieve and/or repair malfunctioning satellites and spacecraft in orbit. The ship has just made a Δv burn and taken new bearings."

Fear comes in RCA color beamed to you via CBS transmitters. She had learned not to worry. She allowed Josh to convince her of the routine nature of orbital flights. But now he was proceeding hundreds of nautical miles into space. *What was a nautical mile? I've got to get hold of Gerald.*

The phone in the study was ringing. That was her private extension. She switched it on still watching the CBS anchor man. It was a message that Gerald was on his way.

Thor arrived before Gerald. "I got it on the car radio," he said bursting in. "Are you okay, Lynn?"

"I don't know. How dangerous is it? They said he's going to rendezvous, to retrieve the other ship."

"Those are the orders, yes."

"But suppose they collide? That could happen, couldn't it?"

"No. It couldn't. That's what the Shuttle has manipulators for—to retrieve a disabled ship."

"What do you suppose could be wrong with it?" Her hands pressed one over the other against her womb, the womb that never bore him. Because there was Josh in living color, looking tan and fit and unconcerned.

Lynn sank onto the settee. Thor poured them each a brandy.

Josh said, "We have radar contact. Are there any other spacecraft in this sector?"

Houston replied, "Negative. We assume you have picked up XSM–2. Transmit bearings and stand by for course correction."

"Won't that take them too deep into space?" Lynn asked. "I thought the Shuttle never went more than three-hundred miles out."

"Not on normal missions. But space itself can't damage it. Space is space, it's all the same." Thor was using a soothing tone, it disturbed rather than reassured her.

"I've got to get myself together," she apologized.

TV coverage had switched to the Jet Propulsion Laboratory, where a spokesman stood beside a mock-up of the XSM–2, playing a flashlight pointer along it. "Sortie Modules were first proposed in the early seventies as scientific observation capsules carried to their stations in the Shuttle's cargo bay. Later versions operate autonymously, that is, they separate from the Shuttle, pursue their own orbits, link up with each other or dock with space labs."

"Switch the channel," Lynn pleaded. "I want to know what's happening to Josh."

Bitterbaum turned the dial, but it was the same figure, now pointing to a painting of Earth, encircled by a cut-away representation of the Van Allen belts. "The XSMs, or Experimental Sortie Modules, are designed for hazardous missions. In this case, mapping the high-energy radiation regions of space, and exploring the Dubna layer discovered by the Russians last year. The XSM–2 is a one-man craft, modified for reentry capability along the lines of the Apollo series. This provides emergency back-up—"

Another voice cut in. "We have a report from Commander Kellogg."

Josh was in front of them again, looking closer and more substantial than the professor at JPL. "Houston, this is Orbiter. We have visual contact with the XSM–2. It's tumbling. We're getting a fix on it now, but it looks to me like low to moderate constant pitch and roll, negligible yaw."

Lynn caught Bitterbaum's arm, digging in with her

fingers. In the middle of the TV globe was a small object. It looked like two paper cups stuck together, rolling slowly over and over.

Bluff and hearty, the voice of the anchor man continued. "Kellogg and Smith have maneuvered the Shuttle into a parallel orbit. You are now looking at XSM–2 through the Shuttle's TV camera. I understand that orders were given to open the cargo hatch and initiate a capture sequence. The remote-controlled manipulators or 'spider arms' are being extruded. If you look closely at the right of your TV globe, you'll see them." There was a lull in the flow of verbiage while the commentator received information on his headset. "Ladies and gentlemen, I have just had word the order has been countermanded. Houston apparently has decided that the XSM–2 is gyrating too rapidly for successful retrieval."

"How can they order a halt? That poor man in there. Josh has got to get him out." Lynn was caught up in it now. She had lost some of her initial fear.

But Bitterbaum's concern was growing. Both Ground Control and Orbiter were trying to reach the disabled module on radio frequencies. "XSM–2, come in, come in. Do you read?"

Josh appeared on the globe. "XSM–2, this is Orbiter. We have you in sight. We are in parallel orbit 12 meters distant. You are tumbling too much for retrieval. Telemetry indicates your port OMS operational. Prepare to make a stabilizing burn at 1605 hours plus or minus 30 seconds. I will transmit data and signal firing time on visob basis."

The network commentator editorialized that Commander Kellogg was proceeding on the theory that the module commander, while not able to send, might possibly receive. "Kellogg is gambling that the trouble may be in the XSM–2's computer. He is therefore relaying to Commander Parker the exact moment to fire the orbital maneuvering engine to stabilize his ship."

The station switched to a direct view of the XSM–2. There was silence. Even the commentator had nothing to say. They waited. Then there was Josh's voice, snapping out the command to fire.

The module hung, sealed and silent, revolving helplessly.

The newscaster took up his soliloquy. "There is no response from XSM–2. Kellogg and Smith are going to use their translation motors to bring the Orbiter closer. The commander is talking to Ground Control, and there is a security blackout on this conversation. This is ABC bringing you a special broadcast. Please stay tuned. You have just witnessed an unsuccessful attempt to communicate with Commander Parker aboard the XSM–2 and have him stabilize his spacecraft. It is not known whether Parker is alive or dead. All regularly scheduled programs have been canceled so that we can bring you live and in color—"

Lynn turned away, hearing G.K.'s car in the driveway.

"Ah, you're here, Bitterbaum," he said, striding to his wife's side. "Good. I'm glad. Things aren't going to be resolved in a minute or two, you know. So we should settle down. That's all we can do."

The enlarged head in living color that hung in the middle of the TV sphere began to speak. "We have just had word from Ground Control. Let me check this. Yes, the word is that Commander Kellogg is going to do an EVA."

Lynn turned a stricken face to G.K. An extravehicular assignment meant a space walk. Only last month two Russian cosmonauts had been lost when their spacecraft inadvertently cut their lifelines.

Gerald took Lynn's hands. "He'll be all right. I know it."

There was a confidence in his tone that made Bitterbaum glance sharply at him. A thought edged into his mind, but it was too monstrous, too fantastic. He pushed it away. But he continued to watch G.K.'s reactions. Either the man had enviable control, or he wasn't worried. Josh was his kid, how could he not be worried? Then he wondered if G.K. had ever thought of him except as his experiment, his passport to history. Certainly this is what Josh felt six years ago when he'd run off.

Bitterbaum was at that age when the past is very clear, more easily and vividly remembered than the present. He recalled even the intonation G.K. had used when he said, "We can't have World War II again."

Perhaps not. But wasn't this a pretty good simulacrum? Josh Kellogg cast in a heroic role before the eyes of the world. It was an insane suspicion. Not even G.K. Kellogg would take such a risk.

The cameras caught it all. Josh lifted the EVA suit, lifeline, and hand-maneuvering unit from beneath the seat where they were stored. The indefatigable commentary went on. "The suit itself is in three layers, an airtight bladder of rubberized nylon which can be inflated to a pressure of 3.5 pounds per square inch, one quarter normal atmospheric pressure. The second layer of fiberglas mesh keeps the bladder cloth from ballooning out. The outer layer is tightly woven glass fabric. Of course none of these layers can protect the commander against the heat of the sun or the dust-size meteorites that whiz through space at 42 miles per second."

"Easy, Lynn," G.K. interposed himself between her and collapse. "He's simply presenting things dramatically. That's his job. You don't think we'd send men up there without adequate protection? Why, one layer alone will absorb the energy of any micrometeorite that might strike. And there are eighteen built into the suit.

She squeezed his hand to let him know he was getting through. But she didn't trust herself to say anything.

"It's going to be astounding, a prodigious thing," G.K. said, "Try to focus on that. The danger is not great, believe me. It is more awesome."

Josh was suited now. He had struggled into this identical paraphernalia dozens of times during brief Keplerian zero-*g* trajectory flights and in six degrees of freedom work stands. Still adhering to routine, he climbed into the transfer tunnel and secured the access door behind him. The pressure began to drop. When it was 2 psi he closed the vent. There would be total vacuum in the tunnel the moment the hatch opened. He checked the biomedical lead that relayed his heartbeat and temperature to earth and got ready to thrust himself through the hatch. Smitty whispered over the intercom, "You're a tube star now, with a number one rating."

Josh smiled from behind the Plexiglas visor. "We're go," he said into the microphone.

"Good luck, sir."

Josh ejected the portable rocket packs and hooked the towline to his belt. He pushed himself and thirty pounds of suit through the opening. He had egressed. His lifeline floated behind him. He was attached to the Shuttle by a three-quarter-inch lead which carried his oxygen. The reference points of his life changed completely.

He knew that his figure on its umbilical cord was being teletransmitted into every home in the United States, possibly the world. But the inside of a man was still private. And although millions of eyes followed his progress, he was alone. Totally alone.

He was a human satellite of earth, a sentient, breathing satellite. The experience hypnotized him. He was born into a sea of space, burnished in the glow of sunset.

He floated on his back, stoned, rapturous. The earth floated as he did in marbled cloud cover and the great flux of seas.

There was no sensation of falling, no disorientation. The amniotic fluid of the universe cradled him. Smitty's voice filled his helmet jarring his mind, recalling him.

That's right, he was here for a reason. There was a job to do. He hauled in the rocket packs he intended to attach to XSM–2 and, using his hand gun, began to maneuver. A new thrill lay hold of him. His giant steps covered the earth. His first was over Hawaii; the next, as the earth turned, was on California. Then Texas,

Florida. An incredible two thousand miles with each step.

All the training techniques of the S–4 Orbital Lab had not prepared him for this. He was preoccupied with the dynamics of his motion. Firing both jet nozzles provided a forward push, a squirt to the right rotated his body through 120 degrees. He pulled himself back into position by tugging on the tether.

Smitty's voice again enveloped his helmet, telling him he was now in full visual from the XSM–2 window. "If Parker's alive, he's got the picture."

From his vantage point Josh was able to make out a suited, helmeted figure in the port. "I see him! He just motioned to me."

Smitty emitted an inappropriate *Whoopee!!* Josh turned his attention to the job at hand. He gestured to Parker, then to the two packs of RCSRs trailing behind him, and indicated he was going to fasten them to the module. He hoped Parker would understand and brace himself against the torque.

Carrying out the procedure was not easy. The Shuttle's computers had performed innumerable triple integrations and come up with the not surprising information that the charges should be attached at maximum moment arms from the center of gravity. That meant one pack at the docking ring to take out the pitch, the other on the aft hull to counteract the roll. But getting them on the gyrating XSM–2 was something else.

Smitty, holding the Orbiter in station-keeping attitude, hollered advice over the intercom. Josh took a breath, fired himself directly at the hatch cover as it came by, and grabbed for the handle. He felt his arm coming out of its socket and prayed that his spacesuit wouldn't split. Now the problem was to prevent the rocket packs following him from clamping on in the wrong place. Once those magnets took hold, they'd never let go. He kicked and punched them away, and clung to the hatch cover until Newton's third law of motion was placated. Then he slithered along the hull to the docking ring, using friction holds to stay with the ship, and gently guided the rocket pack in. After that he crawled aft and clamped on the No. 2 pack.

"Stand by to fire remote-controlled stabilizing rockets," he instructed Smitty. "But first let me get back where I can hang on to something."

The rockets worked. Only a slight wobble was left in the XSM-2.

"Beautiful!" Smitty called. "Are you going in after Parker?"

"Negative. I don't dare open up this tin can unless he's fully suited up. Let's get this ship into our cargo bay."

"Got you. Deploy manipulator arms and commence retrieval," Smitty instructed the specialists at the payload handling station. Then, to Josh, "Hey, are you going to ride that thing down?"

"No thanks," Josh laughed, "I'll come in on my own. Just don't foul my lifeline with the spider arms." He bent his knees to push off from the XSM-2, when something caught his eye. The Sortie Module's hatch was opening.

"Hold everything!"

Heavily, but without sound, the steel cover swung back. A helmet and one shoulder of an EVA suit emerged, then gradually sank back. Josh started toward the opening. A gloved arm appeared. There was no mistaking the motion. "Parker's signaling. He needs help. I'm going in. Stand by to cut the umbilical."

"Acknowledge. Computer readout confirms you have 37 minutes' oxygen supply in your back-up life support. We'll start the clock on you the moment you disconnect."

Reaching the access hatch, Josh ran his own check on his autonomous LSS, switched over, notified Smitty, and flipped the umbilical release lever. As his lifeline drifted away, to be reeled into the Orbiter, he felt a slight chill. But it was purely psychological; Smitty notified him cheerfully that all vital signs read within normal limits.

Josh struggled to squeeze himself and his gear inside the XSM–2 and button it up. The ratchet cranking the hatch against the airseal malfunctioned. He worked it back and forth, finally able to deflate the seal and achieve an airtight lock.

The first thing he noticed was the blackened console. There appeared to have been a fire. He spot-checked the repressurizing controls. Miraculously, the system was operational. Parker slumped in his seat made feeble gestures of greeting. Josh signed to him to stay suited up until ambient cabin pressure was normal and O_2/CO_2 levels checked out.

Guidance, navigation, and control instruments were recording; the electric power system was okay; there were no warning lights indicating malfunction in the propulsion systems. Fire damage seemed to be confined to communications.

Josh removed his helmet and gloves and helped the

other man out of his suit. He saw bandages on Parker's hands and a patch of gauze taped across his forehead. "Commander Kellogg, sir. Here to effect transfer. Are you badly hurt?"

"Short in encryption unit. Fire broke out. Knocked out communications."

"What about you, sir?"

"Burned my hands putting it out. Clumsy. Can't work the damn controls."

"Well, we'll fix you up. In about fifteen minutes Smitty will have us inside the Orbiter." He turned to get Parker a drink of water. Life-support systems, he noted, had suffered no damage. Through the window he saw one huge seven-jointed manipulator arm, groping toward them like some giant, blind insect.

"Any other injuries?" Josh asked, detaching a small drinking container and inserting a flex straw. But the man collapsed in his seat. He lurched against the console, firing the thrusters. Josh found himself flattened against a bulkhead.

"My God!" He pulled himself over to read the instrument panel. They were plunging toward earth. They would reenter the sensible atmosphere in 3:15 minutes at a speed of 24,911 mph.

Josh tried for contact with the Orbiter.

Nothing.

Ground Control. No go.

He transferred his effort to the short-range transmitter in his helmet. There was some kind of reply. A voice with harsh static overlay. He couldn't make it out. At that moment while he was busy with the radio, the Module commander fired the port reaction control engine increasing the distance between them and the Shuttle.

"What's the idea?" Josh yelled at him.

"The only chance is to make it on our own now," Parker answered.

Josh was furious, that should have been a joint decision. But it was too late. There was nothing for it but to prepare for reentry and splashdown. Deorbiting was accomplished with a 10-second burn of the 24,000-pound thrust propulsion system engine at an altitude of 180 miles. The burn decreased their orbital velocity 300 fps.

Aim point was lat. 27°38′ N, long. 64°10′ W. That would put them somewhere southeast of Bermuda.

Mission Control came in suddenly on the battery radio confirming position and velocity vectors. Entry angle, 7.08 degrees. Speed, 37,537 fps. Heating rate, 622 BTU per square foot per second. Heat load, 38,000 BTU per square foot. Transmission cut out as they hit the ionizing layer. On reentry exterior temperature showed 5000°F during the high-load-factor attitude of atmospheric braking.

The ship was yawing, throwing the injured man about. Josh strapped him into the pilot seat. He inactivated Parker's controls and transferred manual mode to the copilot console. He then deployed two drogue parachutes to orient and slow the craft. At twenty-three thousand feet, after jettisoning the forward heat shield, he opened the main chutes, producing an enormous tug.

There wasn't going to be much time to worry. Ground Control probably had a fix on them. They'd be searching the area by helicopter and boat as soon as they could get craft into the area. That close to Bermuda there should be something to dispatch on a search and rescue. The water, if they were forced to evacuate, would be mild. Survival outside, possible. If Parker wasn't too bad.

He hadn't had time to ascertain just what his condition was, or how extensive his burns. He bent over him, but the man's head rolled back. He was unconscious. He felt for a pulse. That was odd, it was as steady as his own.

In those moments before splashdown, suspicion seized him that the man was malingering. But why? To what purpose? He could make no sense of it. But he was suddenly convinced that the distress had been a fake, the bandages a fake. He remembered the way Parker had beckoned him from the cockpit hatch. And the fall against the instrument panel that had initiated the separation. He was morally certain that under the bandages the man's skin was whole and unburned. But he had no time to indulge his scepticism.

Splashdown conditions were not ideal. The oscillation of the parachute descent made him seasick. It could result in a landing with high sideways *g*-loads. "This is it," he told himself.

They impacted in the Atlantic 145 miles east northeast of Grand Bahama Island. They hit squarely resulting in an eight-*g* force on the shield. The capsule's side seam burst.

Visibility was fifteen hundred feet. The wind westerly at twenty knots. Wave action was heavy. Josh activated three flotation bags in an effort to keep the craft afloat. This was the first chance he had to get out of his cumbersome spacesuit. It looked as though they might have to swim for it.

He checked his partner who seemed to have revived sufficiently to unstrap himself. The capsule was drifting under its parachute and swamping. Water poured in through the sprung seam.

Parker struggled to the hatch and began pulling at it. The defective seal stuck. He yelled at Josh. "Give me a hand."

The man's recovery had been altogether too fast. "Not until you tell me what this is all about."

"Give me a hand or we're for it."

Josh didn't move. The water was waist deep and rising. Parker put his shoulder against the hatch. It didn't budge. He pried frantically at the lock.

The side paneling split. A metal fragment struck Josh, the discs of his spine folded in on each other, and he fell into time and black water.

Waves crashed. A light seared the ocean. There was a delay while his brain translated what had happened.

Were there flares? Or was the sharp pain turning into light? He seemed to have lost the boundary of inside-outside. He no longer knew where events were located. The sense of *self* as opposed to *other* was muddled.

There were moments when he realized Parker supported him, that they clung to a floating remnant of capsule. At other times the sea pulsed through him.

They united two human strengths, two human wills into a primitive survival struggle. A single organism intent on not sinking.

But the inner space of the sea slid over him. The

light they always tell you is at the end of the tunnel, that's pain. You have to choose it deliberately. It's easier to slip away, slide back. You have to choose that cutting light cleaving your brain in two. You had to choose it, and Parker's voice telling you to hold on.

Something of the exultation of the space walk translated to those watching. "Look at him haul on that tether," G.K. said, "like he's pulling in a three-pound trout."

"I can't believe it's Josh. What must it be like not on any world?"

That was before he ingressed into the interior of the noncooperative XSM–2. They waited. ABC put on a panel of newsmen to discuss what might be holding things up. They speculated that Commander Parker was too severely disabled to bring out, or the possibility that he was dead through heart attack or accident.

The cameras switched to relayed pictures of the module's exterior. The Shuttle reported an attempted communication. Commander Smith believed he had caught the word *fire.* It was his belief that there was a fire aboard the XSM-2. But this was conjecture and not certain.

The module took on a harsh, forbidding look. Nothing seemed to stir inside. The hatch cover did not move. Commander Kellogg did not reemerge. Lynn shredded a tissue in her hand.

The newsmen were driven to a discussion of the manipulators which would grasp the XSM-2 and deposit it in the Shuttle's capacious bay; how the operator, utilizing direct and TV viewing, commands three axis rates of the effectors in translation and rotation.

Sudden turmoil struck out of camera range. They switched to Ground Control.

". . . has begun to accelerate earthward without warning. We have lost contact."

Lynn's scream tore through both men. Delia started forward, but G.K. motioned her back. The servants had gathered in a knot at the back of the room. One of them rushed for the bathroom and could be heard retching.

"How long will it take him to die?" Lynn asked distractedly. "Do you die from falling, or when you hit?"

"He's not going to die," G.K. said, "all they're saying is that at the moment they are not able to track. But they will. He'll be all right."

"You know that?" Bitterbaum asked him. "You have some sort of advance word from God?"

"I know it because I'm using my head."

Ground Control had just received a message from a station in West Germany which had picked up the module. Lynn, whose lips moved in prayer, was suddenly still. Bitterbaum long ago decided that she didn't think in words, but in great outpourings of emotion which she translated into words. He himself was an extremely verbal person. Not only did he think in words, but in sentences, complete with paragraphs and punctuation. In all his vocabulary, however, there was nothing that could give her comfort.

It was a time of waiting. A time to be gotten through. He wouldn't allow himself to calculate Josh's chances. In the first place he hadn't enough information. And then there was a vaguely superstitious feeling that it might bring bad luck. Better to hibernate mentally and allow the major networks to assault your ears and eyes and hopes with their pomposity. Josh meant nothing to them. It was easy enough for them to speculate, plot the trajectory, the reentry, the maximum temperature the capsule could withstand.

He was glad to see Lynn's lips moving again. He didn't believe in prayers, but he believed in hers. Ground Control was not only tracking, but plotting the impact site and cross ranges to the nearest standby vessels and planes, which were dispatched to an area northeast of the Bahamas. Time stretched like a globule of water hanging from a faucet, elongating itself unbelievably before it falls. He was as imprisoned by it as Josh in the capsule.

The wait continued. The viscosity of the moment thinned. He hung in it, and Lynn and G.K. with him, and the room too. The room was the cocoon around which time wrapped itself, the picture imprinted infinitely in the distended moment.

There was sudden pandemonium among the newsmen in Ground Control. Splashdown had been effected. They had a fix. Six cruisers steamed toward the spot, helicopters were already zeroing in. Television cameras swept an empty sea. A sharp slapping chop rippled the surface. It would interfere with rescue operations, make spotting difficult. Bitterbaum winced not from pain, but from the possibility of a pain he could not handle.

Searchlights played over the troughs and across the churned movement. "Negative. Sighting negative," was the report from the planes. Bitterbaum wondered if they would, from the comfort of their living room, watch in living color the living death of Josh.

Negative, the word skimmed the water. Were they already at the bottom? There was no sign of the module.

Two men, only one able to hold onto the flotation collar, were difficult to spot. But a light, crisscrossing the area, halted and jerked back. Something had been sighted. The light began a slow sweep, stopped, and the S-3 copter dropped down to take a look. One of the men in the water waved his hand.

It wasn't Josh. Josh hung barely conscious in his harness which was tied to Parker. G.K. rose to his feet. He hadn't displayed this kind of emotion at the retrieval failures, or during the space walk, or waiting for Josh to reappear from the module. Not even that instant when the XSM-2 shot out of the Shuttle's line of sight, disappearing into space, had G.K. evinced such frustration, sorrow, and pain. "My God, do you see that? Josh is out. What rotten luck. What incredibly rotten luck!"

Lynn looked at him with incomprehension. But Bitterbaum understood. "It was World War II all over again. A mock-up. A simulation. Only the wrong guy is the hero. A guy called Parker."

G.K. groaned into his hands. Lynn's head turned from one to the other as though she were watching a tennis match. Her eyes betrayed complete and total bewilderment. "What's happening? Josh is going to be all right, isn't he?"

"Sure he is," Gerald said. She intercepted the furious glance he sent Thor. She had never understood the roots of this friendship. There was at best of times a tension between them. Temperamentally they were not suited. Thor with his penetrating and bitter strain of sarcasm was forever offending Gerald's sensibilities. She often wondered what formed the bond. Gerald certainly took more from Thor than from any other human being. But now the canker erupted. What a moment to natter at each other with Josh still in the water and no one knowing how badly he was injured.

Frogmen were lowered from the copter by rope ladder. They swam to the men and untied Josh who seemed to rouse slightly. He was lifted aboard. A medic pronounced his condition stable. That was what Lynn had been waiting for. She left to lie down, to be by herself, and to thank God. Delia settled her and the other servants drifted back to their tasks.

The two men confronted each other.

"You risked everything," Bitterbaum said, "including his life."

"We agreed. Twenty-five years ago we agreed. Besides, it wasn't as risky as it looked. Parker knew where he was. At no time was the vehicle out of control."

"And what about Lynn, who didn't know this? And me?"

"Rough, I grant you. But we're forging a very special human being. The furnace has got to be hot."

"What do you hope for Josh? Do you want to make him President?"

"Listen, Bitterbaum, this has cost me twenty-five years of my life. Yes, I'm going to make him President. Why else do you think I went into this? It's different with you. You're a scientist, you've accomplished your ends. Your experiment is a success. It's worked. I haven't batted a hundred, but I haven't done badly. I wanted Josh to have the type of experience the original had in the South Pacific. I think it came close. After today every man, woman, and child in the country will know of Commander Joshua Francis Kellogg."

"Josh was right," Bitterbaum said. "All you wanted from him was a payoff. He never touched you at all as a person." He saw that he was not communicating and broke off. "Well, I can't stop you. But for God's sake proceed with a little compassion. I don't know if Lynn could take another episode like this. And we still don't know how badly Josh is hurt."

"I don't like it any better than you do, Bitterbaum. But we bred a champion and we raised a champion. There's nothing wrong with that. How can you find anything wrong with a person reaching his full potential?"

The Thor part of him wanted to slug G.K. with mailed fist. The Jewish part wanted to demonstrate by casuistry and argument how wrong he was. But exhaustion won out. Bitterbaum flung up his hands and left.

G.K. was right about the publicity. Cards, telegrams, letters poured in from around the world. Some were sent in care of his publishers, others were forwarded from the Space Corps to the Santa Monica hospital where Josh underwent a laminectomy and spinal fusion.

The neurological portion of the operation was performed at the Mayo Clinic by TV monitor. The surgeon worked at console controls relaying orders to the micromanipulators three thousand miles away, which did the fine detail under magnification with infinitely greater precision than the clumsy hand techniques of the past. But pain was as old-fashioned as ever. Josh woke from coma and anesthetic to hellish days. For the next seven months he would lie absolutely flat. He was lifted and maneuvered by means of a taut sheet, for bathing, for linen changes, and occasionally transferred onto carts for trips to the X-ray machine. He knew that his career in the Space Corps was over.

He tried not to think too much about it. The job of being an invalid was full time. After the morning bath the therapist worked his legs, massaging them. From breakfast on the procession included the medicine nurse, the orderly with tomorrow's menus, the nurse to take the inevitable blood sample, and about that time the doctors made rounds. There was the usual kidding, behind which he tried to read the prognosis. The priest came and enumerated the prayers he was offering for his recovery. He also had a few jokes in his repertoire.

There were stacks of magazines and books, but he tired holding them over his head. The sister in charge of the floor brought him a machine that threw the print on the ceiling, but he found this disorienting. Besides it required too much effort. Many times, sleeping, drowsing, he was out there trailing his golden lead, looking at the world, striding over it, floating rapturously, by definition a satellite of earth.

Satellite first; man second. He was drunk on his environment, he gloried in it, wallowed in it. Smitty's voice was an intrusion, reminding him he wasn't here to leap-frog continents, but to proceed to the non-cooperative target. The rattling of the lunch tray woke him. The mood of the dream remained. He felt that he had become something else, that he was reacting, thinking, feeling in a way unrelated to himself.

His mother and Uncle Thor were there every day. G.K. came when he was in town. Jer flew in from Rutgers where he had been appointed to an assistant professorship. The girls came from school. Victoria had a job with a paper and was doing well. Josh was fond of his sisters. They were charming, attractive young ladies. He was proud of them and glad to see them.

Commander Parker dropped by, and all sorts of memories churned in him. He remembered his suspicion that the bandages had concealed healthy skin; his conviction that the man was malingering. One moment he was rolling helplessly in his seat and the next pulling at the hatch with the strength of a bull. Even now, coming into the room, an impression of vigor entered with him.

Josh decided he was mistaken. He recalled the heady, exhilirating sensation of being loose in space, and wondered if he had been quite rational at the time. His senses could easily have played tricks on him. Parker had saved his life, tied his harness to his own body so that they would sink together or be saved. Besides, what possible cause was served by chicanery? All that had happened was an unscheduled splash-down and the loss of the module. Still the matter was not resolved to his satisfaction.

"Tell me," he said to Parker, "did anything in my actions strike you as peculiar?"

Parker hesitated. "Not at first. Of course I wasn't looking for anything. But you refused to help me with the hatch, do you remember?"

"You got away pretty lucky, didn't you?" Josh asked. "No scars."

"That's right. It was only a flash burn, first degree." Parker laughed. "Looking back, I can see you were high, like a diver, you know. I figured it affected your judgment. If the whole thing hadn't blown, I think we would have gone down with her."

The visit took a toll. It was considered advisable to lower the frequency of the patient's brain waves to the theta level. Josh cooperated. He had learned to use an auto-monitor in the standard bio-feedback course given Space Corps trainees. His old personal cue came back to him, riding his Apaloosa into the surf. Soon the oscilloscope indicated a relaxed, subjective consciousness, and he was allowed to regulate his own

EEG output. During this time he became interested in his mail. Kids wrote, girls with crushes, boys who wanted to be commanders someday, people offering prayers for his safety, and people who felt they knew him through his book. He answered each one via a tape recorder, and hired a secretary to transcribe them.

It was in a pile with others. He noticed the address was Los Angeles, but nothing warned him. No ESP indications. The letter said what most of them said: *I watched the entire thing on television.*

Then it changed: *I could hardly bring myself to realize it was happening to someone I knew. I did know you at one time. Do you remember Lefty? Once before I was concerned about you, that summer on Santa Cruz when you nearly drowned. But you were lucky then and I know you will be this time too. I wish you the very fastest recovery and I'll be watching the papers for reports on how you're doing. I suppose you will get a lot more writing done while you are convalescent. It seems a good time for it. I am quite a fan. For old time's sake I'll sign this—Lefty.* P.S. *Do you know there is no one who calls me that anymore?* P.P.S. *Glad to see you finally got the braces off.*

Josh peered at the postmark and turned the envelope over. There was no return address. It took him an hour to remember her last name. It finally came to him, Compton. Leticia Compton.

He phoned his secretary and asked him to try every Compton in the book until he located the one who lived in Latigo Canyon ten years ago. He was back in beta and determined to handle it. A technician came to take measurements for a brace. He questioned him carefully. It took about a week to manufacture.

"And then what happens, will I be able to walk?" He

figured he had a better chance prying information from this man than from the doctors.

"A young fellow like you, a month from now you'll be going around like normal."

Things seemed to be opening out again. The phone rang and he knocked over a glass of water in his anxiety to reach it.

"Hello."

It was Ned with the information. Andrew Compton. Josh took down the phone number. "Thanks." He clicked to break the connection and dialed immediately.

A maid answered. Mr. Compton was deceased. Mrs. Compton was in Europe and not expected for another month. Leticia? She didn't know if she should give out her number.

He explained they were old friends, neighbors. The woman relented and he copied down the address and phone number. "And her name now is Mrs. William Trenton."

"Thank you," he said, but he said it after he tuned out. It was a hard thing to take in. What did he expect? The world didn't stand still. He knew, having looked at it from out there, that each step was two thousand miles. How could it be that he was the only one whose life changed and that things happened to?

That evening when the doctor told him he planned to get him up, he responded listlessly and without enthusiasm. He stopped answering his mail and turned it over to Ned. He stared out the window by the hour. His view was a triangle of sky and the other wing of the hospital.

What kind of woman had Lefty turned into? He

knew that he had always wondered. He remembered his habit of falling in love from a distance. As soon as he was close to the girl, the charm was gone. Because it wasn't Lefty.

Was this love, he wondered, or an impediment to love? He realized that he compared every girl he knew to Lefty. But was it Lefty? or some paragon of his own devising? He might phone her for old time's sake, invite her and her husband—but he never got further than that.

The brace was a cage of aluminum and leather. It was attached by a shoulder harness. The ribs came up over his own as far as his armpits and extended down to the pelvic girdle. To get into it he rolled as far to the side as he could and reaching behind his prone body shoved the brace under himself; rocking back into it he pulled it tight and fastened the straps. This had to be done by feel, as he was not able to raise his head until the brace was firmly in place. Then once again rolling on his side, he got an arm under him and for the first time in months pushed himself to a sitting position.

What effort. It was incredible. He was wringing wet. Holding to the bed rail, he got to his feet. He found it easier to stand than sit. Sitting compressed the spine, and brought on muscular spasms. The brace held him in a vise, so upright that it was impossible to see his own feet. He moved about for two or three minutes and then let himself down into bed.

Once he was flat, the reverse procedure was necessary to remove the brace. A nurse tried to help him, but he insisted on doing it himself. When he had pulled free, he dropped it on the floor.

The nurse had the last word. "How are you going to reach it next time you want to get up?"

He thought of what Lefty had said in her letter, her assumption that he would undertake a new book, make this time of recovery and convalescence count. But he couldn't organize his thoughts. "I'm still orbiting," he told himself. He couldn't seem to zero in on anything. He couldn't even make a decision about his future. He preferred to look at the angle of sky and the adjacent hospital wing.

They added wet packs to his therapy treatment, and he was permitted to go home. He left by ambulance as he was unable to sit up the requisite amount of time in his brace. He was used to whizzing along the corridors on his cart looking at the acoustical green tiles of the ceiling. This time they passed X-ray and therapy. Every back patient should be issued a can of spray paint. As they rode the halls, they could create a ceiling masterpiece. It might not rival the Sistine Chapel, but it would be something to look at besides yards and yards of acoustical green punch-hole tile.

The ambulance attendants transferred him by blanket to a stretcher. For one dazzling moment he was out in the sun. But it was so bright it turned black. That was all right, its warmth remained on his eyelids. He had been shut away from so much.

Uncle Thor rode with him. As long as he could remember there had always been Uncle Thor. "Swimming is the best possible exercise. Your body is largely supported in water. Even in your brace I think it's a good idea. How would you like to spend a week or two at Poipu Beach?"

"The bathtub," Josh said, and laughed. They called

it that because it was sheltered and warm. He had dived and snorkeled among schools of small tropical fish, like the celluloid ones in the bath when he was a child. But he knew he wouldn't go to Poipu. He planned to work out in the gym and the pool, and in a week or two he would drive to Beverly Hills and—

—Rodeo Drive. He had long since memorized the address. It would be in the next block, the other side of the street. There it was, a large, Spanish-style two-story house set well back.

He parked and got out. It took him a moment. He was still awkward in his brace. Since his build was slight, it was hard to detect except by his excessively upright, military posture. He walked up the flagged path not knowing what he would say. He had imagined it so many ways that they jumbled in his mind.

From the side of the house, in kilts, sandals, a paper harness top, a garden trowel in her hand, came Lefty. They stopped and looked at each other. He observed that the freckles still showed.

"Josh!"

"Yeah," he said.

She came toward him.

"I happened to be passing."

She laughed and took him into the house, trekking

through the formal entry, living and dining rooms, to the kitchen. That was a large, pleasant, sunny room looking onto the garden. She began washing off dirt under the faucet. "I'll pour you a cup of coffee in a minute. How are you feeling? You look a little thin. That must have been an ordeal. I couldn't stand to think of you lying on your back day in and day out. That's why I wrote."

"I'm glad you did. I never liked the way you disappeared out of my life."

"Didn't you?" She felt the coffee pot. "It's still hot." She poured two cups. "Let's take it outdoors, shall we?"

He followed her up a rockery to an iron table under a shade tree. "This is a nice spot."

"I love my garden. I've set out tomatoes, lettuce, and chives. Oh yes, and a patch of mint. I thought I might put in a whole herb garden, rosemary, thyme, oregano." She fell suddenly silent. "It's a long time, Josh."

"Yes."

"You didn't answer my letters. Why?"

"I never got them."

"You never got them? I don't understand."

"Neither do I exactly. But I never did. I wrote you anyway."

"You did?"

"Maybe it was some sort of prank or joke."

"You mean the boys? Or your sisters? I don't believe that."

"I guess I don't either."

"Well, obviously someone was protecting you from

me. They were quite right too. I very definitely had my cap set for you." She laughed a bit shakily.

"And then you met your husband," he said.

"Well, not exactly then. It was the summer I was nineteen. Six months later we were married. Two years after that he was dead."

"Dead?" His exclamation fell between them.

"Didn't you know?" She glanced up quickly. "Yes, we'd just made application to the Directory for Genetic Screening. A week after his death the clearance came through. We had been selected for parenthood."

"What happened?"

She looked at him without change of expression. "Doesn't the name Trenton mean anything to you?"

"You don't mean Bill Trenton who was lost in the weather satellite explosion? God, I'm sorry, Lefty. I trained with him for six weeks, we were in the same lab division. I had no idea—Were you married then?"

She nodded. "So now you know the story of my life. Too bad we can't jump on our horses and ride away from everything into the surf."

"Why can't we?"

She smiled, but her eyes were sad. "No, Josh, when you're twelve you can pound bare heels against your horse's sides and kick her into a trot. You can ride through reality and come out the other side. That magic is called childhood. But we're not children, Josh. The moment came and went and cast us up in different lives. Can I get you another cup of coffee?"

"No," he said, and immediately wished he had said yes. Because she took his refusal as a sign that he would go. She stood up, smiled at him, and extended her hand. He took it, small boned and sun browned, in his. "Can I see you again, Lefty?"

She pulled her hand from his and continued to smile. But the warmth was gone. She had thrown up barricades. "I don't see the point, Josh. I enjoyed your coming by. I really did. But I think it's best if we leave it here. Okay?"

He shook his head. "Not okay."

"Really, Josh, you can't come barging into someone's life from left field somewhere."

"It was farther than that," he reminded her. He felt her relent a bit.

"Yes, it was. I'm flattered, Josh, and touched. But I'm not ready for an involvement."

"Who said anything about an involvement? The only issue is dinner. Friday night. I'll pick you up at seven thirty."

"I'd forgotten how stubborn you can be. All right." But she phoned the next day leaving word that she couldn't make it.

Josh ignored this communication and appeared at her door at seven thirty Friday. "Oh," she said a bit breathlessly, "didn't you get my message?"

"I got it," he admitted.

"Well, then you know I'm going out. I'm taking a class at UCLA Extension that meets three nights a week."

"Let me drive you. We can talk."

"Josh, this is embarrassing."

He stood his ground adamantly, not looking embarrassed in the least.

"All right, I'll get my sweater." She left him there and was back in a minute with a sweater over her shoulder and a notebook. He drove to the freeway and punched for a hookup in the through lane. With the car on automatic, he turned his attention to her. "Now let's have it, Lefty. You want me out of your life. Why? Are you going with someone?"

"No."

"Well then—?"

"Well then, what?" Her voice was tight. "It doesn't occur to you that I might not be interested or looking. That maybe I'm trying to build a certain kind of life for myself. Twelve more units and I'll be a qualified clinical psychologist. I'll have a career. I'll have independence."

"And that's what you want?"

"That's what I want."

He pressed for uncoupling and they were egressed at the university intersection. "Which building?"

"You can drop me anywhere here. I don't mind a walk. I'm sorry, Josh."

"Is it because I'm also in the Space Corps?"

"That's part of it. Yes. I just haven't the courage to, well, open myself to that kind of tension again."

He didn't comment. "What time are you through? I'll pick you up."

"That won't be necessary, Josh. I'd rather you didn't."

"Lefty, I'm washed out. I'll never pilot anything more dangerous for Space Corps than a swivel chair." They had pulled into a parking area; she got out and began walking away. When he caught up to her he saw that she was crying. He pulled her to him and she began to laugh somewhat hysterically. "You're a man of iron," she said and, unbuttoning his shirt, spread it apart to see the brace. "I didn't know you were in that kind of a thing. How long do you have to wear it?"

"Six months."

"It's so heavy. It must be terribly uncomfortable."

"Not really. Actually I'm rather attached to it—no pun intended. It allows me to be mobile, to get around, to be with you. Space Corps, that was what was bothering you, wasn't it, Lefty?"

"This is the building," she said, but made no move toward it. He took her hand and pulled her past it as though it offered a threat.

"That's not all of it," she said, "I've been a year and a half getting it together, getting myself together. The last few months I knew who I was again, and I figured out where I was going."

"Then I barged in."

"Then you barged in. And I saw how fragile everything was that I'd stuck back together. It was like writing a life plan on paper, the first wind that comes along blows it away. And you came along, a wind out of nowhere. I'm very frightened, Josh."

"If it were possible," he said bending over her, "to protect a life, I'd protect yours. Even against myself. But it doesn't work that way. If we reject involvements, commitments, we reject life. You have to find courage for it again."

She held onto him, pressing herself against the aluminum cage that separated her from his body.

There weren't formal dates. But their lives began to join. She accompanied him to the club almost every morning for hydrotherapy. Soon she knew the exercises and was helping him extend them, doing them along with him. His progress was rapid. Generally they stayed on and had lunch.

She brought ink and brushes and taught him the art of sumi-e. "It helped me tremendously. The approach is simply to study something, a rock, a tree, a wave breaking, until you feel you have entered into it. Then you dip your brush and in a few strokes try to capture, what to you is the essence, the character, the soul."

"You've already captured mine. How many strokes did you use?"

"I'm still in the initial stage with you. There are too many possibilities. Don't you feel that, Josh? That there are many ways for you to go?"

"No. There's only one way." They were in a beach cabana lying on soft beach furniture that took on the press of their bodies.

He reached over and untied her bra, and just as deliberately rolled down the bikini. She herself kicked it off her legs. They had not been together before. He was still in the brace.

He kissed her systematically, eyes, lips, nipples. His hands bridged and readied her. "Climb on the table,

Lefty. This is going to take some doing." He slung a canvas pillow and arranged her on it. Then, standing, he placed his hands on her hips and penetrated.

It happened to them. Their bodies were separate, their warmth separate, yet each contraction spurred him deeper until the warmth had one center and her body grew from the stem of his.

He began taking Lefty to the pool at the Latigo estate. Lynn was delighted with her. She managed to get Josh to one side. "She's a marvelous girl, Josh. Don't let too much time go by. Move in on her."

Josh swung his mother off her feet and kissed her. "It's already been attended to. She's decided to join us Kelloggs."

Lefty cabled her mother the news. Mrs. Compton flew back to what was to be an engagement supper. But it wasn't possible to keep to this intention. G.K. insisted on a lavish affair with pavilions set up on the grounds, an orchestra, and a guest list of celebrities.

The press took it up, and wherever they went photographers lay in wait. An artist's sketch was reprinted of Josh minus his beard. It shook everyone. The next edition carried two photographs; one of Josh and one of the former President. Speculation came very close to being actionable.

Josh decided to get it out in the open. He told Lefty. "I'm his natural son. Does it make a difference to you?"

"How'd you find out?"

"I still don't know the details, just the facts. And not all of those either."

"Do you know who your mother is?"

"No."

"Probably some glamorous creature." She patted his arm. "It's better not to probe. Lynn's your mother and we don't want anyone hurt. Right?"

He agreed with her.

Lefty's other big rooter was Uncle Thor. "She has more sense than you ever did," he told Josh, "she keeps both feet on the ground." He had never approved Josh's career in space. "That kind of job is for the technician type without the imagination to be scared."

"You're wrong. What better place for a poet than space? You're stoned on photons. But I'm afraid I'm not a poet. If I were I couldn't keep from writing. In fact that's one of the things I want to talk about: where I'll go, what I should point for. I want to be doing something that I think is important."

"You could stay on in the program."

"In a desk job? I wouldn't want that."

"Well, marry your girl. Go off for a couple of weeks and we'll talk when you come back."

Lefty waved from across the room as she made her way toward them. "I hope no one yells fire. Listen, Josh, you've got to ask mother for a dance, and that will give me a chance to find out why no smart girl ever snagged your Uncle Thor."

Josh went off with what grace he could muster to find Mrs. Compton.

"Now we can talk about him," Lefty said. "He's a wonderful person, isn't he? Unexpected. I mean he's shy and at the same time daring and adventurous."

"Josh is a private person. It's odd in a way, brought up in a large family, surrounded by people."

"I know what you mean. He has an easy manner with people. They like him. But they don't know him. I have a feeling that you know him better than anyone."

"Perhaps."

"If I need an ally, I want to count on you."

"Of course, but why do you say that?"

"I don't know. It's something in Josh. There's a sense of drama about him, of purpose. It's probably what attracts me to him and yet I worry. I know whose son he is. He told me. That sets him apart too. But it's more than that. Walking in space marked him, but it isn't that either. I can't explain, but certain things crackle with static. I almost expect Josh to do that."

Bitterbaum's reply was to put a champagne glass into her hand and to laugh gently at her exaggerations. But lightning looking for a passage from ground to cloud could at any moment discharge a pilot streamer, and then a stepped leader traveling the ionized air, striking and consuming.

Cindy was flying in on Air France from boarding school. The flight was delayed and Josh had a beer watching the field, the scurrying of porters with luggage carts, the portable refueling stations, the taxiing maneuvers, and takeoff. He paid for the beer and glanced at the clock.

Twenty minutes yet. He decided to walk around. Avoiding the moving sidewalk, he entered a stream of deplaning passengers. Then it struck, the bolt that Bitterbaum dreaded. Ground to cloud, a dart leader congealing his brain, ripping his senses. Just ahead of him, traveling the moving platform, was his dead cousin.

Josh kept moving; his legs kept on. His brain turned off. It couldn't get a thought through. But he kept pace with him, in fact, gained.

Steve!

It didn't come out. It caught in the interstices of his mind.

Steve!

It was a whisper, a breath.

He took hold of his arm and turned him around.

Steve looked into his face. The sidewalk moved him on and Josh on the other side of the railing had to keep walking. There were tears all over his face. He couldn't get his breath.

"Steve."

Steve tore himself free and began running along the moving strip. Josh jumped the railing, fell, picked himself up but couldn't maintain his balance on the heaving rollers. He crashed into two or three people trying to keep Steve in sight. A guard yelled for him to stop, another tackled him.

Josh struggled, then all at once caved in. He felt sick. The same way he'd felt when he'd heard that Steve was dead. It wasn't an ache or a pain, it was emptiness. It grew out of the pit of your stomach, filling you with hollowness, with nothing, scooping you out, reaming away emotions, feelings, thoughts, not leaving anything. Not even self.

He was functioning again, giving his I.D., making an explanation, saying he thought he'd seen an old friend. Finally they let him go. Except he couldn't go. His back went into spasm. He tried to remain on his feet but his body was pulled into a bow. The men who had been interrogating him lowered him to a bench. His back muscles knotted like crumpled girders, he was completely covered by sweat. At this moment Cindy paged him.

"It's my sister. I—I don't want her to see me like this. Would you tell her I've been delayed and to take a cab directly home."

His request was countermanded. Cindy was contacted and directed to him. She was a capable fifteen and took immediate charge. Josh was carried by stretcher to a waiting cab.

He was almost grateful for the back episode. It provided a cover. It was natural that he shut himself in his room, allow no one in, talk to no one. They made excuses for him; a relapse is a discouraging thing.

Josh lay on top of his bed. He hadn't moved his head to look out the window. The landscape he saw was one of lies and betrayal. It was easier to understand the world when one was separated from it, when one looked and saw a beach ball engraved with a familiar map, that turned, presenting all sides and features. But on reentry you discovered the main features were cruelty and dissembling. The logic, the reason, that guided you between worlds, was no good here. There was no way to chart a course when there were no fixed points. The people you loved, your own family, were frauds, they perpetrated terrible hoaxes. There was no one to trust. No one to ask.

Was it possible that it was not Steve? He wanted to believe that. If Steve were dead and he mistaken, he could stuff back his guts, his organs, his mind, and take up his life again. But he had touched him, actually touched him. His hand had held his arm. They looked into each other's face. And because there was nothing he could say, no forgiveness to expect, he had torn himself out of his grasp.

There was no possibility that he was mistaken. There was another possibility, however. There was a high probability that he was mad. A hallucination was reality to a madman.

The odd thing was that nothing led up to it. There was no other evidence that his mind was giving way. There were no instances that he could recall where he had seen impossible or unlikely things. The occurrence at the airport stood out as a solitary, unrelated happening. He examined his life for some trauma to explain it. There was nothing.

He was happy. He was in love. He was going to be married. He veered sharply. He continued to search for an underlying etiology. If he were going to hallucinate Steve, why didn't he do it six years ago at the time of his death? Why now?

The only alternative was to believe in a conspiracy. He might be mad. But he wasn't paranoid. Still, he was his father's son. It was conceivable there was something afoot, some scheme to—to what?

And why reach out to Steve, pretend he had died? What purpose could that serve? What rationale was behind it? And who was in on it?

Steve, obviously. And who?

His father? Uncle Thor? His mother?

—It was better to be mad.

He refused to see anyone. His mother came in and he repeated that he was all right. What could he say —*I saw Steve yesterday at the airport?*

She strapped him into his brace, and he let her think that was the problem.

"I don't understand why you won't see Lefty," Lynn said. "She's been ringing up three or four times a day. I do think you should talk to her."

"No."

"You mustn't be so sensitive about your back, Josh. Everybody has disabilities. After all, she's going to be your wife."

"No. This has changed everything. I'm not going to let her marry an invalid."

"Josh, you'll get over this. It's a setback, but the doctors agree you'll be out of the brace in a matter of months."

He couldn't argue medical opinion and his intransigence appeared unreasonable.

She turned at the door. "It's awfully hard on Lefty, being shut out this way. Won't you—"

"No, no I won't," he said violently.

Lynn looked startled. "We'll talk about it later," she said quietly, and quietly shut the door.

The position he had adopted was indefensible. He realized that. But he didn't see any way open to him. If he consulted a psychiatrist he'd be committed. You couldn't walk around loose if you saw your dead cousin at L.A. International.

"I'm sorry, Josh."

He hadn't heard her come in. He had thrown himself across the bed and put a pillowcase over his eyes. He didn't move. He didn't take away the pillowcase.

"I was downstairs when your mother came up. I've been talking to her. I know you don't want to see me. Is it me, or is it everybody?"

"I didn't want this."

"Why?" She marched up to the bed. "Will you for goodness' sake take that ridiculous pillowcase off your face?" She snatched at it and let it fall on the floor. "There'll be plenty of times you'll have to hold my hand. I mean, a marriage isn't a series of dates with each of us looking our best. That's why I can't understand your behavior, I really can't. It's too bad that you had that fall and that your back is involved again. But it's not that big a deal, Josh."

"I'm afraid I disagree with you." He held her off with politeness. "This has changed things. I thought I was recovered. Now I see I've got to reckon with the fact that I'll always be a semi-invalid."

She looked down at him, the pupils of her eyes dilated, swallowing her vision. "I'm hearing you say that you no longer want to marry me. Is that what you're saying, Josh?"

"I'm saying that I can't marry you. That it wouldn't be right, or fair, or the decent thing to do."

"And what is the right and fair and decent thing to do? To cower in bed with a pillowcase over your head, refuse to return my calls, refuse to talk to me on the phone or let me see you? Is this the hero that walked in space, the man with the courage to stand between worlds? I can't believe it. Does the prospect of pain demoralize you so completely that you're no longer capable of planning a life?"

"I suppose," he said slowly, "I might have put it a little differently. I might have said that I was thinking of you. But there is undoubtedly truth in both versions. So take your version and go home, Lefty."

"You bastard," she yelled, saw the impact on him, realized what she had done, and in despair left the room.

So that was that. Another penalty of seeing your dead cousin. His hand searched for the fallen pillowcase and he placed it once more across his eyes. Cut off from light, cut off from life. He hung between worlds.

Sanity and insanity, reason and unreason. His mind swung delicately balanced between polarities.

His father, too, had a session with him. He flew back from two weeks of salmon fishing in British Columbia. He came into Josh's room and delivered himself of a monolog. Hardly in the Shakespearean tradition, it dealt mainly in banalities. "They can't keep a good man down." "You'll be up and about in no time." "Things will look different to you."

Josh suffered through it. He kept the pillowcase over his face.

"You've been through worse than this. You've got to call on that old fighting spirit. And for God's sake take that dust rag off your face."

Josh complied, holding it in his hand so he could put it across his eyes again when his father left.

"That's better," G.K. said. "You've got to face up to things. You have a problem, but it's nothing you can't lick. I expect you down for dinner."

"I can't, sir. I'm not up to it."

"You heard me, dinner."

"The boy's got to make an effort," he told Lynn who was hovering outside the door. Josh replaced the pillowcase. The dinner hour came and went. His mother phoned Bitterbaum who was at a medical convention in Miami.

Josh's resistance was eroded by the series of family confrontations. "I see it's your turn," he greeted Uncle Thor. "What did I do to deserve this?"

"What *did* you do, Josh? That's what I'm here to find out."

"You want to know? You really want to know?"

"I really want to know."

Josh threw back his head and laughed. Then he

reached for the pillowcase which he put across his eyes hoping that would terminate the conversation.

"What's that supposed to be?" Uncle Thor asked.

"The light hurts my eyes."

"Nonsense, there's nothing wrong with your eyes. We can't have any kind of talk with you buried under that thing."

"That's the idea," Josh said.

"Look, I interrupted business in Miami to see you."

"So you've seen me." Then, repenting this churlishness, he removed the blindfold. "All right, but there's nothing to say."

"There must be a great deal to say. This isn't like anything I know about you, Josh. And I know you as well as anyone."

"What is there to discuss? I reinjured my back. And I want to be left alone."

"How did you happen to fall?"

"I don't remember. I must have slipped on something."

"Joshua Francis Kellogg, varsity football, tennis champ, star athlete, slips and falls at the airport. I checked it out, Josh. I spoke to the guard who detained you. He remembers it very well. As long as he's been there, which is fifteen years, he never saw anyone vault the rail onto the moving sidewalk. Who was the man you were chasing?"

"It was Steve."

Bitterbaum sagged in every part of him. His long frame folded onto the bed. "What did you say?" His voice seemed not to issue from his throat, but from his solar plexus.

"It was Steve," Josh repeated doggedly.

"You mean someone in the crowd who for a moment you took to be Steve?"

"No. It was Steve."

Bitterbaum laughed shakily. "You know that's impossible. You know he's been dead six years."

"I held his arm, Uncle Thor. He looked at me and I looked at him. You think I could be mistaken? And then he ran. That's when I jumped the railing. I think I fell then, or maybe it was later. I bumped into someone."

Bitterbaum shook his head, denying everything. "You've got to have imagined this."

"I didn't imagine it," Josh gave emphasis to each word. "But it is possible it didn't happen. I don't see how it could have happened. In which case I'm out of my skull, I'm crazy."

"Hold on, Josh. It's possible to hallucinate without being insane."

"But I hadn't been thinking about him. If it had happened six years ago. I brooded a lot about it then. But it didn't. It happened now, out of the blue, a propos of nothing. Uncle Thor, I had him by the arm."

A groan escaped Bitterbaum. "Oh my God," he said and he said it over and over.

"Uncle Thor?"

The face that Bitterbaum raised had a fallen-in look to it, the craggy features presented a fragmented, almost broken appearance. "Hold on a bit, Josh. There's something I have to verify before we can straighten this out. But you're not crazy, you can believe that."

"There's no other explanation."

"Perhaps," Bitterbaum said, "perhaps." He patted Josh absently. Already Thor was rising up in outrage.

The long frame straightened, the chin seemed more prominent, the eyes, which he marked hazel on his driver's license, dartled a strange green.

Thor strode out of the room, down the hall, and through the rooms one by one until he discovered Kellogg.

"Well," said G.K. glancing up from a tax form. He broke off. Bitterbaum looked somehow swollen. He had never realized his height. He stood over six feet. He towered. And his eyes held a peculiar expression. The figure before his desk hardly resembled Bitterbaum. "Bitterbaum?" he said, trying to quell a sudden nervousness.

Thor tossed his thunderbolt. "Steve is alive."

G.K.'s mouth opened.

Thor reached across the barricade of the desk, grabbed his collar and by it lifted him to his feet. "He's alive. Josh saw him. And you're goddamned well going to admit it." He eased up on the collar to make this possible.

"Yes, all right. You're choking me. What do you want me to say? He's alive. All right, okay. I admit it."

Thor released him with a spinning motion that sent him crashing backward into the chair. G.K. put both hands to his throat. "What's got into you, Bitterbaum? Have you lost your mind?"

Thor ignored this. "The facts, G.K. Just the facts."

"All right. I'd planned to simulate the death of the ex-president's brother later on. But I was forced to play it out then. If you remember, it was the period when Josh left home. It was the only thing I could think of to bring him back."

"Steve would never have agreed. He wouldn't do a thing like that to Josh, to any of us."

"That's right. I had a problem there. I put it to Steve that I'd brought him up, educated him, taken care of his mother. He owed me."

Bitterbaum repeated stubbornly, "Steve wouldn't do it."

"I had a great deal of trouble on that score. I asked him to trust me." G.K. broke off, cleared his throat and began again. "You're not going to like this, Bitterbaum. I told him. I had to. It was the only way I could get him to go along. Once he saw it was for Josh's good, that's when he agreed."

Bitterbaum shook his head in an effort to continue denying, but it no longer worked. "How could you do it, G.K.?"

"Very simply, I made him see that through his sacrifice Josh would reach the position he was being groomed for, become the man he had it in him to be. The deal was he would communicate with no member of the family or anyone who knew them. He was to change his name, and as far as the Kelloggs were concerned, he was dead. The thing I really worried about was you, Bitterbaum. I was afraid you'd smell a rat."

Thor began to crumple into Bitterbaum.

"It was the only way I could think of," G.K. said. "Besides, it was a necessary imprinting, one of the crucial formative experiences, like the episode in space. Remember, Bitterbaum, I went into this for one purpose only, to prepare Josh to resume the life that was cut off. I intend to see him President."

"President! What you almost saw was Josh in a padded cell with his shoelaces taken away." He let himself down slowly into the straight chair across from G.K.

G.K. regarded him with concern. "I realize I had no right taking Steve into my confidence without consulting you. But under the circumstances—"

"Shut up," Bitterbaum said wearily. "What's the point apologizing for the wrong thing? Fix me a drink, will you? A double Scotch."

"But you never drink at this hour. The sun is—"

"The hell with the sun. The hell with the hour. Give me a double Scotch."

G.K. went to the swing-out bar.

Bitterbaum drank, coughed, and got up. "Well, come on," he said looking around at G.K.

"Come on where?"

"We've got to tell Josh."

"Are you serious?"

"Of course I'm serious."

"We can't do that. The time isn't ripe."

"I don't know what you call ripe. You have left him with two choices. Number one: he is mad. Number two: he is a clonee. I vote for number two."

"Wait, Bitterbaum, you can't just go in there and tell him a thing like that. In the first place he won't believe it. This has to be handled with finesse."

"I'm open to suggestion," Bitterbaum said.

G.K. put his head in his hands.

Josh, strapped into his brace, leaned against the window listening with an impatience he tried to hide. Was this Uncle Thor's idea of therapy? Was he trying to take his mind off things with some farfetched scientific account? How could it possibly interest him that thirty years ago someone called Watson and someone called Crick said, "We wish to suggest a structure for the salt of DNA."? That twenty years ago the AMA lobbied through a bill outlawing research in microbiology which would lead to cloning, and that this stand was subsequently reversed?

Well, well. What do you know? Fascinating.

Uncle Thor departed from his technical account. Suddenly Josh was alert. With not the slightest pause in his narrative, Bitterbaum was discussing the day almost twenty-five years ago when the President was assassinated.

He had been there. He spoke of it with total recall. Everything was recorded on his mind. He devoted the same time to describing a worn spot in the linoleum tile as he did to an analysis of the throat wound. Shock had made differentiation impossible. It all came out as he remembered it, with equal emphasis on the crucial events and on the trivial.

By now, Josh was intrigued. He wondered why Uncle Thor had never told this story. He didn't understand the long preamble on cloning or what it had to do with that day. But Uncle Thor had achieved his objective, for this moment at least he was not brooding on his own problems. His mind was actively trying to make a connection. The clues were there. Bitterbaum had been present at the death of the President, his actual father. It was a tenuous thread, and what had it to do with fusion of cellular matter?

"I couldn't stand the thought that he was gone," Bitterbaum said. "Someone lifted his wife up from the floor, she'd been kneeling in blood. Her private physician felt his pulse. Things were confused, but I was functioning clearly. Later, it would hit me. But then there were things to do. I approached the body to remove the nasogastric tube. Using one of the scalpels lying on the table I scooped a minute quantity of cellular material from the throat wound. I went out of the Trauma Room, down the hall to the supply room where I located a portable case of liquid nitrogen. I immersed the test tube containing the cellular material." Bitterbaum paused and looked at Josh.

Josh was resistant to this silent communication. A thought did cross his mind, but it was so utterly fantastic he didn't bother to formulate it. Still he felt uneasy. All this in some way concerned him.

"Shall I go on, Josh?"

His hand tightened on the frame of the window. "Yes."

"I came out here to California. I needed the support of a wealthy and influential man. G.K. and I got together."

"Are you telling me, are you telling me—?" Josh turned from Bitterbaum to Kellogg and back again.

Their features looked as though they'd been put in a blender and mixed with the room. Nothing was confined to itself but ran together, nose and curtains, desk and ears. He remembered the tune Smitty liked to hum: "I do not die of death, I die of vertigo." He tried to sort things out in this reeling room, and in his mind that wanted to dissociate itself, to retreat. "I may be crazy," he said, "it's a possibility we were discussing before. But I think you're saying to me—I think you're saying you grew me from the President's cellular matter, from the neck wound. That can't be right, can it? You'll have to lock me up after all. I'm mad as a hatter."

Bitterbaum put his hand on his shoulder. "As far as I know, Josh, you are the first successfully cloned person."

"You mean I'm not myself. I'm him?"

"We don't know exactly. No one does. You are his biological duplicate. You were raised as nearly like the prototype as possible. Now you can understand about Steve. The original lost a brother. This was to be a simulated experience. Steve *is* alive. By accident, you saw him. You see, the death of the President's brother had a great deal to do with forming his character."

Josh was still struggling to take in what he was hearing. Acceptance was something else. "So I've been brought up in a test tube, all my experiences calculated to duplicate what I'd had the first time around? What shall I call it, my other incarnation? And Steve agreed to do that? Did he know? Does everyone know? Am I the only one who wasn't told?"

G.K. hadn't said a word. He spoke now. "No one knows, Josh. Not even the biologist who did the actual cloning, or the woman who carried you. Only Bitterbaum and I. And I had to tell Steve to force him to carry out his part of it. At the proper time we intended to tell you and the world. We were forced to disclose it now because of the chance circumstance of your running into Steve."

G.K. cleared his throat, words didn't seem to be getting through, perhaps a raucous growl would. "And one more thing. Bitterbaum here had nothing to do with the Steve business. I knew he was too emotionally involved to go along. But I felt justified, that was the original plan, that was the understanding on which I was brought into it. If it was a test-tube atmosphere, it was never intended to be harmful to you in any way. We are both concerned for your welfare. I happen to believe the best thing for you and the country is for you to be the man you were. I don't think you'll find any villains here, Josh. There aren't any bad guys. You mean a great deal to us, there's a bond that —well, I feel as though you are a son. At the same time, knowing who you are, I have great anticipation that—"

"Knowing who I am?" Josh cut in. "If you know that, for Christ's sake tell me."

"You are," Kellogg said, "a replication of one of the great men of this century."

"Am I?" Josh turned to Bitterbaum and asked the same question. "Am I? The President was not cloned. I was. A copy is never an original. Why do collectors hunt for first editions and value them? Up to the moment of seeing Steve alive, I might have been a replication, a nearly identical copy. But then I saw Steve. That never happened to *him. He* never doubted his sanity. And *he* was never told that he was a cloned human, the first man in the world without a mother. I was conceived, not out of passion or love, but asexually from the cells of my own dying body. My first womb was a test tube, my amniotic fluid liquid nitrogen. I was nurtured in a stranger's body. The service bought and paid for, I assume.

"Okay. Until I knew this, I grant you, I might have been his duplicate. But now these differences separate me from him. Biologically I am the late President. But psychologically, emotionally, mentally, who and what am I? Do you know, Uncle Thor? Do you have any answers for me?"

Bitterbaum had been casting back in his mind; the regression was a long one. "Some answers, Josh. We know your biological and hereditary makeup. We know the first time around it produced a leader without peer. That's one side. On the other hand, we know you. You distinguished yourself as a political writer, and as a commander in the Space Corps. That takes intelligence, integrity, and guts. I think with the ability you've demonstrated you'll be able to handle this. In fact, once you get used to the idea, reconciled to it, it may give you an edge. After all, you are aware of your potential. The rest of us are not."

Josh started to laugh. They could see that he was trying to stop, but it took several shuddering breaths before the paroxysm was over. "You're something else, Uncle Thor, you really are. The silver lining and all that. And G.K., you're even more hyper. What was it Martin Luther King said, 'I have a dream'? Well, you had a nightmare, and I'm it."

"I realize it will take getting used to," G.K. said, "I

think under the circumstances your reaction is natural."

"How the hell would you know? How would anyone know? No one in the history of the human race ever had to react to this before."

"Take it easy, Josh. After you've rested we'll talk again." Bitterbaum nodded to G.K. They got as far as the door.

"One thing, G.K. . . ."

Kellogg turned, "Yes?"

"Let me know when you think the country's ready for me."

When he was alone, he did a human thing. He cried. There were no tears when he thought he was dying, not any when he plunged toward earth in a damaged capsule, or later when he hung half-conscious in the water. What he expected then was the common fate of all men. But this was something no one else had to cope with. It set him off, gave him a special destiny.

Man born of woman. But he wasn't born of woman. He was born out of his own sex, out of himself; out of a dead man. Don't beat around the bush, *out of my dead self.* Did the cell that incubated him *remember?* Was there somewhere in his body the first accurate and actual memory of death?

Would it be possible by delving inside himself to feel the bullet penetrate his throat? Had he raised his hand, tried to speak, tell his wife? Had the pain blocked out knowledge of what was happening? Or did he know? The sound of the rifle filled his head with blood and knowledge.

Did I hear the next explosion that ended it all, that carried off the top of my head? Somewhere his pronouns had changed. *I, I,* he thought.

And he thought, *my wife is still living, a grandmother, married again and widowed again, while I am a young man.*

Madness was easier than this. Madness was an interior thing. But in this instance he was sane and the externals were out of sync, the time sequence confused, and yes, it was a fair judgment, the parameters of his life were aberrant, disordered, and insane.

The question was, within such a framework was it possible to bring back normalcy and order? He thought of suicide. But he had been raised a Catholic. He wondered if the church would extend itself to him or whether he was outside the pale. He wondered if he'd been given another soul or was he going on a retread of the old? Or was it possible that he had not been granted one at all?

He was Lazarus. His swaddling clothes smelled of the grave. Were there others? Experiments like him, walking around? Should he contact them? Advertise? Form a club? *Clonees Anonymous.*

What would the reaction be, if people knew? The mailman, Delia, the garage mechanic? Lefty, what would she think? What would she say?

He had no one. He was like no one. He was born an orphan. Dying flesh, that's what he was made of. *Ashes to ashes. Dust to dust.* But a single cell escaped.

Josh went into retreat. He asked that no mail be forwarded, and that no effort be made to contact him. As a concession to Bitterbaum he left an emergency number, that was all. The spot he chose was a cabin in Estes, Colorado.

A stream moved by, rushing, turbulent, pouring aerated jets over moss rocks. Spreading, it became calm, moving placidly, catching light filtered through pines and aspen. Each day he brought a book which he never opened. He stared instead into the water, allowing himself to be mesmerized. It spoke simultaneously in different tongues; the deep, booming pulse that carried from its source found its voice in precipitous downhill stretches, but was muted in the broad pools where contrapuntal splashing and dripping could be heard.

His own life had been squeezed into rapids, too quick, too fast, pouring out its energy. He longed to broaden it.

He reached his hand into the water and allowed it to braid around his fingers. A child is baptized in water. He let it wash his spirit and lave his soul, until he was able to let go of the sense of personal doom. His thoughts spilled out of tight confines and spread and freed themselves. He was able to lay aside the lump of agony that seemed to have replaced his organs, and to move his thought in a new direction.

If he had the courage to write an account of it, stripping himself, exposing himself as a human clone, perhaps some of the fear and hysteria that surrounded the subject could be put to rest. He turned it over for some days in his mind. The implications reached from the biological to the political to the legal. Implicit in the idea of cloning was the vision of man as unfinished. Man's striving for self-perfection was at stake. And society's right to clone certain men and women in each generation.

Monogenic surgery was now being employed on an experimental basis to correct homozygous defects, and a great deal of research money had been funneled into polygenic therapy. But it was far behind the optimistic timetable predicted in the sixties. The complexity of human physiological systems seemed orders of magnitude beyond the best efforts of science. Also this direction was barred by the full weight of legal, ecclesiastical, and popular opinion. People were suspicious of intellectual superiority. They didn't want to be "monkeyed with" themselves, and they didn't want to raise children smarter than they were. As one columnist put it, "The generation gap would then be institutionalized." Fundamentalists believed it was interfering with God's plan for the natural development of man.

The conclusion was inescapable. It was simpler to start with the best genotypes available and duplicate them. But if the idea of cloned genes caused such a furor, a cloned man would be an outrage.

There were occasional Sunday-supplement articles to the effect that China was cloning an army bred for fighter instincts, to overrun the world. But such accounts could hardly be taken seriously in a system where each birth must be applied for. Cloning on a mass scale would never be the answer as it would curtail the diversity that random breeding provided. But shouldn't it have its place? Would society preserve, if it could, its Einsteins, Bachs, Picassos, even certain statesmen? Of course there was the danger that dictators, key figures in military juntas, even presidents would desire to perpetuate themselves.

Who would decide? Who would make the rules?

There was the gruesome possibility of clonees being kept as organ banks. This persuaded him. He made the decision in the affirmative. It was necessary to stand before the world as a clonal man. Let them see him as a human being, in no way distinguishable from any other.

Would they disenfranchise him, deny him his rights under the Constitution? Then let them do it to his face, let them meet him in debate, refute him, deny his right to exist, to procreate. If they felt he should be incarcerated and held as a donor, his organs cut out of him one by one, let them say so.

He was caught up in his crusade. He began jotting down the thoughts of other men to bolster his own. The first entry was Cudworth: *The truths of morality are as evident as those of mathematics.*

He became dedicated to his task, exploring the various possibilities that cloning raised. Months slipped away. The mountain cabin was cold and uncomfortable. He kept the wood stove going. He didn't want to move. He couldn't disturb his papers. Filed in an apple box was a card catalog of medical and biochemical information. He was in the process of typing a hand-written first draft. In the field of law he had amassed an additional two hundred cards. Revisions were paper-clipped to each other. Pages of inserts and pages of deletions, all had their proper place. In the disorder of the room was meticulous order. He knew what each pile contained, and where to find the quote to buttress his thought. He could locate anything in a matter of seconds.

He bought a cord of firewood and stacked it against the exterior of the cabin. He had an arrangement with the local grocery to replenish and deliver supplies each week. He spent six hours a day in typing. He was not proficient, but banged out pages relentlessly.

When his fingers were stiff, blue, and swollen, he realized he had let the fire go out. Rather than interrupt his train of thought, he put on sweaters.

That was how Bitterbaum found him, in an icy room, plugging at the typewriter. "Good God, you'll have double pneumonia before the day's over."

Josh apologized and set about rekindling the stove, a skill which Bitterbaum wondered at.

"I'll have coffee in a moment. How did you find me?" he asked. Although they both recognized the question was, *why?*

"Don't ask. The roads are terrible. Roads? Goat tracks. The car broke down and . . . I'll recount my misadventures another time. Tell me about yourself, Josh." He was about to move a pile of papers from a chair.

"Wait," Josh stopped him, "let me do that. They're filed there." He lifted the sheaf carefully and deposited it on the far end of the table.

"What are you working on, another book?"

"Yes."

"That's good, that's really good. That means you've made peace with yourself, if you're able to work."

"I think I have."

"What's it about?"

"Oh, no," Josh said, "no capsule description. You'll have to read it. In fact I'd like you to see the first draft, give me some advice on it."

"Great. Can I get accommodations in that town of eight hundred pop. back there?"

"Bunk here. You can have the bedroom."

"What about you?"

"I sleep on the floor in a sleeping bag. It helps my back."

"It's settled, then. Incidentally, I'm your mailman. I brought a packet of stuff that accumulated."

"Good. I was running low on newspapers. We'll feed the fire."

Bitterbaum stopped him. "There's a letter from Lefty."

Josh continued with his original intention and placed the entire packet of mail on the coals. Bitterbaum looked upset.

"I know what kind of letter Lefty wrote," Josh said quietly, "understanding. But how can she understand when she doesn't know what it's about? It's a big muddle, Uncle Thor. And it has to remain that way. I'm a pariah."

"Why are you a pariah? No one knows. No one need ever know."

"That obviates the whole experiment, doesn't it? I was raised like the original, even to the point of enacting that whole death thing with Steve. The purpose is disclosure. I mean, that's the whole idea. I'm to take my place on the political scene."

"G.K. and I have been talking. That *was* the plan. But the climate doesn't seem right. We'd be letting you destroy yourself. We feel you should retain your anonymity, write your books, marry Lefty, settle down."

Josh's face softened. It held an expression he hadn't seen on it in a long time. "Did G. K. agree to that?"

"Yes, he did. Your welfare comes first with both of us."

"I didn't know that," Josh said slowly. "I really didn't know that."

"Well," Bitterbaum said, "that's settled."

"Not quite. Better read the book."

"That's my next job. Any beer in the fridge?"

"Help yourself. As a matter of fact, that's where I've stacked the revised chapters one through four, on top of the refrigerator."

"Is this masterpiece titled?"

"Not yet. Maybe you can help me think of something."

Bitterbaum took the can of beer and the first chapters to the bedroom. He left the door open for warmth, flopped down on the cot, pulled up the covers and stacked the pillows behind him. "This is my idea of an office," he called in.

Silence descended except for the uneven rhythm of Josh's typewriter. "I like your style, Josh. It isn't straight reporting. It's as hard-hitting as the first book, but you've developed a feel for words."

"I've been doing a lot of reading," Josh said. "Maybe that shows." He switched on a lamp and continued typing. He worked perhaps an hour more when he was conscious of a blocking of light. He looked up. Bitterbaum stood over him, his Adam's apple working in his throat. "You can't do it, Josh. For Christ's sake, tear it up, burn it."

Josh smiled slightly. "That would be a self-immolation, Uncle Thor."

"But this, this is a crucifixion. You can't do it, Josh."

"If my life has any meaning, it's in those pages."

"Once this is in print, you're marked, exposed, and absolutely helpless. There'd be no retreating, no place to hide."

"I take exception to the word helpless. I'm not helpless. If I'm an outcast from the human race, at least I'm a vocal one. I'll fight their prejudice in court. I'll fight as I'm doing here, with books. They may not consider me quite human, but I've had lavished on me the best human preparation. I can fight them with their own tools, turn their logic against them, debate them. This was your plan for me, yours and G.K.'s. Why back away from it?"

"Because, damn it, you're more important than a plan. Your life, your future will be destroyed. And you could do so much."

"How? By hiding what I am and who I am? Who taught me *courage is the quality that guarantees the rest?* You were right, you and G.K., to bring me up to a tradition. I thought I could never forgive him over Steve. But at least I understand what he was trying to do. So now, at the moment I've joined you actively, you want to turn back."

"Can you really conceive what it will be, Josh, to have the world pointing at you? Humanity has never been kind to those who are different. Can you imagine what it will do to you?"

"I'm tough, Uncle Thor. You and G.K. have seen to that. I'm going to stand up and make a claim. The claim to my humanity. The possibility that the race has recoiled from for twenty-five years has matured in me. I want a place among them, I want them to give me that place. I want them to accept me and future clonees. I want to be accorded the same rights, privileges, and responsibilities as anyone else."

"The world isn't ready, Josh. I was mad to ever think it was. Someday, but not now."

Josh shook his head. "That's what they always said to men who fought for the things I'm fighting for. *The time is not yet. Someday, but not now.* But John Brown stood at Harper's Ferry, and in the sixties college students stood with blacks in the South. You can't be cautious, you can't be prudent. If you had been either of those things, Uncle Thor, we would not be having this conversation."

"Don't take me as a model, God forgive me."

"Do you really mean that, God forgive you? Do you believe that what you did was against nature, that I should never have been born?"

"No, I don't," Bitterbaum said in a burst of anger.

"Then stand with me, Uncle Thor. Defend yourself and me."

Bitterbaum took stock. Thor's gauntlet of iron was rusted with time. A slight pot belly made it troublesome to fasten on the belt of warrior strength. He hadn't recently lifted his club. And while he still bowled Wednesday evenings, it was not with a bolt of thunder but a size-16 ball which he sent none too accurately down lane eight. "If you're determined on kamikaze tactics, if I can't dissuade you, then I'll attempt to launch a thunderbolt or two."

"Great. You've just given me my title. *A Thunderbolt or Two.*"

Bitterbaum nodded; his red beard now streaked with gray moved up and down. "Let's hope they're not boomerangs."

The book was kept so secret it was not given to a professional typist. Josh and Bitterbaum sweated over the final copy before showing it to G.K. It was dynamite and they knew it. There was no immediate response from G.K., so Josh submitted the manuscript to his publisher. Five days later the senior editor phoned to inquire if he was prepared to go ahead with the manuscript in its present form.

Josh understood that anonymity was being offered. He recognized his father's technique. G.K., working through the editor, was giving him a chance to back out.

"It's only effective," he pointed out, "if I stand behind it."

"Then it's not a hoax? It's true. And you actually are a—"

"Clonee," Josh supplied the word. "The whole purport of the book is that I am."

He had returned to the Latigo home to wait for publication, which was being expedited to avoid leaks. Also the family had to be told. Since even G.K. was uneasy, Josh decided the best way to break it to the others was by the carefully thought out presentation in his book. He distributed galleys, and G.K. proposed they meet in the library the following morning. But no one waited for morning. His mother knocked on his door sometime after midnight. "Is this true, Josh? It can't be true."

He put his arms around her. "Is it so terrible, mother?"

"For you, yes. Your whole life is ruined once this is out."

"Yet it had to come out. You see that?"

"I suppose so, knowing you. Yet it's all so monstrous. I can't forgive your father or Thor."

"You use the word monstrous. That's the crux of it. Is the idea monstrous, or am I monstrous?"

"You? Oh, Josh, what an idea. You're just like, well, who you are. And I didn't see it. They kept you in those heavy braces. And then you hid yourself with the beard." She put her arms around him. "You're my son. What difference does it make how a person is conceived?"

"That's exactly the point of my book," he said gently.

"But Josh, I know you. I raised you. I love you. The world won't give you a chance, they'll tear you limb from limb."

"I don't think so, mother. You taught me to have

faith. We must have more faith in people than that."

She raised her head. "I know."

"If you believe I have an immortal soul, then you must believe that it is not against God's plan for man to modify and take a hand in his own development."

"Of course you have an immortal soul. Don't blaspheme, Josh."

"But if you didn't know me? If you were told in a theoretic way about cloning humans, you might feel they were not men in the sight of God. And I must demonstrate that I *am* a man, a human being like any other. I need you. I need all my family. The world has to see that you accept me."

"Did you ever doubt that we'd stand with you, your brother, your sisters, and I?"

Cindy was the next visitor. She had a special knock, a rapid staccato tapping of fingernails. Without waiting for a reply she burst in and threw her arms about him. "It's fantastic. The most exciting thing I've ever heard. It gives me gooseflesh. But why should it make any difference to anyone? I'd love you if you were the Loch Ness monster."

"Thanks," Josh said.

"Oh, you know what I mean."

Her visit wasn't the last. Vicki, who had flown in from Paris where she was a subeditor for *Le Monde,* read the manuscript through and went into Ann's room to discuss it with her. They came in together. "I think it's very distinguished," Vicki said, "being the clonee of one of the most important men of modern times. The world is going to come to you for leadership."

"That's an interesting prediction," Josh said. "I'll

file it along with being torn limb from limb, and compared to the Loch Ness monster."

"But the whole world mourned when you—mourned your predecessor when he died. In every capital of Europe the feeling was the same, that a statesman had been lost. Someone with a broad view, and the humanity to hold things together, is so rare. Oh, Josh, I'm proud to be your sister, but it doesn't stop me from feeling awe for what you are."

"Awe that I'm a clonee? Or awe that I'm a particular clonee?"

"That you're a particular clonee. *His* clonee. Will you give me permission to phone my editor? This is the scoop of the year."

"You'll have to wait until publication. Then it's yours. What about you, Ann? How will this affect that Count Whatshisname the columns have you skiing with?"

"Vassily? Why should it matter to him? Except he'd think we're a whole nest of clonees. I wouldn't mind, but I know it's not true. I've seen my birth certificate."

"People may feel odd at first," Vicki said, "until they get used to the idea. That's why the family has to rally around. If it's adverse, there's a lot of Kelloggs. And however they treat you, they treat us. We'll ride it out."

Josh kissed them each. "Now stop standing by me long enough for me to get some sleep. Okay? We'll meet in the morning and map strategy." But before his cohorts could be sent to bed Jer appeared in robe and slippers with the galleys under his arm.

"This is the most hyper stuff I've read in my life. There's not a word of truth in it. Right? But the way you wrote it you had me almost convinced. Then common sense took hold, you know? What do you think of it, Vicki, you're the journalist?"

"Can't you see that every word is true?" Ann burst out at him. "How could Josh invent something like that? All those details, to say nothing of his state of mind? And how could he invent looking exactly like *him?*"

Jer was befuddled, completely at a loss. "I thought the resemblance maybe gave you the idea. You mean it's true, you are actually a cloned human being?"

"That's right."

"My God," Jer sat down abruptly on the edge of the bed. "Grown from cellular matter, that's what it says here, cellular matter, asexually. But you were always just like anyone else. You were always just an average guy."

Josh smiled slightly.

"But it's true. Good God, it's incredible that father could have been a party to this."

"Why do you say that?"

"Well, it's immoral. Who gave him the right, or Uncle Thor the right, to tamper with human reproduction? You were conceived from your dead self. Was that God's will? It was Uncle Thor's will, but was it God's? We've got to ask that. *Any cell,* you say here, Josh. Does that mean I can be reconstructed from my fingernail paring? And should I be? Should I plan on having kids in the regular way, or should I bring up a family of *me,* cloned, and my wife, cloned? What do you say, Josh? What's it like?"

"Like anything else, what people make of it. If they insist I'm something different, treat me that way, yes

I could become ingrown, odd, peculiar, who knows, even insane or murderous. But it would have nothing to do with the fact that I was implanted in a donor womb."

"But if there's no way to distinguish! I mean, even in your case, you are the clonee of a famous person and no one suspects. If there were a lot of clonees, how would you tell?"

"You mean your daughter might marry one?"

"Don't laugh, Josh. Wouldn't I have the right to know?"

"I don't think so. It's an invasion of privacy. And it's not your business."

"But in a world where everyone did their own thing, brought up clones of their favorite people along with natural children—well, I mean, someone would have to keep track so as to maintain the diversity you speak about, in the gene pool."

"That could be done if the knowledge were kept privileged like a person's bank statements and tax payments. It could be made available at a premarriage counseling session or when you take out parenthood application."

"Let's talk all this out in the morning," Vicki begged. "My head's going around. At this moment there aren't other clonees, there's only Josh."

"Maybe," Ann said. "Besides, he's so successful, I don't see why you should go on having babies in the old-fashioned way, not knowing what you're going to get."

"I don't think it's anything to joke about," Jer admonished her.

"Who's joking?"

"Look," Vicki jumped in, "we came from Newport Beach, Paris, and Tomahawk to let Josh know we're with him. So let's not get into a hassle the first night."

"Second the motion," Jer said. He waved the manuscript at Josh. "One thing I can predict, this will outsell the Bible."

In his dreams that night the clock was set back. They were children playing a game, holding hands, marching in a circle. He was holding Jer's hand and Ann's and they were all going around together. Then all of a sudden he was pushed into the center of the ring.

"The cheese stands alone, the cheese stands alone." His brother and sisters faded into stars, planets, galaxies, and he floated free, the first cloned man, a human satellite hanging from an umbilical cord to his bogus mother ship, just as he had been attached to another bogus mother.

Other men took drugs. His high was on loneliness. The intoxicant was the edge of madness when there is no awareness. Molecular impulses, flying meteorites, the generation of heat, these are the forces that keep you company. But the sun doesn't bleed, volcanic rock is not subject to pain, and only he asked, *Where are others of my kind?*

Or did all men speak through him, cry through him, fear through him?

The cheese stood between worlds. The moon was made of green cheese. When Americans looked closely they saw the man in the moon. When Japanese gave it their scrutiny, they saw a rabbit.

Who saw the spaceman? Closed-circuit television, of course. The world watched his loneliness.

Rocked in the amniotic soup which spewed out worlds, the human factor contained in the visor of his mind slipped away. Thought dissipated. He would snap the leash and find his own orbit. But he was wired and connected to voices giving signals and commands that demanded response.

The voices faded. He was folded in on himself timewise. Out of the putrefaction of his own death he was regenerated. The lizard regenerates its tail, and he created himself *in vitro*.

Did God know what was going on? Was He a modern god? Had He kept up with the times? Was He familiar with the cloning process? Did He approve cell fusion? Did He give His blessing to the cloning of a frog? Animals? What about Joshua Francis Kellogg? Had He foreseen this? Had He planned to bring man to the stage where he would take a hand in fashioning his own genetic structure, in redesigning his own blueprint? Was God ready with extra souls to inhabit bodies grown on scrubbed countertops?

Or was there no place for him in heaven, hell, earth, or space?

The circle reformed; the galaxies held hands. He stood at the center, isolated. His dream emptied until there was nothing in it but himself. His voice called over a desolate tundra, filling his own ears. His eyes swallowed and regulated the featureless void of his own projecting.

The light of morning reinforced his sense of being apart. His family would gather around him loyally. Far from asking it, should he allow it? Wasn't it his place to move out, meet whatever was brewing headlong and on his own? Had he any right to jeopardize their future? Their love for him demanded that they fly to his side, pledge loyalty, allegiance, and a fight. His love for them made opposite demands; that he cut all ties, not allow them to go down in the general holocaust.

The dream was prescience, he should be guided by it, not use the name Kellogg, but simply be Joshua. He would sign the book Commander Joshua, so that there was no question of his identity.

Joshua son of Nun. Joshua son of none.

When a man went into battle he stripped down. Nothing that encumbered, nothing that held you back. No women, no family; not friends, not possessions. Naked, light, and alone he would blow the ram's horn and shout unto the Lord, and the wall would fall down flat. He would charge and take the city, depending on his own prowess, the swiftness and accuracy of his thrusts, the nimbleness of his parries.

Joshua commanded, and the sun stood still.

He went to his bookshelf and picked up the Bible, opening to Joshua 10: *. . . in the sight of the children of Israel, he said before them: Move not, O sun, toward Gabaon, nor thou, O moon, toward the valley of Ajalon. . . . So the sun stood still in the midst of heaven, and hasted not to go down* *the space of one day. There was not before or after so long a day, the Lord obeying the voice of a man . . .*

He needed such a miracle, that God hear his voice and guide him. Then he too by the power of his will could force victory. He mounted his assault from a strong position. He had respect and recognition as an author; as a member of the Baker's Dozen that had walked in space he was a national hero. Millions of people had gasped as he fell out of range of the Shuttle's electronic sights. Millions had not deserted their posts at their TV spheres until the rescue operations were underway and he was picked up.

And now having won their admiration, sympathy, and prayers, he would stand defrocked of his humanity, demanding acceptance into the human tribe, without mother or father to speak for him. His task appeared to him more onerous than his namesake's. It seemed to him more difficult to influence the minds of men and move them to compassion than to command an inert body like the moon or halt the volatile sun.

The first battle was the one he faced downstairs, to be waged against those who loved him, and whom he loved. He began his campaign in the bathroom. With a straight blade he hacked off the beard that camouflaged his features and followed up with a meticulous shave.

Satisfied that his statement was made, he went into the hall and descended the stairs. They were all gathered below. When they saw him there was an audible stir of shock and surprise.

With a single impulse, they stood.

His hand searched for the banister and gripped.

Lefty was there with the others. She came toward him up the stairs, took his hand, and led him down.

He was surrounded, hugged, kissed, his hand shaken. His resolve drained away. That sere, desolate landscape he imagined for himself was populated after all. They wouldn't allow him to go solitary and alone. They insisted on their right to add their voices, a mighty cumulative shout. Joshua had the legions of Israel.

How good and warm and sweet-tasting was this first breach in his defense. A victory would have been a harsh, bitter thing. He stood defeated in his purpose, and happier than he had ever been in his life.

A brunch had been prepared on the terrace, kippers and caviar, pancakes and sour cream, Ozark bacon, eggs and hash browns.

While the others heaped their plates, Josh took Lefty aside. "How did you know about the family council of war?"

"Easy. I have my spies and allies. Your mother called me last night. She told me the whole thing. With Lynn in my corner, there's no point trying to hold out."

"Have you given it enough thought, Lefty? At countdown you'd be right on target with me. I can't protect you. I can love you, but I can't protect you."

"You explained that once before. If protection means safely out of your life, I don't want it. I'm willing to take my chances. Okay, Josh?"

"Okay." They came together and the sun did stand still, and time, and the world.

The book impacted. Publication day removed the safety from the percussion-activated explosive system. The charge was triggered.

Joshua and Lefty were caught cross range of aim point. With splendid disregard for consequences, Lefty insisted their marriage be celebrated at St. Patrick's Cathedral, New York.

Advance word leaked out. Rumor took over. An extra was on the stands. Crowds began lining the sidewalk before dawn. A detail of police and Secret Service men were assigned to the area.

Lefty wore her mother's bridal dress, a gown of hand-crafted lace over a sheath of satin. As she walked down the aisle, a tomato splattered against the filmy bodice and oozed down the skirt.

"Why don't you marry that?" a man shouted. "It was grown the same way he was!"

The Kelloggs and the red-bearded Jew were on their feet crying, "Shame! Shame!" from their pews. The spectators were divided. A fist fight broke out as the police removed the man. Only the appearance of the cardinal quieted the throng. He held up his hand and there was submission.

Outside, the crowd was a jostling sea, well-wishers and hecklers coming together to form an apex of turbulence.

Inside, kneeling, Josh and Lefty repeated their vows, and he slipped the ring on her finger. The great stained-glass windows reverberated. It seemed that the holy figures themselves were murmuring.

Josh kissed his wife, and asked an usher to show them the back way.

They made their escape through the chancel. "This is it, Lefty. Do you think you can keep your nose cone above water?"

"Things will calm down. We won't get married every day. You won't publish an autobiography every day. And things will keep happening in a world that requires headlines. You'll be back-page news after awhile."

"Pray for it," he whispered.

The home he took her to was a condominium overlooking the marina with anchorage for a sloop called *Lefty.* She loved sailing. Sometimes they'd take the run down to Malibu and swim off the deck. Sometimes they didn't bother to untie, but lay side by side soaking up sun.

"I'm glad we didn't go anywhere or do anything," she told him again and again. "This is perfect."

In the first weeks they didn't discuss or plan anything more complicated than a dinner menu. Their conversation was of two kinds. Monosyllabic: "Me too." Or pragmatic: "Any suntan oil left?"

Gradually this began to change. One day they set out to find his old neighborhood. But condominiums and luxury hotels now lined the beach front.

Josh became thoughtful. "I wonder what became of them?"

"Who?" Lefty wanted to know.

But he didn't answer, not directly. He seemed absentminded and abstracted. He took to circling items in the editorial page of the paper. He invited his father and Bitterbaum aboard and there were long political arguments. The phrase *the politics of despair* kept cropping up as characterizing the incumbent administration.

G.K. was adviser to the Democratic National Committee. But he too declared himself discouraged. "The vote is meaningless if there's no real choice. It's machine politics in both camps. All cut and dried."

"Well," Josh stretched his agile brown body, "why don't we find out?"

"Find out what?" Bitterbaum asked, sensing a recklessness behind Josh's casual question.

"The fuss and fury have abated, the question of the clonee and his special problems have been aired in the press and on the media. I've presented my side, and judging by sales, everyone in the country has read it. I say it's time to find out what the consensus is. And the way to do that is to run for office."

"For an elective office?" Bitterbaum was aghast.

"I was thinking of running for Congress."

The announcement lay there.

"Okay," Josh said, "by the count of ten I'm out. But I won't accept that. I'll never know if I've convinced anybody until it's put to a vote. And that's what I intend to do. So I am running for the Twenty-eighth Congressional seat and I'd like your support."

G.K. was on his feet. "I couldn't take it in, Josh. But you know what this means to me. It's the culmination of my whole life." He wrung Josh's hand, tears stood in his eyes. Lefty and Bitterbaum exchanged helpless glances. By tacitly assuming they were with him, Josh swept them along. On the spot the family group became an organization. G.K. explained that it cost him two hundred and fifty thousand per year in excess of his salary when he held office. But that the exchequer was open to Josh, and he personally would underwrite the expense of the campaign.

The absent members of the family were recalled. Josh broached the subject of Steve. "I want him with me."

But Lynn refused to allow it. The hoax had been terrible for her to comprehend. "He's dead. We mourned him. And he's dead to this family."

"You forgave G.K.," Josh pointed out.

It was true. She excused Gerald his part in it. He was her delinquent child, more difficult than any she had raised, and harder to love.

"You've got to understand," Josh told her, "that Steve did it for me. As terrible as it was and as wrong as it was, he did it for me. We can't go on excommunicating him. Have you forgotten Santa Cruz?"

Lynn gave in reluctantly. "I'll never feel the same about him."

Josh kissed her. "You will."

G.K. knew where Steve could be found. He was with a law firm in South Bend, Indiana. The name he had taken was Kalish. He was married with a modest home in the suburbs and a fenced yard.

Marian opened the door, a pleasant girl, but busy. Something was boiling in the kitchen and it was time to get the baby down for his nap.

Josh said he was an old friend, he'd wait. She

brought him a glass of orange juice and explained that Josh was having one too.

The name startled him. He sat and thought about Steve, cut off, starting his own life. Then there he was, coming up the front walk, opening the door. Marian called, "Someone to see you."

They faced each other. The grave stretched between them and several lifetimes.

Josh meant to shake hands, instead he held him by the shoulders, pulling him into a close grasp.

"Josh?"

Josh understood the question. But it was better ignored.

"I need you with me, Steve. That's why I'm here. I'm running for Congress, and the family has got to back me. I want you to drop everything and take over the campaign. Okay? I want you to manage things."

"Does G.K. know you're here?"

Josh nodded.

"And Uncle Thor?"

"Yes."

"What about Lynn?"

"Lynn says, come."

He grinned. He blew his nose. "Hey, I saw that you married Lefty. That's great. Did you meet Marian and little Josh?"

So Josh gathered the family around him. They set about building grass-roots support. "One volunteer is worth ten hirelings," Josh said.

Lynn, Lefty, Jer, and the girls all pitched in. They were joined by college students going door-to-door distributing literature, selling Kellogg buttons and bumper stickers. They held rallies, spoke at fund-raising dinners, breakfast clubs, addressed civic and business groups as well as union meetings, canvassed everywhere for votes, shook thousands upon thousands of hands.

They were received at times with hostility, driven off steps and from property. Bodyguards became necessary to deal with the threat of violence. But G.K.'s privately conducted polls showed they were gaining ground.

Steve and Josh held long strategy sessions. Josh's picture on a poster evoked the *other,* who was still idolized throughout the country. His face and name had become legend. The cult had never died, and indeed was strongest among the young who themselves had never known his short tenure.

"There is such an aura about that man," Lefty said, and then added, "and Josh, it extends to you. They see you as him, through the miracle of science restored to them. Some even see it religiously, as the hand of God working to restore what should have been. It's spooky." She shivered a bit. "But I don't care how crazy people are, or what their reasons, as long as they vote for you."

They did.

Joshua Francis Kellogg was elected by a landslide. The change in their lives was signaled when they left the flags of the regattas, the green-and-red running lights of moored vessels, and moved to the sober environs of Washington.

Josh's familiar face created a furor in that city. He was worshiped, lionized, and adored. Lefty ran interference for him. She learned the art of declining gracefully, selecting from among invitations with restraint.

But the detractors were there, hidden. There were threatening and obscene phone calls. A bomb exploded, having been dug into the rhododendron bed. One evening, in spite of guards at the gates and dogs on the grounds, a rock crashed through the living room window.

These isolated instances aside, Josh had won his battle for personal acceptance. But he was not content to have it rest there. "Let's get it on record," he thundered into batteries of TV cameras. "I don't advocate cloning as a substitute for natural reproduction. But it has a place. It should be considered in the future when we lose a great artist, or scientist, or religious leader. And we must continue through genetic research to attain physical and mental improvement in the gene pool."

At every opportunity he said, "I won't owe my position to who I am, or who I'm cloned from. I want for those like myself, who come after me in the future, the same liberties accorded me."

He struck down statutes proposed in the legislature prohibiting marriage with a cloned person. "That is classing me and my kind with the hopelessly insane." The measure was defeated.

But all this was simply a way of taking the offensive. For as far as anyone knew, the constituency for which he fought consisted only of himself. His real strength was in dealing with major issues. He took a position on China, a position regarding America's role in space. He jammed his speeches with facts and figures. Yet the problems were simply stated. "The country's standing still. We can do better than this. We can move ahead."

He contested the seat of James Peabody for the U.S.

Senate. Again the family marshaled its forces. With Steve directing, they participated actively in the campaign. Opponents predicted he would peak too early, receive too much exposure, run out of gas. But Josh stepped up his TV coverage, press conferences, and nonstop speaking tours. He brought his reform plan to labor, stressed his belief in business. "Smart money will bet on the future of this country." The result was a spectacular and overwhelming win.

"Now I'll never see you," Lefty lamented.

Josh agreed, "It's a hell of a way to make a living."

It amazed her that he could remain simply Josh. People went wild when he spoke; they packed the gallery and stood for blocks for a sight of him or even his car. Hands reached out to touch him.

The mystique surrounding him grew. Cloning in the popular version was equated with reincarnation. He was returned. He belonged to the people and the people claimed him.

But Lefty found moments. She came up behind him as he worked late over the documents he brought home in his battered, bulging briefcase. Uncle Thor bought him a new case, but he clung to the old one.

It was Lefty who smoothed lines from his forehead, and stroked his temples and flattened the rufous strands of hair. "What about dinner and a show a week from Wednesday with the Allisons, accept or decline?"

"Decline."

She made a face.

"I'm sorry, Lefty. I haven't been much good for anything but work lately."

"That's not quite accurate. I am two months' pregnant."

"What, in the regular old-fashioned way?"

"I am a regular, old-fashioned girl. And that is exactly the way I am pregnant." She was pulled into his lap, and for that night at least, the papers remained in the briefcase.

But the respite was one of hours only. A crisis was precipitated by a series of explosions, which destroyed the recently orbited Chinese satellites. At the highest diplomatic level the United States government was charged with responsibility.

Tension in the country mounted. The Democratic convention took the unprecedented step of convening early. The city was Cincinnati, Ohio. The quarters, prefab bubble structures. The world watched.

The presidential contenders, having stalked the length and breadth of the land, laid their candidacy before the delegates. Josh was there to take his part in the proceedings. He was known for his liberal views regarding China, and his first book espousing rapprochement with that country was much quoted. For this reason he was asked to make the nominating speech.

Lefty, afraid of being jostled by crowds, remained at home and watched on television. The rest of the family were on hand. Politics had become a way of life. Josh's astonishing rise whetted their appetites. The Kelloggs were seated on the floor to hear his speech in favor of the candidate from Illinois.

When he appeared on the podium and was recognized, a kind of fever seized the delegates. A stamping began, and rhythmic hand-clapping. Those holding standards for the states pounded them against the floor. Josh stood before them, waiting. But the noise did not subside. Instead the assembly came to its feet.

They were orderly. They didn't attempt to storm the podium, but they would not give way. Their voices rose in a chant. The words became decipherable. "Kellogg! Kellogg! We want Kellogg!"

They would not be silenced. The chairman pounded his gavel. The tumult continued, five minutes, seven, ten. They surged forward; the Secret Service people couldn't hold them. They crowded the base of the speaker's platform.

Josh held his hand up. He took the mike and started to speak. The amplified sound of his voice met the wall of sound which broke before him. They wanted to hear.

"Ladies and gentlemen, thank you." A roar blanketed his words. People had been moving on the floor, passing the word.

The word was: "Draft Kellogg!"

It was taken up with one thunderous voice. Josh stood before them like a reed. And the wind of their will blew upon him. He turned to the chair. The party brass huddled. Labor was seen, the black leaders, and the militant young. Regional bosses, the muscle of the party, caucused then and there on the podium with TV cameras highlighting the event, picking up even the beads of sweat.

At last they faced the packed auditorium and a large lettered sign was passed up to them. The chairman raised it.

DRAFT KELLOGG!

The hall exploded. Pandemonium swept it. Bitterbaum's body was a microcosm of the mass excitement. His heart engorged, seeming to fill his chest cavity. His circulatory system expanded, blood burst his arteries. I'm having a coronary, he thought. And then he thought, It's worth it.

A glass of water set him straight. Palpitations ceased, respiration returned to normal. By that time the delegate vote had proceeded to the *N*s.

"New Hampshire casts eleven votes for Joshua Francis Kellogg."

"New Jersey, forty-one votes for the next President of the United States, Joshua Francis Kellogg."

"New Mexico, with seventeen votes, goes for Kellogg."

"The sovereign state of New York, one hundred and fourteen votes, casts a unanimous ballot for Joshua F. Kellogg."

A half hour later, Wyoming, the last state, was heard from. "Wyoming, fifteen votes for Joshua Francis Kellogg, spontaneously drafted as the presidential nominee of the Democratic party."

The NBC cameras were diverted from the jubilation, banner waving, and snake dancing on the floor to Secret Service men hustling out a man with a revolver. The man was sobbing hysterically, "What is he? He's not a man, he's a vegetable! We've turned the United States of America over to a vegetable!"

Lefty, watching all this, had false labor pains and was taken to the hospital.

Josh was now speaking to those in the stadium and to the country. He spoke to a vast stillness. There was no rhetoric. He spoke as though to one person. And they were like one in their attentive eagerness.

"I ran for president of my class at college. I didn't make it. There is nothing in my life, nothing has ever happened to me to prepare me for this. One doesn't remember through a single cell. I wish I had the experience of the man from whom I was cloned. I don't. I hope I have his courage, his potential to learn, and his will and determination to aid in the betterment of man's condition where it can be legislated.

"I don't have a speech in my pocket. But I don't think you want to hear a speech. What you want to know is how I will respond to the need of my country.

"I say this nation must set sail on a new sea. Citizens of America, in this generation you are citizens of the world. If I have my way, the People's Republic of China will be a full partner in space. And instead of viewing the earth as they did in the seventies as a closed circuit, I take the position that it is once again an open system. And that spaceship Earth will sail it freely, exploring stars and harvesting knowledge. Once again we can expand, if not our birthrate, our explorations.

"I see the future as open under the creative governance of man. I see man in control of his biological future and of farflung environments. I see him mining new ores, jettisoning pollutants to be consumed in the sun's corona. I see the end of war and a retrograde burn on terrorism. Technology has forced morality on us. Technology has made civilized brutes of us.

"We have tools. It remains for us to pick them up and use them, and use them in a good cause. That cause is the people of earth. Let us cooperate, stand together as brothers. The earth is small when you look down at it as I have. From out there it looks like a beach ball. Certainly it is too small for divisiveness and insularity and fear.

"We are one stock, the human race, and we all survive or all perish on this third planet from the sun. Our future is open if we open ourselves, our technology and our world. The future is *now,* and *now* determines the future. Therefore choose life." He paused, he looked into half a million eyes, like phosphoresence that lights the sea. "Damned if I didn't make a speech after all. It must go with being nominated."

A roar burst from the densely massed assemblage. The first-aid stations were filled with those overcome by heat, by excitement, or who had been jostled, pushed, and stepped on. There were several heart attacks and a birth.

Josh had the impression of being removed from all this by shoulders. They blotted out the auditorium and he was walked to the side, and funneled down some steps. A door closed behind him, and there was Bitterbaum holding out a glass of water. That first, before the handclasp of congratulation.

"Do you realize what's happened?" Josh asked him.

Newsmen burst in followed by a coterie of party officials, G.K., kingmaker, in their midst. Steve ran interference, let no one at Josh, fielded all questions while Bitterbaum and the shoulders got him out of the building into a waiting car.

"Drive around," were Bitterbaum's instructions, "just drive."

The city sped by a blur of massed geometric solids trimmed in blinking neon. Then it opened into country, fields of clover were borne to them and the musty sweet smell of cattle. Bitterbaum was pressed in on himself, his long frame jack-knifed. He said nothing, but waited for Josh to sort it through.

"I know it's nonsense," Josh said finally. "I mean, I know it can't be. But I have a feeling that it's all happened before. I seem to remember. I know it's a memory built out of news clips and the millions of words written about it. The trouble is, I can't convince myself of that. I know this is an hour of great triumph, perhaps the greatest in my life. And yet I carry a sense of doom. As though nothing I could do or say from this point on would stop for one second or change by one fraction the course of events. I can't escape success.

"And success for me culminates in quick death. It's the reverse side of the coin. The eternal flame burns in memoriam, and the airport, and the cultural center, the wildlife sanctuary, the causeway and parkway, and the three acres set aside in England as a shrine, and the mountain in Canada. What does it all mean? It means that he's dead. Bitterbaum, we're replaying the same tape. My fate is locked up in me. I'm homozygous for assassination, blood-typed for murder."

"What can I say?" Bitterbaum replied after awhile. "You admit you're talking nonsense."

"Yes."

"Do you really feel confident about winning the Presidency?"

"I'm convinced I'll win it."

"I don't know. The incumbent will accelerate the crisis on the theory that in a major emergency the public won't dare effect a change."

"Yes, that will be his ploy," Josh said.

"But you don't think it will work?"

"How can it? It's not part of the pattern."

Josh instructed the driver to return to the hotel. They rode back toward the city in silence. On impulse Josh turned to him. There was an expression on his face that Bitterbaum had never seen before. It was a look that comes after resignation, when knowing the conditions of the game, one moves from a position of strength. There was a zest and a ring in his voice when he said, "Did you hear them out there, Bitterbaum? It was a fantastic thing to happen. All those people, so sure you can do something for them and for the country. I guess we both realize that no one can do what they're hoping for. But I'd like to have the chance to try."

"I believe you're going to have that chance. And it's not any inexorably woven package. The Presidency does not mean your death. As I said to you once before, I did not clone your assassin."

Josh smiled. "You witnessed an acute episode in a chronic condition known as Self-Doubt. I suffer from it as other people suffer from hemorrhoids. But it's under control now. And something else that maybe needs saying. If I were evaluating my life on a scale from one to ten, it's ten. Bitterbaum, look at you. You're twice my age, but you haven't walked in space, you haven't written books, you haven't been nominated for the Presidency. Why, you haven't even gotten married. But you'd rate your life as worthwhile. Right? Come on, honestly. On a scale from one to ten, where would you put Thor Bitterbaum?"

"That's easy. Either one *or* ten. As you pointed out, I seem to have missed the usual things. No wife, no kids, no home, no family. But I've had my work, and in a way, a rather unique way I admit, you're my family, Josh."

He had never been this outspoken about his feelings and he waited with some misgivings for Josh's reaction. "That's right," Josh said, as though the idea was not new to him. "I took it for granted. The girls said I was your favorite, and I knew that was true. I never asked why. It didn't occur to me it was on my account you never took the normal course, never led a normal life. I see that now.

"Bitterbaum, I'm going to need you as I never have before. Just looking into that ugly, red-bearded face of yours reminds me of the miracles we've pulled off to date. And there may be a couple more in us. What do you say, Uncle Thor?"

The forest of Ragnarok swallowed the city of Cincinnati. Thor swung his club over his head and the circle it described beat stars from their orbit. But Uncle Thor couldn't get any words out.

Everything Joshua Francis Kellogg did and everything he said was a headline. The daughter born to Lefty was a headline: CLONEE NOMINEE OPTS FOR TRIED-AND-TRUE METHOD OF PROCREATION. Along with the telegrams, letters, and phone calls of congratulations, there was hate mail. His secretary attempted to keep this from Lefty, but an occasional one slipped through.

"I can't believe it," there were tears on her face,

"that anyone would write such filth when a baby is born."

Josh brushed it off. "In an avalanche of publicity, you're bound to hear from the cranks too."

Dr. George Rudolph Demsdale, Nobel Prize-winning biologist, captured a headline of his own with the disclosure that it was he who more than thirty years before had cloned the Democratic candidate.

G.K. phoned Bitterbaum. "He finally figured it out." They arranged to lunch with the old gentleman for the express purpose of giving him details on how they had outwitted him.

But there weren't many light moments. Congress met in special session to lower the age at which a man might assume the highest office. The administration attempted to block and filibuster this vote. But it came to the floor, was carried, and subsequently ratified.

The infighting was dirty. Criticism reached back to the early sixties. The mistakes in Cuba were rehashed and the debacle of the Bay of Pigs. The clone of such a man could be counted on to make the same errors of judgment. How could you put the government in the hands of a dilettante the second time? Was a pattern of monarchy to be established in our democracy?

There were signs and posters everywhere: *Don't turn the country over to a clonee. He will ban people. We need a man, not a vegetable. Is it a man, is it a bird, what exactly is it?*

Josh sloughed off the invective, relying on a superb organization to canvass voters and get his proposals before the people. He wrote his own speeches, working from notes jotted during the day in conference with labor, in meetings with students, businessmen, blacks, Chicanos, women.

The searchlight of publicity was trained on his life. It was disclosed that he had been bred for the office by G. K. Kellogg. His relationship with Steve was ferreted out. The fact that he owed his life to his cousin was written up and played up. David and Jonathan they called them and made much of their mutual devotion.

To retain his sanity Josh kept Bitterbaum close to him, using Thor's caustic observations as leaven to lighten the atmosphere of tension under which he lived.

G.K. had come into his own. He was the pro. His opinion was sought and his influence made use of. Also, when contributions ran low, the coffers were replenished from his personal fortune. It was his son who would be President. A Kellogg. He had guessed right on a lot of issues, followed hunches that more often than not paid off. But no investment had ever returned such lavish dividends.

Several dozen women, each claiming to be Millicent Ash, sold their stories to the papers. It didn't matter. None of the jibes mattered. There was a general euphoria in the country. November 7 the incumbent would be dumped and Josh Kellogg would be running things.

It was Steve's idea to dig out old photographs of the martyred President and use these rather than taking any of Josh. In this way they identified and fused him further with the still-vivid memory. The hero who had been torn from them and given back.

None too soon. The country, indeed the world, had a decision to make. If Josh Kellogg had his way, the men of earth, standing together, would break through the radiation belts, the gravitational fields of space.

Heavy industry would orbit a pollution-free world, and the quest to replenish the terrestrial supply of minerals would continue. The unmanned missions to Jupiter were heavily backed by Joshua and his party. He pointed out that the most stringent retrenchment could only delay the day man would deplete his planet. There was no choice but to reach out.

The opposition said, *retrench.* Use the research funds for defense. Gird to protect investments and territory. Ring the burgeoning populations spilling over the boundaries of other continents.

Irresponsible, Kellogg replied sternly from prime time. *We must prepare for the twenty-first century. Therefore, choose life.*

The nation agreed. From the time the first precincts were polled and the first scattered returns tabulated, it became clear that the country had gone Kellogg.

More was happening than could be taken in. More congratulations, more telegrams, more phone calls, more decisions, more documents, more briefings, more meetings. He sorted out impressions at odd moments. His brain cells seemed to possess a specific configuration for time lag. Sensitive to some things, oblique to others. During a conference with his top fiscal adviser he remembered a wistful expression that had crossed Lefty's face the night before. The impression inserted itself into the meeting on economic stability. He wrote her name on a pad that contained figures on the GNP and a tax proposal. His secretary buzzed to inform him he was running ten minutes late and the Israeli envoy was waiting to brief him on the Middle East. He went into the anteroom himself to escort him in. The man reminded him of Bitterbaum.

He must see to it that Bitterbaum was not forced from his side by the new routine and work load.

Mornings were given over to an ordering of priorities and long range planning.

Committee meetings, decision making, perusal of proposals, this was midday. He scrawled a memo to himself, "The disposables." He wanted to be President to all the people, the low riders and the old ladies in paisley wraparounds.

Evenings were reserved for functions. Visiting dignitaries, men of influence sought him out at these times.

Strangers. Strangers smiling, strangers shaking hands. He looked around this crowded living room for Lefty. He recalled one of their early dates. She decided to prepare a special dinner, and they shopped in East Los Angeles at a Japanese grocery. Lefty filled her basket with dried shrimp, taro chips, bamboo sprouts, and jars whose exotic and unrecognizable contents intrigued her.

At the checkout stand an old Japanese lady beamed kindly. As she looked over the items, her face broadened into smiling templets. "No, missy, no, no," she said, putting her purchases back on the shelves. She had decided that "missy" would "no like," and that was that. They left with fortune cookies.

He watched her moving with grace and ease among the guests. He had to find more time.

But not yet. The duties of the Chief Executive were formidable. He was still trying to grasp the dimensions of the job, bring himself to an understanding of the delicate nuances that were an extension of agreements. Tentacles reached in subterranean fashion into a dozen areas. In addition to evaluating all this, his inauguration speech was on his mind.

He carried a crumpled draft around with him, and took it out at odd moments to revise the wording, make a deletion, or add a thought. Once he was sworn in and the ceremony was behind him, things would ease off. He spotted Bitterbaum at the punch bowl. He was holding forth to a senator and a naval attache, quoting Aristotle. " 'One cannot practice virtue if one leads the life of an artisan or labors for wages.' That's why you can trust the President. Right, Mr. President? He's never labored for wages."

Josh took his arm in an attempt to lead him off, but Bitterbaum wasn't to be budged. "This is the President-elect of the United States," he told the embarrassed naval officer, "and I knew him when he was reading *Billy Whiskers,* that's right, *Billy Whiskers.*"

Josh piloted him with a firm hand.

"I remember another time, do you remember this, Josh? We were at dinner, and G.K. discovered that you and Steve had been fooling around during the regatta, and that's why you lost the race. He sent you from the table, do you remember that?"

Josh smiled. "Yes, I do." He steered him up the stairs, waving off help from servants, and led him into the first guest bedroom. "Sit down, Uncle Thor, and I'll pull your shoes off."

"You remember *Billy Whiskers?*" Bitterbaum asked anxiously.

"Oh yes."

"And the fountains of Rome. Remember how you ran around every damn one of them?"

Josh laughed out loud and pulled the comforter over him.

Bitterbaum caught his hands and said urgently, "Josh, what if I asked you for a blanket forgiveness? Would you give it to me, not knowing whether it was for opposing G.K. or for cloning you in the first place? Tell me, Josh in your opinion, which should it be for? If G.K. had listened to me, you never would have become President. I've stood in your way, Josh, been a stumbling block. That's a terrible thing.

"G.K. was right all along and I couldn't see it. This is what you were meant to do, to save us all. I felt it once, when I did what I did. But I let my personal feelings for you get in the way. I began to be persuaded by the very thing I have most contempt for, a superstitious fear. Because things happened a certain way before, I felt them driving on us like a fast squall and that we would be drenched a second time in blood. I know now that's wrong, Josh.

"Initially I had the vision. G.K. kept it. I didn't. Greatness, the opportunity to guide the destiny of the world, I put this aside. It meant nothing to me compared with your welfare, Josh. But now I see it differently. The punch bowl has given me back the golden image, and I see that it's wrong to deny a man his potential. You're standing where you're meant to stand, Josh. And this time you'll make it. It's a different world. There have been a few thousand revolutions of the globe, and man is at another place now. They're counting on you, Josh. And me too, I'm counting on you.

"Tell me, Josh, what do you think I should ask forgiveness for? This is not a rhetorical question, Josh. I have a feeling I haven't hit on the right crime. You see, I'm turning into an old Jew after all. I have a need to atone.

"You know something, Josh? I wouldn't do it now. I couldn't do it. If it were up to me again, no. Never. The ancient god in me grows old. And I grow old.

"It was a terrible burden, I confess it, Josh. And a terrible joy, a joy that illumined my life. So right or wrong, Josh, I don't ask forgiveness for that. Just for not always being able to sustain it."

Josh smiled at him. "Who can always sustain his life, Uncle Thor?"

"We're going to make it this time around, Josh."

"Shhh, go to sleep." He stood still for the count of ten. Bitterbaum's breathing was regular. Josh turned and walked quietly toward the door.

As he reached it Bitterbaum's eyes flew open and he declaimed in a stentorian voice: "I wish I loved the Human Race. I wish I loved its silly face. I wish I liked the way it walks; I wish I liked the way it talks. And when I'm introduced to one, I wish I thought what jolly fun." His eyes closed and instantly he was asleep.

Josh went downstairs to meet the majority leader.

—I wish I thought what jolly fun.

When the evening ended and the last guest had departed, Lefty fixed him a cup of coffee and they sat together in the kitchen. He took out the draft of his inaugural.

"Oh, Josh," she protested, "you never relax when you're relaxing."

"I want your opinion. Tell me if it gets wordy or high-flown. I want to keep it simple and direct." He started to read.

She sat without moving. The coffee grew cold, she forgot to taste it. She delighted in the intense enthusiasm with which he infused every word, lending it his stamina and vitality. There was a great welling in her and words gathered at the periphery of her consciousness which she refused. Instead she brought her husband's hands to her lips and kissed them.

He pulled her onto his knees and she continued kissing him. From this more intimate position she concentrated on the hollow of his neck where she felt the pulse of his life beating.

The details of the inauguration were carefully worked out. The ceremony was to be performed in the Rotunda, following in every respect the investiture of 1961, even to the ride afterward along Pennsylvania Avenue.

Bitterbaum fretted over security. To placate him Josh arranged that he attend planning sessions between Steve and the FBI, where the most elaborate precautions were discussed and implemented. The bullet-proof bubble top was to be up during the motorcade procession. During the swearing in, Josh and the chief justice were to stand behind a Plexiglas barrier.

There were Secret Service men spotted in key positions with an unobstructed view of the area. Bitterbaum seemed satisfied. "It's foolproof," he admitted to Steve. And from that moment began to really worry.

The evening before Josh was to take office was set aside for a final honing of what he hoped would be an historic speech.

Lefty came in about eleven thirty, and whispered, "Luck."

"Did you decide on your dress?"

"Poor love, you've got the whole-entire world on your mind, plus my dress. I'm wearing the beige and my birthday pearls. Will you be very late?"

But he was already back at work. She kissed the top of his head and left. Three hours later he looked up. He had promised himself not to work so long. He took a shower to relax. Lefty was sleeping holding onto his pillow, a habit she had developed during many lonely nights. He got in carefully so as not to wake her.

The luminous face of the bedside clock read three. *Read twelve.* Noon sharp. *Sharply noon.* There were maps of the route printed in all the papers. And there was an *X* at the spot where they would kill him.

It was hard sitting in the car, having it move street by street closer to the intersection where it would happen. The route was planned to take forty-five minutes. He would be dead in thirty.

The sun danced in his eyes hotly. The signs, the stores, Thom McAn Shoes, Hallmark Cards, Walgreen Drugstore, it was all slipping past. If he concentrated he would see the Mercantile Building on the left and a department store, Neiman-Marcus.

Twelve twenty-eight, the neighborhood began to deteriorate, bars, bailbond signs, a public gym, the county jail, dingy courthouse, records building, a warehouse. The heavy Lincoln slowed for the turn into Elm. The plaza was in front of him and the railway overpass.

The tunnel looked cool, looked dark and cool. And the faces, smiling. Hands stretched toward him, waving, V for peace, for victory.

He was looking directly ahead into the tunnel. There was an afterimage in his mind of the red, white, and blue Hertz sign and the time and temperature electrically dispensed from the top of the bank. He knew it was twelve thirty, Central Standard time.

Time to die.

The alarm tore through his head. He opened his eyes. He had been reprieved. This was to be his day. The day the sun and the moon stood still for Joshua.

A hush descended as Joshua Francis Kellogg placed his left hand on the Bible and, raising his right, took the oath of office. As he pledged his allegiance to his country and its people, a shot exploded.

On the grandstand to the left of the Rotunda where the President's family was gathered, a man crumpled to the ground. It was Steve.

Bitterbaum reached for the carotid. He was alive. Bitterbaum waved at the podium in an effort to communicate this. A great cry was torn from him: "No, Josh!" For he saw the President, as if driving off-tackle, shoulder aside the FBI and Secret Service, and leaving the bullet-proof platform, charge through the crowd to Steve's side.

This was their strategy; Bitterbaum knew it instantly. Josh, exposed and unprotected, was the target. He was cut almost in two by repeated shotgun blasts.

Bitterbaum accompanied the still-breathing body in a nightmare of repetition. There was no pulse, no blood pressure, no discernible respiration. The eyes deviated outward, fixed and sightless. The chest was racked by efforts to breathe.

Another woman accompanied him this time. It was Lefty beside the stretcher, Lefty who got into the ambulance. Bitterbaum also crowded in. Blood was seeping around the tourniquet. He tightened it. He had pushed organs back in, more for decency's sake than any other reason.

It was no use, no use, but it must all be gone through. Like an ancient pagan ritual.

Josh was carried into the hospital, into emergency. Measures were initiated that would not be tried were he anyone else. He was hooked to an electrocardiograph. The heart still labored. Bilateral tubes were inserted into the pleural cavity to prevent lung collapse. A solution of lactated Ringer's was fed into his leg by catheter. A tracheotomy was performed. Bitterbaum thrust in a nasogastric tube. None of the procedures worked.

The bleeding stopped. Bitterbaum, while he functioned as a doctor, mourned as a man. Josh was gone. "Lefty . . ." he said.

She had not allowed herself to be separated from him. "I know," she brushed aside words of comfort. "Bring him a priest."

The EKG had gone flat. But the future was still possible. Life was possible instead of death. A man with training and knowledge takes the scalpel, the one lying there, and lifts a small amount of matter from the wound.

I wish I loved the human race. . . . That was the trouble, he did. Too well. Thor raised his anvil and transmitted the tissue to a test tube. Red Beard swung his club and goats and wild boar ran at his side. In the Ragnarok, in the forest of Thorsmorsk he brandished Mjellnir, and shrove and hallowed the dead that they would rise.

Thor, Red Beard, sat under the windswept tree and pondered the runic lore set in stone.

It was over.

The nightmare of death was ended.

Man could live again and again, forever if he wished. In this century he had come out of the forest. In this century he had gone to Caltech. In this century he had killed death.